D1369496

SISTER BETTY SAYS I DO

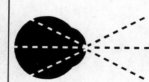

This Large Print Book carries the
Seal of Approval of N.A.V.H.

SISTER BETTY
SAYS I DO

PAT G'ORGE-WALKER

THORNDIKE PRESS
A part of Gale, Cengage Learning

GALE
CENGAGE Learning·

Detroit • New York • San Francisco • New Haven, Conn • Waterville, Maine • London

GALE
CENGAGE Learning

LIBRARY OF CONGRESS CATALOGING-IN-PUBLICATION DATA

G'Orge-Walker, Pat.
    Sister Betty Says I Do / By Pat G'Orge-Walker. — Large Print edition.
        pages cm. — (A Sister Betty Novel Series) (Thorndike Press Large Print
    African-American)
    ISBN 978-1-4104-6278-7 (hardcover) — ISBN 1-4104-6278-1 (hardcover) 1.
African Americans—Fiction. 2. African American churches—Fiction. 3.
Christian fiction, American. 4. Large type books. I. Title.
PS3607.O597S59 2013
813'.6—dc23
                                                                        2013030311

Published in 2013 by arrangement with Dafina Books, an imprint of
Kensington Publishing Corp.

Printed in Mexico
1 2 3 4 5 6 7 17 16 15 14 13

ACKNOWLEDGMENTS

To every thing there is a season, and a time to every purpose under the heaven.

Ecclesiastes 3:1 (KJV)

My beloved spake, and said unto me, Rise up, my love, my fair one, and come away. For, lo, the winter is past, the rain is over and gone.

Song of Solomon 2:10–11 (KJV)

I give sincere thanks and appreciation to the town folks of Williamston, Belton, Anderson, Piedmont, and especially Pelzer, South Carolina. My childhood memories went a long way into creating the Sister Betty character.

"On Christ the solid rock I stand, all other ground is sinking sand." I give all praises to my Lord and Savior Jesus Christ; to my husband, Rob, a constant prayer warrior who always covers me and the family with so much love and prayer; my beautiful daughters, Gizel Dan-Yette, Ingrid, and Marisa; along with my grandchildren, great-grandchildren, and, forever in my heart, my twin great-granddaughters, Livi and Serene, whom God saw fit to take back to heaven no sooner than they had arrived. My ninth great-grandchild has also arrived; welcome Nolan Gary Brewer . . . what happens at great-grandma's house stays at great-grandma's house.

As always, I remain sustained by prayers and support from those too numerous to name. I thank them all.

I am eternally grateful to my beloved bishop John L. and Lady Laura L. Smith, and to my entire St. Paul's Tabernacle City of Lights Ministry congregation, pastored by Reverend James D. Tucker and Co-Pastor Evangelist Phyllis Johnson. Many thanks to Bishop Paul M. Morton whose song "Finally" from the album "Sacred Love Songs" became Sister Betty and Freddie's theme song. My unconditional appreciation goes to numerous supportive churches and organizations.

Deep gratitude and appreciation to my editor, Selena James, and the Dafina Books/Kensington Publishing family, and to long-time friend and attorney Christopher R.

Whent, Esq., and my wonderful physician, Dr. Karl Deratus.

Without a doubt, I thank my online and off-line readers, my supporters, family, friends, numerous book clubs, my beloved friend Carol Mackey and my adopted sorority, the Deltas along with the many fellow author friends who share prayers and encouragement and offer wonderful virtual hugs.

A very special thank-you goes to Elder Lamar L. Moore, affectionately called Mr. Church-All-By-Himself. You will always be my prophetic son.

What a lackluster world this would be without the wisdom, humor, and in-your-face spirit of motivational speaker and founder of the E.S.T.H.E.R. Ministry (Empowering Sisters to Have Eternal Relationships) and author of *Tell Prince Charming to Keep That Slipper: I'm Standing on My Own Two Feet,* the incomparable relationship minister/coach Livi Stith-Bynum. I treasure your insight regarding Sister Betty's, Ima's, and Sharvon's reactions. It will make many women and men hit the reset button in their lives. I can't imagine having a book published without involving the PR skills of Ella Curry, BAN, and Ty Moody. And, of course, the wonderfully creative promotional items by Debra Owsley of Simply Said. Thank you ladies for all you do and have done for my literary career.

In 2012 and 2013 I lost my ninety-one-year-old mother-in-law, Rosalie Walker. My mother-in-law was a bundle of energy with a surplus of chutzpah. I also lost my last remaining aunt who never had a chance to return to her native Cuba, mi tia Bertha Martha; and my fellow authors Dee Stewart and Rachel Berry. I've no words for the deep hole left in my heart by the departure of Dee Stewart and Rachel Berry, two amazing women of literature and God.

www.patgorgewalker.com
www.sisterbetty.com
www.Twitter.com/pgorgewalker
www.facebook.com/sisterbetty

PROLOGUE

A year ago . . .

"Sister Betty," Trustee Freddie Noel whispered, his bony, hairless chest pushing in and out. Adding to what was apparently a moment of uncertainty, he swallowed hard, nearly tripping as a leg hit the edge of the ottoman.

Feeling somewhat embarrassed from the near fall, he bit his bottom lip before announcing, "I need to say something." He fumbled around inside the pocket of his suit jacket and retrieved a small box tied with a blue silk ribbon. "You know I ain't the most romantic being on the planet. . . ." Freddie quickly lowered his eyes. His shoulders slumped as he took a deep breath, while at the same time raising his free hand and pulling at a small sprig of silver hair that resembled a Mohawk in training. It was a nervous habit formed twenty-five years ago, when he turned forty-five.

9

His cheeks, turning almost a bright red, contrasting sharply with his lemon-yellow complexion, slowly began shrinking, freeing the air seconds ago trapped inside his lungs. Now, with the untied box in hand, Freddie's fragile body knelt at Sister Betty's feet. He slowly raised his head. His tired and now tearing brown eyes, embedded in deep sockets, began darting between the opened box and the huge fourteen-carat, pear-shaped diamond ring he now held between two trembling fingers. "Betty . . . Sarah . . . Becton, would you pretty please marry me?"

Sister Betty, almost a foot shorter than Freddie, could feel a hot sensation flooding throughout her small brown-skinned body. She felt as though she'd suddenly turned into the head of a lit match. If that was the case, then her sudden rush of tears would quickly douse its flame.

"Yes," she replied, smiling, then giggling like a child who received what she'd always wanted on Christmas morning. She allowed him to slip the diamond engagement ring upon her finger. And, just as the man kneeling before her had done moments ago, she quickly took a deep breath, struggling to form the words through her smile. Finally, she added, "Yes, Freddie, I will marry you."

That was late spring of 2010. It was a first

for them in marriage, and as far as carnal matters went, perhaps for Freddie more so than for Betty. She'd lain with a young man once in her youth, an ill-advised sexual act committed inside her parents' South Carolina barn that ultimately produced a stillborn son. Freddie, on the other hand, had had several missteps, which had caused most women seeking fulfillment to shun him. He ultimately learned to do without the pleasure of a woman.

They were overjoyed now, having lived into their twilight years, to finally jump the broom. Their future looked so bright, they'd begun wearing sunglasses every day.

"Honey Bee, what do you think about honeymooning in Aruba?" He'd not bothered to tell her that it was a place he'd always dreamt about going. He could've gone more than a year ago, when he won over a hundred million dollars from South Carolina's Mega Millions lottery. Instead of traveling and living the high life, he'd given most of it to the beloved Crossing Over Sanctuary Church, where he and Sister Betty attended, because it was in deep financial trouble.

He didn't wait for her to answer before laying out upon her living room coffee table several brochures detailing cruises and land vacations in the Caribbean. "Just take your pick," he told her. "Anywhere you wanna go . . . And if none of these tickle your fancy, we can visit a travel agent and see what else there is."

On that beautiful sunny day, when all things seemed possible, the date was set and the wedding planning was about to go into full swing.

Of course, ole Satan wasn't on the guest list but decided he'd send a gift or two, anyway.

CHAPTER 1

One year later . . .

It was barely sunrise when she awoke on this blazing hot Saturday morning. For much of her adult life, Sister Betty had been up by eight o'clock and praising her God by nine. The sun rays poured through every window in the five-bedroom Tudor home in the ritzy section of Pelzer. And added to her discomfort was the fact that she'd not slept well at all.

During the night she'd had visions. That was nothing new. She always had visions. She also had a keen sense of discernment. When she was on her knees, praying and speaking in tongues were her lines of communication to heaven. But last night her visions weren't clear, and by the way she'd tossed and turned, waking with her knees feeling as though she'd used them to run instead of her feet, she knew God was trying to warn her about something. Or at the very least, He had something for her to do, as usual. Either way, at that moment she was way past too tired to figure it out.

For the better part of her sixty-something years, she'd been committed to a fervent prayer life. Sister Betty, a five-foot-two brown ball of fire, was a no-nonsense prayer warrior who some believed prayerfully aggravated God to the point of Him needing aspirin. She was free to praise her God in song with her tinny voice until the angel Gabriel would tell her to shut up, or to shout the victory until she wore a hole in the plush carpeting, which covered every floor but the one in the kitchen and bathrooms.

Yet despite her tiredness, she lifted her arms toward heaven. "Thank ya, God, for yo grace and mercy." Of course, a woman of her seasoned years had many uncertainties that caused her to give extra praise. She never knew what to expect after crawling into bed, taking off her wig and revealing her natural hair, braided to resemble micro rows of natty gray threads, and tossing her partials into the water jar on the nightstand. She didn't know whether she'd see another sunrise. *The last thing I want is for anybody to find me bald-headed and bald-mouthed.*

One thing was for certain — everyone in

her small hometown of Pelzer, South Carolina, knew about her unusual encounter with the "Almighty."

It'd been almost thirty years since God had surprised her with a phone call drafting her into His holy army. One phone call that interrupted her favorite pastime of watching soap operas had also disrupted her quiet life. God had turned her world upside down and had taken her out of her comfort zone. Once the word got around about the very unusual telephone call, everyone in her hometown finally had their proof, calling her eccentric and laughing behind her back, saying, "Sister Betty Sarah Becton has lost her ever-loving mind."

Drinnggg! It sounded as though an elephant had placed all its weight on her doorbell. Sister Betty grabbed her wig and, still dressed in her nightgown, trudged down her hallway. She warily opened her front door a few inches. "Sweet Jesus," she murmured as the uninvited guests, church mothers Sasha Pray Onn and Bea Blister, barged inside. The two bothersome church mothers had sat on the same pew for more than thirty years, and for reasons long forgotten by both, neither one could stand the other. Yet they always hung together. When asked why that was, they'd simply say, separately, "I'm keeping my friends close and that heifer closer."

Without saying "Good morning," and almost stepping on her feet, they headed down the hallway and on into her living room.

"What now!" Betty felt her praying hands morphing into fists. She'd known the two women for most of her adult life, and they'd been a boil on her nervous system and a threat to her salvation for most of it.

Sasha Pray Onn was the main culprit and leader of the *unwelcome* committee. She was petite yet deadly, and her hair, a mound of gray pulled into a tight bun on top of her head, resembled a puff of smoke. Sasha was a pecan-complexioned aggravation, and her entire family was a rowdy bunch. "Satan keeps them on earth because they'd cause too much confusion in hell," most said with a straight face.

Bea Blister, the other aggravation, was physically a remarkable sight. She was dark like an overripe raisin. She had a back shaped like the letter *C,* caused by years of bad posture, although many believed she had pulled a back muscle from years of peeking through keyholes and had never recovered. Bea also favored multicolored wigs. She was at least three times the weight of Sasha and almost twice as tall on those occasions when she could straighten up.

Within seconds of entering the living room, Sasha stood with her nose in the air, defiant, as though it was Sister Betty who had defiled her personal space. Sister Betty, frowning, looked her up and down. Sasha also had skinny chicken legs shaped like a pair of parentheses, seeming ill-suited to keep her taupe-colored knee-highs from falling down. Yet somehow the twisted knot she'd tied above the knee stayed put. She also wore white orthopedic Hush Puppies, and her serrated-edged Bible and a cane dangling from her wrist completed her holier-than-thou outfit. Her slanted brown eyes, hidden behind square-shaped spectacles, scanned the room before she began complaining.

"This here a big old mansion," Sasha whined, fanning with her free hand, "and you ain't got no central air-conditioning? That's a sin before God." After a moment she added angrily, "When He made you rich, He didn't mean for you to take all that money to your grave or make people feel uncomfortable when they come to make a Christian call."

As she looked Sasha up and down, the smile on Sister Betty's usually smiling face morphed into a sneer, which she didn't try to hide. "Sasha," Sister Betty hissed, "get to your point, and then hurry and leave." Without waiting for Sasha to respond, she quickly turned to Bea, who hadn't said much at all. Looking Bea squarely in her eyes, Sister Betty added, "I'm in no mood for neither of y'all's silliness today. I'm fasting, and you two are making me lose my prayer points."

Bea groaned slightly, trying to force an aura of innocence. "Sister Betty, never let anyone or anything mess up your salvation." She pivoted and pointed at Sasha. "Do you think I'd ever let this Smurf monkey holding a Bible put my soul in jeopardy of hellfire?" Bea suddenly reached out and grabbed Sister Betty's hands, turning her ring finger back and forth. "This engagement ring is just gorgeous," Bea said, smiling. "It'd be a shame to have to slap Sasha hard enough with it to leave a pear-shaped mark on her mug."

Sister Betty jerked away her hand. "Bea, you do understand that I meant you, too, don't you?"

Bea said nothing, choosing instead to stare at Sasha's contorted face before returning her eyes to Sister Betty and sighing. "I guess it's the company I've been keeping that makes you hafta throw me in the mix with Sasha." Bea winked. "I know if it was just me and you standing here, you'd have thought otherwise, especially since you'll need my help in finishing up plans for your wedding reception."

No, I wouldn't! Sister Betty wanted to speak her thoughts aloud, but Sasha spoke up too fast.

"Watch it, she-rilla!" Sasha snapped at Bea. "I'm not invisible. You'd better be glad my blessed Jesus holds me and Sister Betty in the middle of His hands. There ain't no way in the world anyone with an ounce of style and grace would let you anywhere near a part of their wedding planning."

Bea spun around from Sister Betty. Waggling her finger in Sasha's face as her dark eyes narrowed, she retorted, "I know He holds Sister Betty, but you act like you must've slipped out of the good Lord's hands and fallen on your head a few times."

"Will you two please stop?" It was her turn to spin around. Sister Betty looked around her living room for her blessed oil spray. "Where did I put it?"

"Ahem," Bea said softly as she stepped in front of Sasha. "I know you're looking for that can of blessed Pam oil spray. Please just open a window or something. Sasha and me sweating like Friday night strippers sitting on Sunday morning church's second pew. I also have things to do, so we need to hurry this chat along."

Betty took a few steps forward and pounded her fireplace mantle.

Sasha stepped from behind Bea. "You're standing there with a look that's unbecoming a saint and a soon-to-be bride."

"I hafta agree," Bea added. "Sister Betty, you do look a might bit pissed off."

Sasha turned and glared at Bea. "That's what I meant!" She then turned back to Sister Betty and continued speaking softly. "We've known you for more than forty years, and we ain't even upset that our wedding *invites* haven't arrived yet. If anyone should be mad," Sasha snapped while poking the carpet with her cane like she was trying to stab a fish with it, "it oughta be us."

"Pay Sasha no mind," Bea added, with one of her heavy paw-shaped hands now sitting upon one hefty hip. "We know how slow the mail moves."

"I'm not going to blame it on the U.S. mail." Sister Betty stared in defiance of their supposed humility. "They were mailed almost a year ago, and not to you."

"We forgive yo bad memory and all," Bea

said, ignoring Sister Betty's comment while at the same time nodding her head in agreement with herself before plopping down upon the sofa. "Besides, we just figured you were all lathered because you was getting married for the first time. I think it's called having the bridal blues or something like that."

"It's called virginity jitters," Sasha murmured, rolling her eyes at the same time as she sat next to Bea.

Bea waved off Sasha's interference with a flip of her hand.

Sister Betty watched Bea's white skirt rise, showing too much of her thick hips and thighs, which resembled sides of old mottled beef. Her calves were tattooed with varicose veins and were dangling off the sofa. Bea opened her mouth to speak; her lips fluttered, making sounds like a car engine gunning.

"When we saw you was trying to hurry past us yesterday in that big car you and Trustee Freddie always riding around in while we was standing outside, sweltering in the heat —"

Sasha didn't wait for Bea to finish. She jumped right in. "We thought you acted like we was low-life heathens. That was just downright rude. Since when do you see

21

good Christian folks standing about outside of Lucifer's Barbeque Pit, and you just gonna drive on by without waving or saying a hello? How you know we wasn't going your way?"

"Oh, Sasha, hush up," Bea said as she turned and smiled at Betty. "I, for one, was a bit more thoughtful. I figured you had the wedding on yo mind." She stopped and pointed at Sasha. "Only an ole she-troll like Sasha would think otherwise."

Lord, please help me before I say or do something to blemish my salvation. Sister Betty took a breath deep enough to make her cheeks appear sunken. Turning away from Bea and Sasha, she looked out of her window and exhaled loudly, startling a robin perched on the windowsill.

Seizing the opportunity of momentary silence, Sister Betty spoke. "Since you two have said all I care to hear, you can leave now. I won't be jealous if you spread your aggravation elsewhere."

Sasha had never been known to bite her tongue, whether her teeth were in or out, and her dentures began making annoying sucking and clacking noises, like her gums had turned into tap shoes. "Please sit down, Sister Betty, so we can get this wedding reception planned. How are we gonna get anything done with you standing over there?"

"It's my wedding, my day, so stay outta my way. Do I need to get a court order —"

"Harrumph," Sasha murmured. She'd cut Sister Betty off and begun jabbing at invisible flies with her cane. "All I know is that it's been almost a year and a half since ya got asked for your wrinkled hand in matrimony, so the sooner we get ya married, the quicker ya will stop playing holier than the rest of us."

Suddenly, Sasha narrowed her eyes, tightened her lips, and began inching away from Bea. She nodded toward Sister Betty, with her loose dentures held captive by the tightening of her mouth, a signal that Sister Betty knew all too well. Sasha was about to tell a lie.

"I'm sharing this with you, Sister Betty, because folks whispering behind your back. They've been saying that since you marrying someone with a lot of money, just like you has, that it has made ya start acting funnier than usual."

"What do you mean, Sasha, by me acting funny?"

"I mean funny, as in how you acting all unusually high and mighty, like Trustee

Noel's ice is colder than everybody else's ice."

Sister Betty found herself searching for a seat in her own living room. It wasn't that she hadn't known for years that folks talked about her. Some had always thought she was extraordinarily close to the Lord. She just couldn't understand why they'd think badly of her because she'd become engaged. She also wanted to sit a bit closer to Sasha to see the depth of her lies or the truth, should she happen to tell it. "Go on, Sasha."

Bea, determined that she be involved in the conversation, urged Sasha on. "Yeah, tell it, Mighty Mouse."

"Don't rush me. This is painful, but I must tell the truth." Sasha laid open her Bible in her lap. It was a move she often used. However, the page she'd turned to was the appendix. "For instance," Sasha continued, "you don't want nobody talking about him or even to him unless it's about the Lord. Y'all together so much, ya act like there's some type of spell or something put on the both of ya." She pointed in Sister Betty's direction. "In fact, I ain't seen you this particular sort of crazy since you snapped a few years back, telling folks the good Lord done called you on the telephone."

"He most certainly did," Betty murmured under her breath.

Sasha then leaned back against the sofa. "So if ya ready to get off that high horse of yourn, we can get started on planning this shindig of a wedding reception."

"Why do you want to do something that I obviously don't want you to do?" Sister Betty asked before adding, "For the last time, neither of you is invited."

Sasha let out a loud sigh, hoping what she was about to say sounded reasonable or, better yet, truthful. "To tell the truth, I'm entering the business world," Sasha confessed. "Perhaps with she-rilla. We're pooling our knowledge of what's trending, and planning upscale events."

As if on cue, Bea raised her head and slowly tried to sit up straight, failing to silence the annoying cracking sound from her back. "That's right. We haven't made up our minds yet, but we're thinking about calling it A B.S. Event." Leaning forward, she explained further, "Those are also our initials." Falling back, she smiled a little and then continued. "We even have a slogan. 'If somebody else plans it, then it's not B.S.' " Bea paused and raised her pen in the air. "I need a little mo' time to work on yo guest list and get yo reception invites hand-printed and into the mail. This time I'm gonna see to it that it's done right, because I'm doing it myself and all by myself."

With her pillbox hat leaning to the side, Sasha boasted, "I'm in charge of finding places to hold the events. That's called venue hunting."

Sister Betty's fingers lifted her wig a little, and she began to scratch her scalp in frustration. She became mute, unable to believe Bea's crazier than normal audacity.

Bea quickly dropped her head. She licked the lead tip of the pencil before she began to scribble something on a yellow legal pad. Suddenly, without warning, she lifted her head and added, "And if Trustee Noel even thinks about getting sick again, so y'all can't get married this time, I gonna whup him so bad, even the good Lord won't recognize him!"

"He was sick!" Sister Betty barked. "And if it didn't bother me none, I don't see why it's anybody's business when and how I get married. . . ."

Sister Betty's eyes moistened as she recalled when her fiancé, Trustee Freddie Noel, collapsed last February. It had happened just a few days shy of their wedding day, after he'd fallen earlier in the week while trying to shovel snow, which was rare

26

in Pelzer. He'd spent a few days in the hospital, which caused them to postpone their wedding day. Freddie had returned home with the cause of the collapse undetermined.

"Your problem is that when you ain't being too uppity, you too nice," Sasha chimed in, interrupting Sister Betty's thoughts. "That's why me or Bea gonna plan this wedding reception for ya!"

"Tell her, Sasha!"

Sasha raised her cane. "Are you deaf or something, Bea? Didn't I just tell her?"

Sister Betty found herself fingering the cross around her neck. As she looked around the living room, her eyes finally landed upon the large red velvet–backed picture of Jesus hanging over the fireplace. All she could do was stare at His peaceful countenance and pray. *Lord, if you don't help me with these aggravating women, I'm gonna need some of your forgiveness for premeditated violence and bail money.*

"At the moment we're almost finished with outlining things," Sasha announced proudly, interrupting Sister Betty's silent prayer. "I've got some great ideas, and Bea thinks she has one or two, as well."

"Yep, I've got it down pat. And this time it'll go off without a hitch," Bea sneered, "despite what place this lil Smurf done thought to hold it."

Throwing up her hands, Sister Betty gritted her teeth. "Are you two back to name-calling and wasting my time?"

"You know these are just our pet names." Sasha winked at Sister Betty before clicking her false teeth, signaling she was lying, again. Sasha then rushed from the sofa and pressed a sheet of paper into Sister Betty's hand. "Now, all you hafta do is look over what I've written and decide which of these here venues is good enough for you. Just make it quick, because I have other things to attend to."

"When ya finish balling up that wad of stupidity," Bea quipped, "ya can take my suggestions and let me run with them."

"I've had enough!" Sister Betty yelled, causing Sasha to retreat back to the sofa. "How many times I need to tell you two that this may be my first marriage, but I've known a carnal nature before, and I've been to a few weddings, too? So for the last time, you two can leave now, because I know what I want and how I want it." Sister Betty watched Sasha, who was not one to tolerate being pushed around, pitifully try to cross her parentheses-shaped arthritic legs.

"That may be," Sasha said coldly, "but

everybody at the church knows your fiancé, Freddie Noel, skinny and as yellow as a number two pencil, ain't ever had the wrapping taken off his old carnal pleasure. . . ."

"What'd you say?" Sister Betty could feel her fist take on a life of its own as it began to ball up again.

Ignoring Sister Betty again, Sasha continued. "You gonna need some advice before Trustee Freddie returns from his monthly prison ministry visits."

"How do you know where my fiancé goes?"

"I know more than you think I do," Sasha replied. "I know another thing, too."

"What?" The veins in Sister Betty's scalp began to pulsate. She could feel the heat rise from her head. She was hot!

Sasha was determined to finish what she thought was a blow to Sister Betty's foolish confidence in matters of a worldly nature. "I know that you know nothing about how to start a life with a man his age who's probably still a virgin. He acts like he's had very little experience in the ways of womanizing."

Sister Betty jammed her hand inside the pocket of her nightgown and felt around for a safety pin or a nail clipper, anything to jab Sasha. "You're going too far, Sasha. I believe I got something, though, that'll bring you back."

"Sister Betty, stop acting shy and extra saved," Sasha snapped while pointing toward Bea, who had remained busy writing on her legal pad throughout their exchange. "At least ask Bea about such sexual matters. Low-life folks she ran with back in her day called her Bea Baby Doll. This ole heifer ran a gambling parlor and a bawdy house. Everybody knows she's done more than just a little prison time, and you know in there they learn new tricks every day. So if anyone can show you how to keep your man happy with more than just baking him a mind-crippling red velvet cake, this ole she-rilla silverback can."

"Betty, how do you spell Becton?" Bea had suddenly turned to face Sister Betty, with her eyes twitching like a pair of Mexican jumping beans. "Is it b-a-c-k-t-u-n? And are you also taking the name Noel?"

Bea quickly dropped her head again. The front of her curly plum-colored wig moved down onto her forehead, leaving her fez slanted. She continued focusing on the legal pad in her lap, with only her dark, plump cheeks blowing in and out showing any sign of life, not acknowledging Sasha's tasteless attempt at promoting her sexual expertise and exploits from her pre- and early Christian past.

Obviously still ignoring Sister Betty's complaint, Bea began pushing her wig back into place and adjusting the fez before she spoke again. "I've been calling ya Sister Betty for more than forty years, and I ain't ever had to spell yo last name. I'm guessing, though, that you'd want it printed on the reception invites. I'm also guessing you'd want to invite them nosy next-door fake detective cousins, Joy and Patience, as well as some of your relatives, like Thurgood and Delilah Pillar from New York."

"Just put all your angst to rest," Sasha told Sister Betty softly, as though she'd not said a mean word in the last two minutes. Then, sitting sideways and with her pointing finger flipped at Bea, she continued. "We can get Porky and Grandma Pudding to cater it. You'll see that idea written on my venue suggestion list. And once the health department gives Porky the go-ahead to reopen the El Diablo Soul Food Shanty, we can hold the reception in the back room." Sasha pointed at the paper in Sister Betty's hands. "You'll see it written down."

"Have mercy." Bea raised one hand and nodded at Sister Betty. She then used her hand to circle her head, indicating what she thought of Sasha's idea. "Look, I got to go

31

and get things started," Bea announced suddenly, before winking at Sister Betty. "All I can say," she added, "is that when you and Freddie show up for the reception, y'all better be wearing sunglasses, 'cause you two gonna look like stars!"

"I believe it's you two nosy, Satan-serving she-witches that'd better be wearing sunglasses to cover the black eyes I'll give you if you come anywhere near me and Betty's wedding day!"

Sister Betty turned around fast enough to cause whiplash. "Freddie! When did you get here?"

CHAPTER 2

"I've been standing in the foyer for the past ten minutes, listening to these two interfering and signifying. Dang busybodies, the both of them. Ain't their business about what should or shouldn't be going on in folks' private bedrooms."

Trustee Freddie Noel's yellowish complexion had turned almost ashen from anger. Before Sister Betty, Sasha, or Bea could say another word, he had already crossed the carpet and stood hovering over Sasha and Bea.

With his long bony fingers waving between the two church mothers, he blasted them further. "Let me tell you two meddlesome she-demons another thing."

Bea tried to rise up to show she wasn't afraid of Freddie. As much as she wanted to do so, all she managed was to move farther back on the sofa.

Sasha's cane kept slipping out of her

hand, so she kept quiet.

"Freddie, please," Sister Betty pleaded. "Neither of them is worth it."

"Don't move a muscle, Honey Bee. I want you to stay right where you are!" He clasped his hands and began cracking his knuckles slowly before shuffling his feet rope-a-dope-style like Muhammad Ali. "When I'm finished with them, you can throw the leavings out into the street."

As he turned around once more to face Bea and Sasha, Freddie's eyes began blinking, alternating between widening and narrowing. "If I catch either of you two over here again, interfering, insinuating, signifying, or bothering my sweet Betty, with so much as a howdy-do about what she and I have or haven't ever done, again —"

Sasha didn't wait for Freddie to finish. "Oh really!" she growled, trying to match his threats with as much masculinity as she could in a desperate act of intimidation. "So then what are you gonna do . . . if we do?"

Freddie bent down and now stood close enough to smell the odor of the snuff Sasha always claimed she never dipped. "I will put my foot so far up your scrawny tail that every time you open your big mouth, folks can see what color drawers you're wearing!" He stood and then added, "That is, if it's a day that you're wearing any. Everybody knows and has seen that you don't always adhere to the feminine trappings of underwear."

It took a few moments for Sister Betty to wrap her head around what had just happened. She'd never seen that side of Freddie, although she could certainly understand Bea and Sasha pushing him to that point. "My God," she murmured.

Without saying another word, besides a unified "Harrumph," Bea and Sasha gathered their belongings. With Betty and Freddie walking close behind, the two stubborn old women took their time heading toward the front door.

Sister Betty knew Sasha wasn't leaving without having the last word.

No sooner had Sasha stepped outside and onto the front porch than she turned toward Freddie. She curled her lips, turned her head, and said boldly to Sister Betty, "We'll see you at Wednesday night prayer meeting."

"That's right," Bea finally chimed in with her own version of false bravado. She began waving her legal pad in Sister Betty's direction. "Perhaps then you'll explain to the people of God how it is that the man you ain't married to yet can come and go into your house, as well as insult good Christian-like folks with good inventions!"

"Intentions, Bea, intentions!" Sasha groaned, correcting her before shaking her head and appearing disgusted.

"Whatever!" Bea snapped. "They are doing sinful things. I just know it! I know a sinner when I see one." Bea then turned to Sasha and quipped, "C'mon, sinner, er . . . Sasha. We gotta figure out which of those dumb ideas you have on where to hold the reception at that we're gonna toss out."

It took only a short time after Sasha and Bea's visit before Freddie led Betty back into her living room. She told him about the unsettling vision she'd had the night before Bea and Sasha's visit. "I should've known God was trying to warn me so they wouldn't pluck my last praying nerve," she said before they both fell to their knees.

Soon after saying a fervent prayer in which they repented and asked God for restoration, the couple, hand in hand, entered Sister Betty's spacious kitchen.

"I feel such peace every time we come in here together," she sighed.

Sister Betty and Freddie had already decided to sell his home once they were married. His house was only around the corner. With that in mind, she'd had her kitchen redecorated. It seemed like a practical idea, seeing as how they both loved to cook and would need extra space. They'd had it remodeled in cherrywood, everything but the sink, stove, and refrigerator. There was also a mirrored ceiling, which reflected the shine from the speckled white marble tiles and the red and white walls. In the center of the kitchen was an island that took up most of the space.

The long center counter was Freddie's idea. He'd said he wanted to look into the saintly eyes of his beautiful Honey Bee each time they cooked.

The night before Bea and Sasha had barged in, Sister Betty had made a pitcher of his favorite lemon-flavored green tea. After pouring the tea they sat for a moment in silence, sipping slowly, while Freddie smiled and embraced her with the gleam in his eyes.

Sister Betty soon rose and began busying herself about the kitchen. "Take this bowl and snap the beans for supper," she told Freddie. "It'll give you something to do. You're making me blush looking at me. I'm not used to that," she teased.

Freddie laughed and replied, "I guess beans will do as a substitute since I couldn't snap Bea's and Sasha's necks."

Sister Betty didn't join in the laughter, as she normally would have. Instead, she silently prayed for wisdom. Despite his praying earlier, she wasn't convinced his overhearing Bea's and Sasha's assaults on his manhood, particularly his possible lack of a lot of female contact, hadn't humiliated him. The way he'd reacted had taken her completely by surprise. Threatening Bea and Sasha in such a manner wasn't how she had expected her shy fiancé to respond.

Deep in thought and prayer, she almost pulled the kitchen drawer out of the cabinet while trying to get at the utensils to ice the cake she'd baked the night before. *Heavenly Father, I need some of your wisdom,* she thought prayerfully. She would one day soon become his wife, and now was as good a time as any to learn how to make him feel more comfortable and manly.

"Freddie," Sister Betty murmured sweetly while placing the cover on the cake plate.

Lifting his head, which he kept down while he snapped the beans, he replied, "Yes, honey?"

Sister Betty wiped her hands on a towel, walked over, and stood behind him. Her slender fingers began instinctively massaging his slightly stooped shoulders, as though she'd done so for many years.

"I know we've gone before the Lord and worked it out with Him, but you made me proud standing up for me and battling those two old, nosy she-demons." She hoped that bringing it back up wouldn't make him feel bad, since she intended on making him feel better. She needed him to know that she felt safe, protected. It didn't matter how much or when was the last time he'd had carnal knowledge. After all, it wasn't like she thought about or cared whether he ever took home the gold from the sex Olympics when she accepted his proposal.

Freddie gently removed her hands and turned to face her. "I know I said it already, but I'll say it again. I'm sorry, Honey Bee. The last thing I wanted to do when I saw your side door open was to walk in here and find those two old crows mouthing off. The truth is that I just need to pray more."

"Well, since we're being truthful," she replied with a strong laugh that caused her shoulders to heave, "one of the last things I'd wanted was for you to walk in here and catch my wig all lopsided."

"Come to think of it," he replied, smiling as he looked her up and down, "you could be completely bald, honey, and it still wouldn't matter."

"Well, since you put it that way, I won't hold that or your anger at those two meddlesome women against you. Fact is, I'd been up since the break of dawn, trying to get the most out of the last day of my prayer fast, when they came by without being invited."

"Well, we won't let them ruin what's left of the day. By the way, isn't that lovely lawyer cousin of yours, Sharvon, returning to Pelzer today?" A smile blanketed Freddie's face, where moments before tired lines had connected his brow to his cheekbones. "It's good she's coming back to stay awhile. Having young folks around can sometimes put more pep in your step."

"I know what you mean. I never thought I'd feel this way about some of my kinfolks, but I just love having her around. I'm just happy that this time she'll be here for more than a few weeks. She may join this big law office. But don't say nothing, because I'm not supposed to jinx it. At least, that's what she believes."

"Young people say the craziest things." His words were followed by a smile. "But I say if it's God's will, then she'll get the partnership." Freddie checked his watch and added, "What time is Sharvon's plane landing?"

Betty turned to look at the kitchen clock. "Oh my. If it's on time, then I've less than an hour to get to the Greenville-Spartanburg airport."

"I'd go with you, but it's my turn to gather books and stamps for the prison ministry."

"I know you would if you could. God's always got a ram in the bush."

"And we thank Him for that," Freddie told her. "So you'd better put a move on before your spiritual son, Reverend Tom, arrives before you're ready."

When Sister Betty returned about fifteen minutes later, she quietly laid her Bible on the counter. "Ahem. Praise the Lord, son."

The thirtysomething reverend Leotis Tom, all six feet five inches of him, laid down the fork he held in midair, cake crumbs falling down. "Praise Him, Sister Betty." Leotis rose and wiped cake crumbs from his mouth with a napkin. "As usual, you've put your foot in this cake and made it beyond scrumptious. I don't care if it's healthy or not."

"I probably should've told him not to touch that cake." Freddie winked at Leotis, while at the same time pushing aside his own saucer littered with cake crumbs.

Leotis turned toward Freddie, returning the wink. "Trustee Noel, here it is you've

41

gotten me in trouble again with my spiritual mama. How many times are you going to make me have to apologize to her?"

Sister Betty said nothing, preferring to pretend that she was very disappointed that they'd cut the cake by shaking her head hard enough to cause her sun hat to slide a little.

Despite the supposed annoyed look on her face, Leotis walked over and kissed her on her cheek before returning to his seat.

"Don't bother trying to soften me up." Sister Betty looked him up and down as though for the first time before she broke out in a smile. "Look at you. I see you're out of uniform today."

There was no turned-around collar or dark-colored clothing, his usual preacher's wardrobe, which often hid the results of a healthy lifestyle, namely, running track and engaging in constant workouts. Instead, he wore a red shirt with short sleeves that seemed to burst at the seams from his huge muscles, along with matching trousers, which were not quite as tight yet revealed chiseled thighs and legs. His dark, curly hair was damp around the edges from perspiration, and there was just a hint of moisture on his caramel-complexioned face and playfulness in his hazel eyes.

"First, you come in here and cut my chocolate cake without asking, and now you standing here, looking at me like I'm Betty dum-dum," she teased. "You see, my fiancé, who's still in trouble, won't stand for that."

"That's right," Freddie chimed in. "Don't let me hafta get someone else to lay hands on ya. I'd do it . . . but I need these paws to lift another forkful of cake."

All three broke out in laughter. It was their ritual. They loved one another just as much as if they had more than just the *blood* of Jesus between them.

"Come on, Mrs. Soon-to-Be Noel," Leotis said, laughing. "Let's go get that gorgeous cousin of yours. I'm sure she's missed you."

"Yeah," Freddie added with a wink, "and I'm sure there's someone in this kitchen who, if *he* tells the truth, will admit he's missed Sharvon, too — and I don't mean in a sisterly fashion, as he claims."

"I know what you're hinting about, but you just worry about getting this one to the altar," Leotis said as he pointed to Sister Betty. "When God sends me the right woman, I'll know it."

"And how will you know it's the right one?" Sister Betty asked as she folded her arms across her chest, staring at him hard, daring him to be more specific.

Leotis folded his massive arms across his chest likewise. Without flinching or giving an inch in tone, he replied, "I'll know because there'll be not just one to choose from, but two." His voice suddenly became more serious in tone. "I'll know because just like King Solomon wisely thought of a way to tell the real mother of the baby in question, God will show me the right choice to make whenever the time comes."

"Good thing you ain't preaching that nonsense to the good people at Crossing Over Sanctuary," Sister Betty teased. "We'd have nothing but bachelors and men trying to get out of marriages. And you know the women would be cranky about it."

Leotis laughed. "I guess they would at that. And speaking of cranky women, I had a call from Mother Pray Onn just as I was leaving."

A look of guilt spread between Sister Betty and Freddie, as though they were expecting a reprimand from their pastor.

"She called to remind me that I promised her two weeks ago that I'd pick up one of her relatives at the airport today. I guess it's a good thing I was going, anyway, because I'd truly forgotten about it."

"Well, a promise is a promise," Sister Betty told him quickly.

Leotis blew a kiss at Sister Betty, causing cake crumbs to scatter. "That's true, and as long as it's someone who's not talking about marriage, we'll have a short but lovely ride back to Pelzer."

"I gotta hand it to ya." Freddie laughed. "When it comes to making up a way to not talk about getting a wife, you take the cake."

"That's right. As a matter of fact, I feel like another slice to take for the road."

As though she hadn't heard him, Sister Betty sighed, "That reminds me. Can we get to the airport?"

She couldn't claim to know all of Sasha's relatives, but she was certain none of the Hellraiser nuts had fallen far from the tree.

CHAPTER 3

"We haven't even arrived at the airport."
Leotis spoke through clenched teeth. "I'll
call you as soon as they are in the car and
we are leaving. This is the third time you've
called. Mother Pray Onn, I need to keep
my eyes on the road and not answer cell
phone calls every five miles. . . . I know what
she'll be wearing. You've told me that three
times, too." He flipped the cover to his cell
phone, turning it off for good.

Sister Betty watched the pained look on
Leotis's face. It was the same expression
he'd had since they left her house and she
reminded him that none of Sasha's relatives,
with the exception of her niece Zipporah,
were sane. "Zipporah was raised from birth
by foster parents," she'd told him. "That's
the only reason she escaped the crazy gene
pool them Hellraisers call a family."

They'd just driven into the Delta arrival
terminal when Sister Betty spotted Sharvon

dressed in a yellow, sleeveless tunic-style dress. A purple sash accentuated her tiny waist. She was waiting by the curb with her luggage. Sharvon appeared engaged in conversation with another young woman, who was shorter. The other woman had long red hair pulled back into a ponytail and was dressed in tight green shorts and a white halter top that would never stop her large bosom, should it decide to escape.

"We'll need to get Sharvon's attention quickly," Leotis told Sister Betty. "The TSA won't allow this car to remain idling too long." With the glare from the hot sun nearly blinding him, he craned his neck out of the car's window, trying to look in Sharvon's direction. "From what little I can see," he said, now using one hand to shield his eyes, "she's not alone. If it's a friend who needs a ride, and it's not too far out of our way, I think we can fit all their luggage in the trunk and squeeze one more person besides Mother Pray Onn's kin inside the car."

Just as Sister Betty's car window began rolling down, she heard her name being called. It wasn't Sharvon, but the woman standing with her.

"Sister Betty!" the woman called out, waving frantically at the car as Sharvon joined in, waving at her, as well.

They had wheeled luggage, and instead of waiting for Leotis's car to come closer, Sharvon and the other woman began racing toward it against the traffic.

When they neared the car, Sister Betty's head jerked toward Leotis and then back at the women. She took a large swallow and moaned, "Oh, Jesus, why give me two of them all in one day?"

"What's wrong?"

"That's Ima Hellraiser with Sharvon!"

"Do you mean Mother Pray Onn's niece Ima? She's the one I'm supposed to pick up." Leotis used both hands to shield his eyes before he blurted, "Wow, she doesn't look anything like the way she was described to me."

"Yes. She's the one and, I thank God, the only one."

"She doesn't look anything like Mother Pray Onn," he said softly, his eyes suddenly appearing brighter. "She's beautiful."

"She's deadly like a snake and sneaky like a scorpion," Sister Betty hissed. "You'd have to watch out for that one."

"Luke ten, nineteen," began Leotis in his baritone preacher's voice. "Behold, I give unto you power to tread on serpents and scorpions, and over all the power of the enemy, and nothing shall by any means hurt you." With both hands now gripping the steering wheel tightly, he smiled, his eyes still locked on Ima as she strode toward the car with Sharvon.

"Harrumph!" Betty replied as she searched her mind for a rebuttal scripture. "Exodus seventeen, two. Why chide ye with me? Wherefore do ye tempt the Lord?"

Before they could continue their back-and-forth, impromptu scripture challenge, Sharvon tapped on the driver's side door.

"Hello, Leotis. Please hurry and open the door." Sharvon quickly pointed to the other woman. "We've got extra company, and we need to get out of this heat."

Ima said nothing as her bright green eyes with specks of brown became like missiles, locking onto Leotis. She smiled appreciatively. "Speak for yourself," Ima told Sharvon, laughing. "Hellraisers live for heat."

Both women piled into the backseat while Leotis placed their luggage inside the trunk, and Sister Betty rubbed her knees, which had suddenly begun to throb. It was a sure sign that God was trying to tell her something using her knee phone or a continuation from her bad night.

"Sister Betty, I thought that was you." Ima laughed and began squirming in the backseat, causing a bit more jiggling from the halter top than necessary. "I heard about your news." Again, she laughed and began humming, "Here comes the bride. Here comes the bride."

"Yes, Ima, it's me. I'm certain I've made your day." Sister Betty turned in her seat, looking Ima straight in her green eyes, which seemed suddenly brighter from the laughter. "We ain't got to worry about no police or nothing, do we? I've got other things to do than go get Sasha to bail you out, especially since I'm not on speaking terms with her." She quickly turned around, letting Ima know that she'd said all she wanted to say and no response was welcomed or needed.

"I didn't know you and my cousin Betty were such old and not-so-dear friends," Sharvon said, slowly hunching her shoulders, with a questioning look upon her face.

"I've known Sister Betty most of my life, and we always tease like that," Ima said softly. Pointing to Leotis, who'd just reentered the car, she added, "But I don't believe I've ever met him."

Not waiting for Sharvon to introduce them, Leotis turned around and extended his hand to Ima. "I'm Reverend Leotis Tom."

"From Crossing Over Sanctuary?" Ima asked. "You mean you're the gentleman who Aunt Sasha got to fetch me?"

"The one and the same," Leotis replied. "I've been Mother Pray Onn's pastor for more than eight years, and yet I don't recall you ever coming to the church."

"Are you certain about that?" Ima purred.

"I'm certain I would have remembered you from among the more than two thousand members."

The immediate and appreciative glances between Leotis and Ima didn't go unnoticed by either Sister Betty or Sharvon.

Sharvon said nothing. She pursed her lips and just stared at the back of Sister Betty's head or looked out the window.

Sister Betty could tell Sharvon felt uncomfortable, because she hadn't said much. She also recalled the conversations she'd had with Sharvon over the past few months, since she'd come to stay after her mother died. She knew Sharvon had more of an attraction to Leotis than she'd let on, yet just like him, she wasn't rushing to enter the dating or matrimony game. "He doesn't seem to be in a hurry, so why should I?" she'd said after she and Leotis had gone out several times to dinner and a movie. "We're just good friends."

Sister Betty fingered her Bible and wondered whether or not she'd approve of Ima becoming the jealousy-driven shove toward Leotis that Sharvon needed.

However, until she made up her mind one way or the other, Sister Betty wasn't about to let any flirtation between Ima and Leotis continue unchecked. And so she reached over and tapped Leotis on his knee and began singing as the car turned onto the highway heading back toward Pelzer. "If you let that Devil ride . . . she's gonna wanna drive."

Smiling at his spiritual mother's obvious insinuation, Leotis looked into his rearview mirror. He did it just in time to catch the unappreciative eye of Sharvon and the flirtatious look from Ima. Now strumming the steering wheel, he could think of but one response to his spiritual mother's warning. It was the words in an old Stevie Wonder song he'd always liked, "Don't You Worry 'Bout a Thing."

Suddenly Leotis felt alive and leery at the same time. It'd been quite some time since he'd been in female company and felt what he was feeling. *Father God, please don't place me between a rock and a hard place. Wisdom and restraint, Lord . . . I need wisdom and restraint.*

Sister Betty, on the other hand, clasped her hands and began silently praying as she queried God. *Father, I've been all up and down and in and out of your holy Word. If there's any situation in that book that is akin to what I know is about to happen if Leotis lets Ima into his world, please show it to me. And, Father, if it be thy will, please slap Leotis upside the head with some wisdom. Amen.*

CHAPTER 4

It was early Friday morning, just a little past dawn, and for days Sister Betty had witnessed Leotis stretch and bend his staunch beliefs on marriage and dating like a Cirque du Soleil contortionist.

She wasn't really surprised. In fact, she'd known for the past week or so of restless sleep, throbbing knees, and the other discomforts that followed Sharvon's return, with Ima in tow, that something would go wrong. Sister Betty just didn't know when, where, what, or how.

She had also missed having Sharvon around to toss around her ideas for the wedding. Eight and a half weeks would pass before she knew it, and there was plenty to decide and to have done. Although they lived in the same house, Sister Betty seldom saw Sharvon. Sharvon would leave before eight in the morning and would not return until almost midnight. She had spent almost the entire past four days at the Singer and Berry law firm, to which soon would be added the name Becton. Sharvon had finally accepted their offer to join. It'd mean long hours, for the most part, until Sharvon became familiar with her various cases and the staff she'd oversee. Sister Betty was pleased because law was something Sharvon loved and had thrown herself into.

In the meanwhile, Sister Betty made up her mind that she wouldn't allow Ima's sexy come-ons to become a reason for any romantic notions between Sharvon and Leotis. *At least Sharvon won't be witnessing the way Ima's gonna just throw herself at Leotis. I just know she will. I can just feel it,* she thought.

Sharvon quietly entered the kitchen and threw her arms around Sister Betty's neck. "I'm about to go for a quick run before I head out to the office this morning."

Sister Betty laughed as she turned to face Sharvon. "Come on, Sharvon. Sit with me for a moment and have some breakfast. If you don't come out of that size four you wear and put on some weight, I'll have to get your maid of honor dress from the toddler department."

"There'll be no buying anything for me in some toddlers' department," Sharvon said as she pulled at the string on her running shorts. "I'm trying to maintain this weight so if I have children one day, I can relax and not worry about gaining too much weight."

Leotis Tom held the reputation as one of Pelzer's most handsome men in and out of a preacher's robe and the fastest. He loved running and had won several local marathons. When he wasn't on his knees, praying and talking to God, he'd have his heavenly chat while running.

He awoke early this Friday morning and found that it was already in the mid-seventies. He wanted to start off his day with a run at a nearby high school. He was soon dressed in one of his usual eye-candy outfits: dark running shorts that showed off long legs with double-dipped muscles, one stacked one upon the other; a white headband to absorb the sweat; and a white tank top that displayed arm muscles resembling the back of an alligator's tail.

Leotis was in the midst of tossing his gym bag onto the backseat of his car when he heard laughter coming from the direction of Sister Betty's house.

"I see great minds are thinking alike this hot and about to be humid morning," Sharvon called out, laughing while she pointed to her outfit. She wore a pair of dark brown gym shorts, a beige tank top, and running shoes. She wore her hair in a ponytail, and it partially covered the backpack dangling off one shoulder. "Are you on your way to Barack Obama High, too?"

Whether he meant to or not, as usual, the way Leotis smiled showed his appreciation for her well-toned body. He was still a man with manly needs, but he was also one who quickly shook his head, rebuking the possibility of a lustful thought. Over the months he'd come to respect and admire Sharvon, and he loved her like the little sister he'd never had. Although they hardly ever planned to run the track together, this wasn't the first time they left their homes at about the same hour to do it before starting their busy days.

"I've already got my things in the car," Leotis called out. "Would you like a ride?" He then laughed and began running in place to challenge her. "I'll give you another opportunity to break my record. Perhaps a fifth try will be the magic."

"In your dreams, but thanks, as usual." Sharvon ran down the sidewalk and into his driveway. "I plan on running only about an hour, so perhaps another time would be better to leave you gasping for breath."

Leotis, with both hands on his hips, looked at Sharvon. He shook his head, laughing. "I guess any excuse is acceptable in this heat. I won't challenge your pride this time."

"Oh, give me a break, Leotis," Sharvon challenged. "I just saved your reputation. Besides, I've got two meetings at the firm this morning, and you know how crazy Fridays can get."

"I know how crazy every day can get," Leotis replied, taking her backpack from her hands. He gently placed it beside his gym bag on the backseat. "It's another reason why I gotta stay fit and prayed up."

It didn't take them long to drive the mile to Barack Obama High School and park inside its lot. Like-minded runners were already rounding the oval track. Minutes after warming up with a few leg stretches, Leotis and Sharvon ran onto the field and blended in with the others. Neither spoke as they ran, preferring to let their challenging speeds and endurance speak for them. They'd just rounded the last lap of the fifth mile when Leotis's head jerked from a tap on his shoulder. He'd never seen her come up behind him, and he was certain Sharvon hadn't this time, either.

"I certainly didn't expect to see either of you out here this morning." Ima's breathing was steady and even as she gently tapped Sharvon on her shoulder. "You guys have room for one more?"

Without waiting for an answer or a return greeting, Ima thrust her long and lean frame between Leotis and Sharvon. She had no problem keeping pace or keeping an eye on Leotis's quick glances tossed her way. She didn't bother looking at Sharvon, knowing that like most other women, she'd be jealous.

As the three slowly walked the last few feet to one of the benches where runners usually ended with a stretch routine, Sharvon spoke first. "Hello, Ima." Without waiting for Ima to reply, she began stretching her long legs, before bending from the waist, showing her flexibility. "Leotis and I were just finishing."

Ima didn't respond directly to Sharvon. Joining in the stretching exhibition, she looked at Leotis, who'd not said a word. She could tell he wasn't disappointed she'd joined them, because he'd not taken his eyes off her. Once she let him have, in her opinion, all his eyes and flesh could handle, with her back still to Sharvon, she purred, "Too bad." As she raised one arm, then grabbed the elbow of the other, stretching from side to side, she added, "I'm just getting started."

Leotis spoke, finally kicking aside the cat that had gotten his tongue. "Ima, it's a pleasure to see you again. I can tell you love to take care of your temple, like I do. I've got to take Sharvon home, but I'm certain we'll run into each other on the track again." He'd said it as though it was a duty to take Sharvon home, and if he didn't have to, he'd stay right there with Ima.

"I'm sure we will," Ima replied. "I was hoping it'd be sometime this week at the Health Nutt." Ima stopped speaking for a moment, using the short pause to bend over, with her backside toward Sharvon, and pretend to tie her sneaker. Knowing Sharvon was still listening, Ima added, "I haven't had an opportunity to tell you just how much I enjoyed our lunch there the other day. It was my first time going there since they opened in Pelzer. You really showed me a good time, Reverend."

The heat from Sharvon's eyes penetrated the side of Leotis's head. She was hot and wanted to singe his brain for what she thought was the dumbest move he could've made with Ima. She couldn't put the words together at that moment and didn't need to, since he'd already turned his head and looked away, but not before she'd seen his guilty look.

And just as quickly as Ima had appeared, instigating and insinuating, separating them as they sped around the race track, she strutted away, leaving her incendiary words to separate Leotis and Sharvon as they rode back to their houses.

As Leotis drove toward his home, with Sharvon still not speaking to him, the old saying "Quieter than cats jumping on cotton" came to mind. She sat in the backseat and slammed her backpack onto the floor and against the car door. He didn't have to look in his rearview mirror to tell her anger hadn't subsided one bit. He fumbled around with the radio dial, but somehow his satellite radio couldn't find a signal. As they neared their houses, he decided he'd not let the Devil win the day.

"Sharvon," he began quickly, glancing in the rearview mirror to see if she even bothered to look his way without smirking. "I'm cutting to the chase. I don't want you to put more into what Ima said than need be."

Sharvon glared at him but said nothing.

"You know the Health Nutt is one of my favorite places to grab a bite. It just happened that Ima had discovered it, too, and we sat down at the same table. Good food and random conversation were all we shared."

Sharvon crossed her legs and her arms and continued glaring.

"I guess I probably should've shut down her insinuations as soon as she began revising the situation," he said as he turned into his driveway and parked. "But I didn't think it'd bother you this much."

Without saying good-bye, Sharvon snatched her backpack and flung it across her shoulder, then hopped out of Leotis's car and speed walked down his driveway, toward Sister Betty's house.

Leotis sat in his car and watched Sharvon storm through Sister Betty's side door. If she'd been surprised at the obvious flirtation coming from Ima, he was just as surprised at his reaction to her anger. He hadn't meant to hurt Sharvon, but then he hadn't thought she cared about him beyond being good friends.

"And this is why I gotta stay in my own lane and out of the oncoming traffic of these females," he murmured as he exited his car and went inside his house.

CHAPTER 5

"Today may be Sunday, but this is the third straight day you've stopped by at this early hour and missed Sharvon," Sister Betty told Leotis. "If I didn't know any better, I'd think you were trying to avoid her."

Leotis gave Sister Betty a weak smile but said nothing.

Sister Betty reached out her hand and tapped his as she chuckled. "I think the winds in Pelzer are changing, and perhaps you might be trying to avoid the love trap."

"You have an active imagination," Leotis replied. "But then again, it's one of the things I admire about you."

Sister Betty then pushed a wrapped plate of steamed vegetables picked fresh from her garden toward him. "Here. Take this plate and eat what's on it later, because you're talking nonsense." She placed her finger on her cheek and smiled. "Now that I think about it, you look like I done stole the truth out your mouth."

"No, you have not," Leotis replied. He began laughing and tapping the side of his thigh, which had begun to jerk slightly, indicating he wanted to change the subject. "I just wanted to get your thoughts about the service the other night. I didn't have a chance to discuss it when it was over. You and the trustee seemed in a hurry."

"Oh, really?" Sister Betty said. "Is that so?"

"Yes, that's so. It's pretty much the same with me right now. I'm in a hurry to meet with a few church elders from the Mount Kneel Down Church in about twenty minutes. They're stopping by on their way to their church. I believe they might want me to preach for Reverend Stepson's upcoming anniversary, among some other business."

"It's no problem," Sister Betty told him. "I've got some thoughts about your message, but they can wait until there's a better time. You just make sure you eat those vegetables while they're fresh. You can come back for more if you want to."

Taking the plate in his hands, Leotis rose, then gave Sister Betty a peck on her cheek. "I always do. I'll be back before long to pick you up for morning service."

As soon as she'd closed the door behind

Leotis, Sister Betty went and sat on her living room sofa. She laid her head back to rest it against the cushion and smiled as she thought about her pastor. This past Thursday night, during the second week of the revival meeting, he'd preached a great sermon. His topic had been "God's Set-Aside Man." The sanctuary had exploded, the churchgoers confirming that they, too, believed their God had some folks anointed and others appointed for His purpose only. Yet no sooner had the church let out than she and Freddie met Leotis outside to make the trip home and saw that his persona had changed.

Instead of asking, "How did you like the sermon?" which was something he'd always ask — as if the rousing shouts of "Preach! You better say that Word, Reverend" hadn't already confirmed it — Leotis had said only, "I didn't see Mother Pray Onn at the revival meeting tonight. Have any of you seen her? Is she sick?"

As much of a hurry as they'd been in, it wasn't lost upon either her or Freddie that Leotis had never asked about Sasha's whereabouts before. Fact was that he had always seemed relieved when she wasn't there to create some ridiculous disturbance. The only conclusion was that he might've been asking about Ima.

Sister Betty heard the phone ringing and pushed aside thoughts of the past Thursday. She rose quickly from the sofa to reach the phone before her answering machine took over the call.

"Hello and praise the Lord."

"You almost ready, Honey Bee?" Freddie asked cheerfully.

As usual, his words were like a balm to her spirit. "Just about ready, Freddie," Sister Betty answered softly. She sounded almost schoolgirl giddy whenever she said something that seemed to rhyme with his name. "I couldn't seem to find the right slip to wear with my dress this morning."

"I'm sure no matter what you decided, you'll look beautiful, Honey Bee."

"Thank you, Freddie."

Sister Betty wondered if she'd ever get used to hearing him call her by the favorite pet name he'd given her. He'd often mentioned how the names Freddie and Betty seemed to roll off the tongue and sometimes sounded a bit "childish." Months ago, she had let him hold her by the hand while she gazed lovingly into his eyes, and she had given him permission to use the endearing term Honey Bee. It wasn't too far-fetched where she was concerned; after all, he'd already begun calling her honey.

"Honey Bee," Freddie said, "I think you might want to get a move on so you can be ready when Leotis picks you up."

"I intend to be," she replied. "But do you know what else would be just as wonderful this morning?"

"What, Honey Bee?"

"Sharvon coming to church with me would be great. But she's already promised she'd work a few Sundays, until she's caught up."

"That office ain't even open on Sundays. She's gonna miss some good preaching," Freddie said. "She's gonna miss out on snatching Leotis, too, if what I've heard from the Bea Blister grapevine is true."

Sister Betty knew he was probably right. She hadn't had a good feeling since Freddie told her how he'd run into Bea at the mall. Bea had acted as though nothing bad had happened a few days before, when he'd threatened her and Sasha. Instead, she'd told him how as soon as Ima laid eyes on Leotis, she'd staked a claim on him.

"Well, Leotis is a grown man and knows the Word of God," Sister Betty told him. "Hopefully, he's gotten over his first impression of Ima."

That was what she said to Freddie, but

she did have a sliver of doubt. There was no denying Ima was beautiful, with her long red hair, green eyes, and to-die-for figure. But she was Sasha's niece and part of the Hellraiser family. To know Ima was to eventually look past her beauty and want to hit her with a brick. Sister Betty hoped it wouldn't get that far.

"Well, I've got to go, Honey Bee. If the trustees weren't having a meeting before the morning service, I'd leave my car at home and walk around the corner to ride with you and Leotis." He let out a soft chuckle before continuing. "You just stay prayed up today. I've a feeling it's going to be a hot service, and I want to shout on the very spot at the altar where I'll make you my bride."

"Me too," Sister Betty replied. She was glad he wasn't there to see the tears welled up in her eyes. Every time he mentioned how much he either loved her or couldn't wait to get married, she wanted to cry.

They said their good-byes, each imagining the other blushing through the telephone. Both were eager to see the other as soon as possible, knowing and appreciating that the gift of love in their season was a gift and favor from God. Each had forfeited their relationships over the years and had been devoted to performing God's will. They'd often said that their finding each other's love was an example of obedience being better than sacrifice.

A short while later Sister Betty had finished dressing, and it was just in time to hear the familiar blast of Leotis's car horn.

Quickly locking the door behind her, Sister Betty turned to go down the steps from her front porch. Because the sun was in her eyes, she thought her eyes were playing tricks on her. But the sun wasn't the trick. She almost slapped herself with her pocketbook when she spied Ima seated in the front seat of Leotis's 2012 black Tahoe. She remembered him saying that his Honda Civic was in the shop, having brake work done.

She began quoting the twenty-third Psalm of David. "Yea, though I walk through the valley of the shadow of death, I will fear no evil —"

Sister Betty repeated the psalm as she walked down her pathway. She opened the back door to the Tahoe and stood her ground, a quickly placed smile upon her face replacing her concern. Speaking loud enough for them to hear, she asked, "How are you two feeling this bright and sunny day that the Lord hath made?"

Leotis, with his hazel eyes appearing like velvety cognac in the sunlight and brighter than usual, stuck his neck outside the car window and chirped, "I'm blessed and highly favored." When Ima said nothing and didn't move an inch, he quickly added, "It's a blessing just to see this gorgeous day."

Still outside the Tahoe, Sister Betty nodded at Leotis. She then shifted her Bible to one hand and reached for the car's support handle with her other as she tried to climb in the backseat. "Don't you move to come around and try to help me, Reverend Tom. I guess you're so used to me sitting where Ima's plopped down that you forgot how high the step is to get inside the back of this thing."

Leotis pulled his head back inside the car, allowing it to fall forward enough for a few of his short curls to touch the steering wheel. Out of the side of one eye he saw Ima twitch slightly. He didn't bother to take a long look over at the big smile now plastered on her face. Looking upward, he murmured, "Father, whatever was I thinking?"

Once she had pushed Leotis's hand aside when he finally offered his help, and had entered the backseat, Sister Betty began thumbing through her Bible. It wasn't for anything in particular. It was something to do with her hands . . . so she didn't reach across the seat and snatch Leotis by his hair. She couldn't believe how angry she'd become in just a few short minutes. But then again, she couldn't believe that her beloved spiritual son and pastor was dumb enough to allow Ima to ride along.

As they drove down the highway, Sister Betty's eyes pierced the back of Leotis's head, while he tried to engage her and Ima in small talk. She was sending him bad vibrations, and she knew he felt them. It was evident by the way he kept swerving in and out of traffic.

"Are you all right, son? Anything happening that's causing you to drive so crazy?" Sister Betty asked.

"Nothing I can't handle with some help from the Lord."

Sister Betty began thinking that if it wasn't her signals that had him nervous, then it must've been something else. Perhaps it was the tiny two-piece neon orange suit Ima wore. She took a moment to pretend she was adjusting her seat belt and leaned forward enough to get a closer look at Ima's barely covered honey-complexioned legs and thighs. It also appeared that her two double-D mares were trying to get out of their bra barn. *Have mercy, Jesus. Ima looks like she shops at Whores"R"Us.*

Sister Betty quickly leaned back and again looked out the passenger window. For the second time since they'd picked up Sharvon and Ima from the airport three weeks ago, she found herself breaking out in song. "Don't let this Devil ride . . . she'll wanna drive."

With all the small talk fallen by the wayside, Sister Betty said nothing more. It was the same with Leotis and Ima, until Leotis finally turned on one of the local gospel stations. Sister Betty hoped he'd done it perhaps to put a foot on the Devil's neck or, as she'd already prayed for, to keep his carnal thoughts in check. She'd seen him glance down toward Ima's uncovered thighs too often for it to be an accident. Besides, he couldn't see the road if he was looking down, or the traffic lights. Traffic lights never killed anyone; oncoming cars almost certainly did.

Sister Betty couldn't take another moment of the quasi silence. She had to speak up, and she intended to put the Devil in its place.

"Ima," she began, "I didn't mention it the last time I saw you, but it's too bad your engagement to Reverend Lyon Lipps didn't work out."

"I'm not sorry," Ima replied curtly. She looked over at Leotis to see if perhaps Sister Betty's mention of her engagement had meant anything. She saw no reaction.

"Really?" Sister Betty replied as she inched closer to the front seat without undoing her seat belt. "I thought the way you chased after the man, and him so seemingly bewitched by you, that there'd surely be a wedding."

Sister Betty fell back in her seat. She could tell by the way Leotis's earlobes suddenly twitched that he was doing a bad job of pretending not to pay attention. So she continued. "Well, perhaps it's not for you to marry or be in a relationship with a man of God. It would be very constricting to your lifestyle, I'm certain."

Wham! She'd laid it out there. If Leotis wasn't aware of Ima's recent past, well, now he was. Sister Betty let a smile appear. *I'm stopping this Devil in its tracks right now.*

Somehow Ima managed to turn around in her seat without unbuckling her seat belt. She was small enough to do so, and when she did, her tiny skirt rose higher.

"Well, Sister Betty . . ." Ima glanced quickly at Leotis. She seemed pleased to see his eyes dashing all over the front seat and zeroing in on her girlish possibilities, and even more pleased when he blurted, "Sweet Jesus!"

"As I was about to say," Ima continued, "I wasn't raised to knowingly commit adultery." She stopped and tapped Leotis on the arm, purring once she felt his hard muscle and happy he'd taken off his suit jacket. "That is against the Word, isn't it?"

"Yes, ma'am. God doesn't approve of such things." A bluish hue had spread across Leotis's fingers from gripping the steering wheel tightly. He suddenly felt as though he were losing his grip on his salvation and his sanity, too. He purposely didn't watch late-night cable television so as to keep his mind uncluttered by carnal things.

Sister Betty took a deep breath. She held her jaw until it began to ache. "What does adultery have to do with anything? As far as I know, you've never been married. So how is it you'd be committing adultery if you married Reverend Lipps? I hope it's not because he expected you to behave and dress like a first lady, and you couldn't see yourself doing so."

Ima fell against her seat; she began clapping before letting out a loud laugh. "Oh, Sister Betty, I didn't know you were so judgmental, despite your ole sanctified self."

Ima gently touched Leotis's muscle, this time through his cotton shirt. She stroked it again for a second before asking, "Did you know your spiritual mother was so judgmental? Do you approve of that, Reverend?"

Without saying a word, Leotis took one hand off the wheel and gently removed Ima's hand before returning his own to the steering wheel.

Although he'd not come along, somehow Sister Betty could feel Freddie tugging at her conscience. Despite his recent outburst and threats to Bea and Sasha, she knew he'd want her to back off, saying that it wasn't nothing but the Devil trying to score a hit.

Freddie wasn't there, and she wasn't about to back off. Instead, Sister Betty craned her neck, sucked her teeth, and said sharply to the back of Ima's neck, "Reverend Tom ain't got nothing to do with this!"

"I never said he did," Ima replied without turning to speak. "I believe you were butting into my business about Reverend Lipps."

"I'm not butting into your business. I'm just trying to have a conversation with you while we're driving to church. You're the one who brought up adultery. I'm sure you got enough sinning on your record without needlessly adding to it. I'm just trying to explain that you couldn't commit adultery, because you ain't ever been married, and even if you had once been married, as long as you weren't married when you remarried, it wouldn't be adultery."

Leotis said nothing, but his jaw began twitching as he listened.

"Well, thank you, most holy Sister Betty." Ima's lips slowly pursed before a smirk spread across her face. "I never said it was about me being married. I said I didn't want to commit adultery. It was your precious Reverend Lyon Lipps who was the one who was married."

Sister Betty sat there, stunned. It took her a moment to recover. She still didn't believe Ima. Reverend Lipps and his twin brother, Lionel, were renowned preachers. Everyone knew Lionel was married. He'd married one of their members, Sister Need Sum. If Lyon was married, too, he'd have certainly mentioned it. . . . Someone in his family would've.

Sister Betty clutched her Bible and held it in front of her, as though she expected Ima to swear by it. "What made you believe that he was married? Perhaps he just wanted to get out of the engagement."

"I didn't believe him at first," Ima began, smiling like a fox hired to watch a henhouse.

"But when his wife showed up with the marriage certificate a week before we were gonna do the deed, and he couldn't produce divorce papers, I sorta figured she had the upper hand. You know me. I don't like a lot of drama."

"You don't?"

"I sure don't. And, of course, Lyon didn't want any public drama, either. He settled real quick for breach of promise and a few other charges I threatened to file against him. Then, once he found out my aunt Sasha's brother, Uncle Brutus, was one of the divorce judges, he threw in a little extra to keep it out of the papers."

Before Sister Betty could reach down and pick her face up off the car mat, Ima had turned back around to face Leotis, whose jaw had dropped but no longer twitched.

Ima suddenly pointed to a large building. "You can let me out on this corner," she told Leotis. "Thank you again for your kindness in allowing me to ride along with you."

"It's not a problem for me," Leotis replied while staring through his rearview mirror at Sister Betty's grim face. "The offer for you to attend tonight's revival service still stands. If you can't get a ride, someone will certainly give you a lift. It's a two-week revival. You can't find but so many excuses not to attend."

Ima threw a smile toward Leotis. "You certainly know how to put a woman in a tight squeeze when it comes down to the church. Let me think on it, and I'll get back to you." Ima then winked at Sister Betty before wiggling her way out of her seat belt and onto the pavement. She said her good-byes and then took a double look at Sister Betty, who still remained plastered against the backseat, looking like she'd been Tasered.

"Sister Betty, are you okay?" Ima asked. "You look surprised. I got a job here the other day. It's something of a civic nature. It's what I do from time to time, in place of going to a morning church service. I'm what you might call a female heart defibrillator passing out books, Jell-O, and a lot of charm to the older men." Laughing again and not waiting for an answer from either Sister Betty or Leotis, Ima strutted away toward a building with the name SERENITY MALE NURSING HOME on its sign.

During the remaining ride to the church, Sister Betty and Leotis prayed, each silently and unknowingly, disappointed and questioning why they had given the Devil an inch. After all, they were on their way to a revival service, and not a moment too soon.

Once they arrived at the church, Leotis went to his study to prepare for the morning service. Sister Betty took the elevator down one floor to Crossing Over Sanctuary's fellowship hall.

To get to the fellowship hall, Sister Betty walked down a long white-paneled hallway. Hanging on the wall were four-teen-karat gold picture frames. President Barack Obama and Dr. Martin Luther King, Jr., were just a sample of those who had visited the church or had had a huge impact on it.

When she finally arrived, Sister Betty found the fellowship hall buzzing with excitement. She then remembered the combined choir was supposed to meet before the morning service. They were going to rehearse a special song selection meant as a surprise for Leotis. He'd said during a service that he'd worn out his Donnie McClurkin *Live in London & More* CD, with its rendition of "Great Is Your Mercy," and wished the choir would learn the track. She didn't have much of a singing voice, but Sister Betty had decided she wanted to be a part of such a blessed surprise.

The choir was singing the last refrain by the time she walked over. However, what she'd heard left no doubt that everyone had fasted and was prayed up, ready for the Lord to rain down the Holy Ghost fire. But, on the other hand, because of how she'd acted on the way to the service, she now felt convicted and unworthy to participate when it was time to sing. Lord, why did I allow Ima to mess with my testimony? she thought. Instead of delivering her normal and often over-the-top greetings of "My God is a good God" and "Ain't no Devil stealing my joy," she walked over to the other side of the fellowship hall with her head down, saying nothing to anyone who looked her way, and found someplace to sit by herself.

Freddie had arrived at the church about an hour ago. He and the other eleven trustees and elders sat at a table in a far back corner of the fellowship hall. The six men and six women, ranging in age from forty to seventy-five, were dressed in their ceremonial black-and-white attire and, from a distance, looked like a colony of penguins. He'd seen Sister Betty walk in, and when he noticed she hadn't spoken to anyone, not even giving a wave in his direction, he knew something was wrong.

Freddie stood up. He quickly closed the binder lying on the table in front of him and said, "Y'all, excuse me for a moment." Pointing to one of the other men, he added, "Elder Batty, keep on discussing the plans for the wedding surprise for Sister Betty. Just don't finalize nothing until I get back. I won't be but for a minute."

Sister Betty saw Freddie headed her way. He was doing his usual gallop, making the limp he'd gotten from a car accident appear more pronounced, and she knew he had something urgent on his mind. It was too late to get up and leave. She inwardly scolded herself for not doing so when she first saw him in the back of the room.

She began fingering the large cross hanging around her neck. She made a motion that looked to be more a comforting gesture than one done out of nervousness. The closer Freddie came, the more Sister Betty didn't like the way he looked. Several times in the past few weeks she'd noticed a dark and sometimes ashen appearance to his normally lemony complexion. And at that moment, it also occurred to her that it looked as though he'd begun losing his hair and the precious sprig he liked to twirl. Now he looked like he'd been in the sun too much. *Hmmm,* she thought. Now that he'd come closer, she looked at his eyes. She leaned her head as though she needed to see him sideways. His eyes . . . there was something about them that didn't set well with her. But just as she'd done for the past few weeks, she'd say nothing. "Criticizing is not a good way to keep a man," she'd always heard.

Sister Betty saw that Freddie was smiling; it seemed like a concerned smile, but it was a smile, nevertheless. Sister Betty took a deep breath, telling herself, *This is probably all in my head. It's good he's in such a good mood.* She needed to believe it, because she knew he'd disapprove once she confessed to what'd happened earlier on the ride to church.

Freddie reached out for Sister Betty, attempting to give her a quick embrace. It was a move the congregation had come to appreciate from such an elderly couple. They'd obliged their fellow church members by exchanging hugs every time they complimented her about her gorgeous and most expensive engagement ring. But this time Sister Betty didn't respond to his outreach as she normally would. She couldn't.

Freddie could almost feel the chill coming off her. "Honey Bee, what's wrong? Have I done something wrong?"

"No," she replied. "I have."

Sister Betty pointed to the empty chair

beside her, and Freddie sat. She told him how unbecoming she'd acted once she spied Ima seated in Leotis's car. She went on to tell him about the Jezebel type of clothing Ima had worn and the concern she had for Leotis's reputation if he continued to escort her about. By the time she finished telling Freddie about that morning's ride, she'd confirmed what she'd known from the start.

"Freddie, I am so ashamed. What if I was called upon to pray for Ima, or anyone, with those types of thoughts on my mind?"

Freddie looked at her, and a smile crept across his face. The furrows in his brow narrowed as he reached for her hand. "Honey Bee, don't be so hard on you."

"But you don't understand. . . ."

"Oh, but I do." Freddie then took her free hand in his. Smiling again, he continued. "Didn't I recently want to kill Bea and Sasha?"

"Yes."

"Did I do it?"

"No."

"Well, now look at it this way," Freddie said softly. "If Jesus got angry, why do you believe you can't? I've heard that one or more of those Hellraisers have angered just about everyone in this community for as long as Pelzer's been around. If you believe that getting angry with them is gonna keep you out of heaven or prevent your prayers from reaching there once you've asked God for forgiveness, then they've won and you've cheated yourself out of the victory. And you ain't giving God much credit for His grace and mercy, either."

Sister Betty began to smile so hard, she risked her partials falling out. His wisdom was one of the things she'd come to truly depend upon and love about him. "Freddie, God sure did right by me when he placed you in my life."

"Ditto, Honey Bee."

Sister Betty placed her Bible beside her on another open seat. She rose, quickly smoothing an invisible wrinkle on her long skirt. She bent over a little and took one of Freddie's hands in hers before whispering sweetly, "Lord, I just want to thank you." And before she could add, "For this great man you've given to me," Freddie's hand slipped from hers. He slumped over the side of his chair and onto the floor in a heap.

"Oh, Jesus!" she wept. "Please don't take him!" She alternated between calling on her God for His mercy and promising Freddie she'd never leave his side.

Chapter 6

The moment they got the news that Freddie had passed out, the intercessory prayer team sprang into action. Its members included several of the church's mothers' board, deacons and deaconesses. They, along with Leotis, raced to Freddie's side. Bea and Sasha, who'd never been on the intercessory prayer team during the entire time they ran the mothers' board, waited on the sidelines.

Sasha was truly speechless for the first few seconds. She then somehow discovered that she wasn't completely devoid of compassion when she asked Bea, "Don't you think we should go over and join them?"

Bea's eyes stayed laser focused upon those who were anointing Freddie with blessed oil, some even speaking in tongues, pointing God in Freddie's direction. Taking into account that everything done on Freddie's behalf was too serious to half step, Bea turned to Sasha. "No, I don't think we need to add to the misery. Wasn't we just talking this morning about getting back at Trustee Noel?"

"You're right, Bea," Sasha conceded with a sigh. "We got grudges against the man. We shouldn't risk God's wrath by pretending we don't by asking God for something on his behalf."

It took the ambulance almost five minutes to reach Crossing Over Sanctuary. During that time, Sister Betty waited and prayed while she coddled Freddie's head in her arms. His skin felt clammy but not ice cold. There was a grayish pallor to his skin and lips, while a bluish hue circled his closed eyes.

Bea and Sasha, along with many of the other onlookers, quickly parted like the Red Sea as soon as the EMT unit dashed into the fellowship hall. With the exception of the EMTs asking questions and barking orders, everyone was quiet.

As long as Sister Betty had lived in Pelzer, she'd never been inside its Anderson General Hospital's emergency room. Nor had she ever sat waiting for as long as she'd done so far today.

She was met with disappointment each

time someone with a stethoscope and a white jacket appeared and she thought, erroneously, that they had news about Freddie. She began squirming in her seat, as though there were a fire lit under her.

Shifting her Bible about in her lap, she suddenly remembered one of the occasions that'd brought her to that hospital. It was several years ago, when her longtime best friend and neighbor, Ma Cile Acker, passed away. She was godmother to Chandler, one of Ma Cile's grandchildren, whom they called June Bug when he was a child. The bad news had come within minutes. As sad as the memory was, she suddenly stopped squirming. *Maybe this is a good sign,* she thought as she squeezed Leotis's hand. If God had decided to take Freddie, surely the doctor would've come out and said something by now.

Now deep in thought, Sister Betty jumped when she suddenly felt Leotis patting her hand with one of his. He used his other hand to cradle her shoulders, pulling her closer to his chest. From the moment they'd left the church, he hadn't left her side.

"God's got this," Leotis whispered. "He didn't bring you and Trustee Noel this far to leave you two." He gently squeezed Sister Betty's shoulders, his way of putting finality to what he'd just said.

"I came as soon as I heard."

Both Leotis and Sister Betty looked up and discovered Sharvon standing before them. Leotis's double take didn't go unnoticed.

The hive of activity took a backseat once Sharvon had entered the room. Everyone, including medical staff, gave her an appreciative look. Her make-up was flawless. She had her long brown hair pulled back into a stylish French pleat. Her size four figure, covered by a chic dark green two-piece suit and a white blouse, looked amazing. The only thing missing from Sharvon was a stethoscope about her neck or a fashion photographer taking pictures. She looked like a cross between a doctor called in for a consultation and a runway model.

Leotis unraveled his arms from around Sister Betty's shoulders and stood. "Please have a seat," he told Sharvon. "I didn't mean that you should drop everything when I called." He lowered his voice, saying, "I've been trying to reach out to you for several days, and I'm glad you took my call this time. I'm sorry for the nine-one-one text, but I just wanted you to know what was happening with Sister Betty."

Sister Betty hadn't given Sharvon a second

thought from the moment Freddie collapsed. Yet she was glad Leotis had had the presence of mind to call the only family she had in Pelzer. "Thank you for coming, Sharvon," she said softly as Sharvon stood over her. "Right now I'm a mess and don't know if I'm coming or going."

Sharvon accepted Leotis's offer of his seat. Placing Sister Betty's hand in hers, she looked her older second cousin directly in the eye. "Listen, Cousin Betty, if I were in Freddie's condition and aware of my situation, I would not worry one bit. You have such an amazing connection to God. . . ."

Leotis hadn't meant to add anything but did. "Yes, you do have a prayer life unlike many I've ever known, and don't you ever forget it."

Leotis and Sharvon spent the next few minutes tag teaming Sister Betty. Leotis quoted scriptures, while Sharvon reminded Sister Betty of the strong love she and Freddie shared. Within a short time she calmed down, but within seconds the tears came flowing down her face, ending in a tiny puddle at the base of her throat.

Before Leotis rode to the hospital in the ambulance with Sister Betty, he'd turned the morning service over to one of the visiting preachers. He was a bright young man,

an up-and-coming preacher with a renowned prophetic gift, named Elder
Lamar L. Moore. He was a member of
Brooklyn, New York's St. Paul's Tabernacle
City of Lights Ministry, as well as a good
friend of Leotis's. Moments ago Elder
Lamar had arrived at the hospital with
about twenty members from Crossing Over
Sanctuary. He told Leotis that the Lord had
laid it upon his heart to give a very short,
fifteen-minute sermonette. He had obeyed
and then had dismissed the church to allow
all who wanted to go to the hospital to see
about Trustee Noel to do so.

As though he'd read Sister Betty's mind,
he treaded where the others had feared to
go. "Hopefully, whatever the problem with
the trustee is this time," Elder Lamar calmly
told Sister Betty as he smiled, "I don't
believe it will affect his ability to walk down
that aisle. I, for one, was so pleased to
receive an invite and can't wait to get back
here for your wedding." He turned in time
to witness the others from the church,
including Sister Betty, nodding in agreement.

Leotis rose, walked toward Elder Lamar,
and tapped him on his shoulder before leading him aside. "Thank you for that. I don't
know why I'd forgotten that the trustee's

health issues have led to the postponement of their first wedding date." He leaned in farther toward the elder, out of earshot of the others, before adding, "I'm not certain how long I'll be here with Sister Betty at the hospital. I don't want your trip here to be in vain. Please do me a favor."

"Certainly. What is it?"

"Preach your scheduled sermon. If you need any help with tonight's revival, I'm certain the deacons' board will be right there to assist."

"Of course I will." In the same quiet manner as he'd arrived, Elder Lamar turned and led those who'd accompanied him out of the waiting room and back to the church.

Sister Betty sat surrounded by several of the church prayer team members. They remained with her while Leotis and Sharvon, who'd also grown impatient, left to see if there was any further word on Freddie's condition. They soon returned with a doctor, but it wasn't one of those who'd seen Freddie when they first arrived.

While the others remained seated, Sister Betty rose to meet them.

"Miss Becton," the doctor began, "under normal circumstances I would not be able to discuss Mr. Noel's condition with you, because you're not a family member."

Sister Betty clutched her Bible to her chest. Her eyes darted about, almost pleading, as she replied, "But I will be soon." Pulling her Bible away from her chest, she extended it as though she wanted the doctor to swear upon it. "I've got to know. . . ."

"Please calm down, Miss Becton." The doctor stopped and pointed at Sharvon. "Your attorney has provided me with a duplicate legal power of attorney, such as the one that was among Mr. Noel's personal property when he arrived. The hospital is well aware that Mr. Noel has no living relatives."

Sister Betty, stunned, gave Sharvon a questioning look. When had she and Freddie drawn up such a document? She was happy they had, but why was it a secret? She didn't have time to dwell upon that. It was what it was.

The doctor was short and very thin and spoke with a noticeable facial tick that, after every few words, made him appear to smile. Dr. Lee Y. Chang was the name on his ID plate. "As I was saying," the doctor continued, "Mr. Noel is resting comfortably. We gave him several tests. Two returned with signs of perhaps old rib injuries. There's bruising that appears to support it. Other than that, none showed any trauma from his fall earlier today and were inconclusive as to its cause. There are other concerns that need addressing by his primary care provider. We've faxed over a report with that information."

Sister Betty took a few steps forward until she was almost nose to nose with the doctor. "Old rib injuries and bruising. I'm not quite sure what to make of it. What does all that mean?" She remained rooted in place, although he'd moved a few steps back. "Is my Freddie gonna be able to come home, or are you keeping him?"

"He's getting dressed as we speak. However, I'm not prepared to say this won't happen again, because we still don't know everything. He'll need further testing, and perhaps his medication may need adjusting."

"Further testing," Sharvon echoed. She was about to say more, but the look upon Leotis's face stopped her cold. Had he read the same thing in the doctor's voice as she had?

"I would suggest, since he lives alone, that you speak to our social services department. It's good that Mr. Noel is financially able to afford what many of our patients cannot. They can recommend or help you find a home attendant. For the time being, he'll need one who is able to spend at least six to eight hours a day with him."

"He won't need social services," Sister Betty said sharply. "I can take good care of him." She turned and pointed to Leotis and Sharvon. "My cousin Sharvon is staying with me. I can depend on her for help if I need it." Sister Betty then pointed at Leotis. "My pastor lives two doors away. I know without a shadow of a doubt, he'll be available to me and Freddie. He always has."

Both Sharvon and Leotis nodded, confirming what Sister Betty had said.

The doctor withdrew a small pad from his breast pocket. "That's good to know." He then began writing something on the pad. "This is a prescription that should for the moment help with his high blood pressure. As I said before, some other meds may need adjusting, but I don't want to do that. Let his private doctor render a more complete diagnosis and make a final decision."

Sister Betty's face fell. "High blood pressure." She looked at Leotis and several others standing about. "A moment ago when you were rattling off a bunch of things, but I didn't hear you say nothing before about any high blood pressure."

"Well, it was very high when he arrived," the doctor said calmly. "I'm just taking precautionary measures until his doctor can get to the root of today's episode."

The doctor pivoted toward Leotis and extended his hand. "It was good seeing you again, Leotis. It's been quite some time since I've visited your medical care center at the Promised Land complex on an on- cology or geriatric visit. I hope we can get together and return to the community outreach the ideas we've shared in the past. I also hope it will be under different circum- stances."

"Of course, Lee," Leotis replied. "Anytime Crossing Over Sanctuary can be of as- sistance, you know we will."

As the doctor walked away, Sister Betty gave Leotis a questioning look.

"I already know what you're thinking," Leotis told her. "And, yes, I know Doctor Chang. He's on the Pelzer community outreach board and comes to the Promised Land twice a month to help treat the resi- dents. It's picked up quite a bit since President Obama's Health Care Reform Act went into effect."

Leotis didn't have a chance to finish explaining. The sound of a familiar purring voice came through the din of the emer- gency room.

Ima raced through the others, knocking

95

them aside like they were bowling pins. She walked quickly toward Sister Betty with her hands extended. Instead of continuing toward Sister Betty, she turned and shoved her body in between Leotis and Sharvon, still wearing the "almost nothing" neon orange outfit from earlier that day.

"Aunt Sasha only told me a short time ago about Sister Betty's fiancé. I rushed right over. Oh my goodness, I am so sorry." Ima immediately reached up and tapped Leotis on one of her favorite parts of his anatomy — his muscular bicep. She directed her eyes toward Sharvon as she continued speaking to Leotis. "I should've never let you and Sister Betty continue on to service without me," she said, pursing her lips. "If I'd come to morning service, like you wanted me to, I probably could've done something to help."

"Like what?" Sharvon snapped. She didn't bother to cover up her annoyance with Ima. "This is a family matter." Sharvon stopped and pointed toward the others, who'd remained out of earshot. "You can join the others if you intend on staying."

Ignoring Sharvon's sharp rebuke, Ima wiggled closer to Leotis. "Reverend Tom, I didn't know you were family, too."

Leotis quickly pulled away from Ima. He

scanned Sharvon's and Sister Betty's faces for help and found nothing but disapproval. He received the same looks from several of his congregation members, too. He prayed for words to say that were stern yet not too harsh. He'd learned in the short time since they'd met that she might have the reputation of being the Devil's spawn, but Ima was still a soul that needed saving. Without meaning to do so, he hastily glanced down, catching a glimpse of her long, lean legs. The smooth caramel skin on her legs still had a honey glow about it. Her legs looked as though they'd been polished with some type of body butter.

He jerked his head away and sighed. *Satan, I rebuke you!* He could imagine the Devil laughing at his fleshly state. He shook his head, as though trying to block the Devil's laugh, and hoped he wasn't in danger of losing his soul while trying to save hers.

Chapter 7

Just as she said she would, Sister Betty cared for Freddie in her home. When Sharvon wasn't working a twelve-hour day at her new law firm, she played nursemaid while Sister Betty napped or needed a ride to the church's food bank. The food bank was started by Sister Betty and Ma Cile years ago, when they'd first come into some extra money. Next to God and Freddie, making sure that others had as much to eat as she had was a priority.

It happened that Leotis had some out-of-town business previously scheduled. He had dropped in only twice since Freddie began staying at Sister Betty's. Yet he called quite often and ended the calls praying with Sister Betty while Freddie listened in on her speakerphone.

All during that first week of Freddie's release from Anderson General, church members flooded Sister Betty's home. Some called ahead, but a lot didn't.

"Praise be to God," most would say as they slowly entered. It didn't go unnoticed to Sister Betty that those who'd been there before went immediately toward her bedroom. "He's not in my bedroom," she'd say while redirecting them to one of the spare guest rooms, where Freddie lay, pretending he was asleep. It usually worked because Sister Betty would whisper, "He's really not up to much company. Y'all know how it is."

Even Bea and Sasha stopped by to say hello but wouldn't stay long. "All's forgiven," they told her. The only concern they truly had was whether or not Freddie looked well enough to go through with the wedding. They needed to see for themselves since they had no intention of not throwing the reception that'd launch their ill-conceived event-planning business. Of course, like the others, they also wanted to see if he was in the same bedroom as Sister Betty, or just how close her bedroom was to his room. They didn't want to plan a reception that wouldn't happen, especially because two old, inexperienced fools did something carnally to cause heart attacks.

On two occasions Ima, dressed in the least amount of clothing legally allowed, came with them. She didn't stay too long once she learned Leotis wasn't there. On one of those occasions Sharvon went out of her way by naming a piece of trash she'd tossed into the garbage Ima.

Oddly enough, the only visitors Freddie seemed happy to receive were the other members of the trustees' board. Although he was a guest in her home, he'd go so far as to have them shut the door so Sister Betty couldn't overhear what they discussed. "Just some old boring trustees' board nonsense," he'd explain. "It's nothing for you to worry about. You do too much already."

"Oh, you're too much, Freddie," she replied on one occasion, before saying, "That's the same excuse you give me when you won't let me go to those doctor visits with you. You've gone twice, and I only have your say-so about what the doctor says."

"Oh, stop worrying, Honey Bee. I've told you that everything is fine. I just need to stop acting like I'm twenty," he told her. "Trust me. God's got my full attention."

Caring for the longtime bachelor didn't come with any particular rewards, as Sister Betty soon learned. He sometimes resented her fussing over him.

"Honey Bee, please stop. I'm not helpless," he'd ranted when, on occasion, she'd

100

try to spoon-feed him. One of those times, she'd made a big pot of chicken noodle soup with bits of vegetables and chicken, thick enough to choke any man three times his size.

Often, during the hottest part of the day, she'd tiptoe into the room and quickly tuck the sheets about him as he slept. He would awaken and look like a mummy, with nothing but his head and a remnant of what was once his sprig showing. "Sorry, Freddie," she'd whisper if she woke him. "I've got to make sure you get well."

He'd somehow quickly free himself from the sheet jail and command, "Then stop trying to kill me with kindness!"

Their usual prayerful atmosphere and playful moods, with such endearing words as "honey" and "Freddie dear," took a downward turn. The couple who'd planned in a few short months to say "I do" and spend their remaining days together couldn't spend one or two weeks under the same roof where either gave an inch.

It all came to a head at the end of the second week of Freddie's stay. He wasn't supposed to drive unless he got the okay from the doctor, and today's visit would, hopefully, give him back his freedom.

However, things went wrong: the Access-a-Ride bus broke down, and another wasn't available until much later. It meant he'd be too late for his doctor's appointment. Leotis wasn't available to take Sister Betty to the food bank or Freddie to his scheduled doctor's visit. Sharvon had called, saying she was stuck at work and wouldn't be taking a lunch hour. She couldn't do it, either.

"We can always take a taxi," Sister Betty suggested, reaching for the pad by the telephone, where she kept frequently dialed numbers. "It could drop me off at the church and take you on to the doctors."

"Nah," Freddie said quickly. "You call a cab for yourself. I'm thinking about calling Elder Batty instead. He don't do nothing anyhow but sit around all day, begging Bea for a slice of her red velvet cake or whatever she's done lately to make him act crazy. He's probably available."

An hour or so before Elder Batty was to arrive, Sister Betty needed to go around the corner to Freddie's house. She wanted to retrieve some things he'd been asking for. Things such as his shaving cream, razor, and solid stick deodorant were high on his list, along with clean underwear, which he'd run out of the day before. She could've washed his underwear, but he wasn't having it.

When she'd earlier suggested he let her buy those things, he wasn't having that, either. "Honey Bee," he'd told her, "how would it look with you buying my drawers and we ain't even married yet? Besides, I'm feeling pretty good, but imagine how much better I'd look and smell if I had those things that I personally bought?"

Sister Betty threw up her hands in surrender. "Just rest a bit in my room until I get back," she'd told him. "I haven't put the clean sheets on your bed yet."

"Okay, Honey Bee," he'd replied, smiling. "I guess it don't make sense to climb atop no clean sheets until I bathe and change from everything I've been wearing for the past day and a half. Don't you rush none, either. You walk slowly. I don't want you passing out in this heat." He chuckled at his attempt at poking fun at his passing out at church.

Sister Betty left Freddie sitting in her room, watching television, and she did what he'd asked. She walked slowly around the corner to his house.

As it happened, Elder Batty arrived early, after she had gone to Freddie's house. He was available but wasn't alone. When he showed up, he brought Bea along.

Sister Betty, in her hurry to get to

Freddie's home and back, left her side door slightly ajar. Seeing that the door was not completely closed, Elder Batty reached for the doorbell. Bea was quicker than he was, and acted as though she lived there, too, and with the full rights of any tenant, Bea reached for the door handle and pushed the door completely in.

"Sister Betty," Elder Batty called out as he followed Bea inside and stopped in the foyer. "I'm a bit early. Where are you?"

Instead of Bea waiting for an answer, she walked quickly through the foyer. She ducked her head inside the kitchen, and when she didn't find Sister Betty there, she headed toward the back of the house, where she knew Sister Betty's bedroom, along with the spare guest rooms, were. Bea waddled just past Sister Betty's bedroom; then she quickly backtracked. Her fat jaw almost dropped to her chest, and the hunch in her back went from looking like the letter *C* to an *I*. Bea came face-to-face with Freddie. He had just stepped out of the shower in preparation for Sister Betty's return and was dressed in nothing but the skin the good Lord gave him.

By the time Sister Betty was two houses away from reaching her own, she heard the yelling. One quick glance at the church van in her driveway told her that Elder Batty had arrived. *What in the world is all that yelling about?* She began picking up speed and rushed inside her house. Inside her living room she found Bea all up in Freddie's face, with her finger pointed at him. Elder Batty was standing with his arms stretched out, trying to separate the two, and Freddie, for whatever reason, was wearing one of her housecoats.

"Bea Blister, what in the world is you doing in my house, acting crazier than usual?" Sister Betty flung the bag she'd carried onto a nearby chair. She immediately went at Bea. "I said, what's going on?"

Bea swallowed hard. She took a few steps back from Freddie but kept her finger waving at him while turning to face Sister Betty. "I believe the real question is, why do you have a naked man in your bedroom? You supposedly so saved. I knew you wasn't nothing but a hypocrite!"

"Calm down, Bea," Elder Batty warned. "This ain't none of your business!"

"Check this old demon before I knock her out!" Freddie yelled but couldn't finish. He had become winded and could barely manage to find his way onto the sofa without falling.

"Bea Blister," Sister Betty shouted as she

raced to Freddie's side. "I don't know what you're talking about, and frankly, I don't care. But if you don't take your . . ." For the first time in her adult life and since she'd given her life to Jesus, Sister Betty wanted to cuss. Instead she snapped, "Big behind out of my house . . ."

Freddie quickly began perspiring, and Sister Betty raced to the kitchen, returning with a cold, wet cloth to wipe his brow.

Freddie swept Sister Betty's hand away. "I'm okay. I don't need that or no babying."

In the meantime the argument that'd started between Bea and Freddie spilled over, and now it was Elder Batty's turn for scolding.

Bea balled up one fat fist. She rammed her fingers through the mauve-colored beehive wig she wore, as though looking for a hidden weapon, before she shot a nasty look at Elder Batty. "That's why you always out of that male-enhancing pill, ain't it?" Bea accused and pointed back at Freddie. "You've been sharing it with this alleged man virgin!"

As soon as the words left Bea's mouth, the temperature in the room chilled to zero degrees. Bea's angry admission of her and Elder Batty's use of Viagra quieted the room.

Sister Betty rose, with her wig now tilted a little to the side and looking like a flower behind her ear. "Say what?"

Freddie reached down from where he sat, and closed the snaps on the housecoat he wore. They'd popped open as he'd prepared to take a swing at Bea, so he couldn't follow through with it.

And Elder Batty's face turned a shade of red that did not make him look good at all.

With nothing left unsaid, and Freddie still needing to get to the doctor's, Freddie grabbed the bag Sister Betty had tossed onto the chair, and left the room to dress.

Elder Batty pulled out his cellular phone. "I'm putting an end to this craziness right now." He turned and gave Bea a nasty side look, while at the same time shaking his head in amazement. "Hello," he said quickly into the phone. "I need a cab in a hurry. . . ."

Bea began railing almost as soon as Elder Batty began dialing for a cab to take her home. "You ain't just gonna call me no cab and think that's the end of this!" Bea turned around to face Sister Betty, and her face turned a darker shade of black as she began rocking from side to side, warming up for what she thought would be a knockout punch. Her wig du jour, which now resembled a possum on her head, slid two inches off her scalp and onto her right ear.

"And you better believe that as much as you may want me to do it" — Bea leaned forward and pointed her finger in Sister Betty's face — "there ain't no way in hell I'm going to give you no wedding reception!"

Sister Betty didn't back away an inch. Vile words rolled from Sister Betty's brain down into her mouth to escape into the open, but her tongue got in the way. Instead of saying something that she'd certainly need to repent for, she allowed her partials the freedom to roam from one side of her mouth to the other while giving off a clicking sound each time. "I never asked you for no wedding reception, and I didn't ask you to come to my house!"

"Well, who else was gonna give your high-and-mighty self a reception? Just name one person who has known you for as long as I have, and can still want to do something nice for ya." Bea tried to straighten her back slowly, so as not to show how much pain she was in, and just as she finished, the sound of the cab honking caused her to lean over again.

Bea went on. "It ain't over. I'm going straight to the church when I leave here. I'm heading for your beloved food bank to shout it out. And I know some of them rehearsing on the senior choir would be very interested in the unholy goings-on in your so-called sanctified house!"

Sister Betty crossed her arms over her breasts and leaned back as she threatened Bea. "You go running that mouth about something you know nothing about, and I've got one word for you in front of the entire congregation that'll make you wish you hadn't."

"Oh, really?" Bea replied. "Just what you got to say that's gonna shut my mouth and stop me from telling the whole world about you being a high-minded hypocrite?"

Sister Betty straightened her wig, and looking Bea square in the eye, she yelled, "Viagra!"

CHAPTER 8

Several days later, after Freddie had seen the doctor and returned with the good news that he could drive again, Sister Betty found time to call Leotis. She could've left a message when she didn't reach him after the hospital fiasco with Ima, but she wanted to say her piece directly to him. A short time later she finally reached him at home. As much as she'd determined she'd fuss at him, she found she couldn't. He seemed in such a good mood, and actually, she was, too.

"Today is so bright, so warm, and just so beautiful, and of course, God is so good," she declared. "I feel the same now as I did the other day, and I could've just shouted for joy right there in my living room. You just can't imagine the relief I felt when Freddie told me that the doctor said the medicine he's taking has his blood pressure under control."

"That's a good thing," Leotis replied with a tone that didn't seem as jubilant as Sister Betty's. "We got to get you two to that altar. We don't want unnecessary stumbles along the way because he doesn't like taking medicine. God gave us doctors for a reason."

"I just hope you continue conveying that message to Freddie. He fights me tooth and nail about taking his medicine and trying to help him get well. He says faith should be all the medicine he needs."

Sister Betty and Leotis chatted a bit longer. She was laughing while complaining about the trustees' stubbornness. She, however, never mentioned the fiasco from Bea's recent visit, as well as her threats. Meanwhile, whenever she talked about how she'd love to see him settle down, too, and give the church a first lady, he avoided her innuendos regarding any possible attraction to Sharvon, or vice versa, as a possibility.

Despite the good-natured conversation they were having, Sister Betty decided she needed to say her original piece, after all. He'd just have to hear her out.

"You know better than to try and make any attempt at soul saving with Ima," she said in a matter-of-fact manner. "God don't want you ending up in no fatal attraction situation." And then, as had become her recent habit of doing, she gave him the same advice she'd give all day, every day. "Just remember what happened to that rabbit in that pot. Ima might make ya hot . . . but you'll burn in hell if you take your hand off of God's plow."

As usual, Leotis laughed it off, hoping to end the call on a good note. "You take care, my wonderfully anointed spiritual mother. I love you, and there's nothing you can do about it."

"You know I feel the same way about you." There was a short pause, however. Sister Betty hadn't hung up yet and neither had Leotis when she suddenly heard a familiar female voice in the background. She couldn't hear or understand everything, but she could feel her face contorting into a disapproving scowl. Was Ima there this entire time?

Her peace of mind quickly plummeted, leaving in its place questions. As if she were his natural mother, she began to worry. *Sweet Jesus, how can he allow her into his home? He's supposed to shun every appearance of evil.*

Even though Leotis had central air-conditioning blasting throughout his home, beads of sweat suddenly peppered his

112

forehead. He almost broke his telephone when he slammed it down, hoping Sister Betty had hung up before Ima came out of his bathroom and began speaking. While there was a grim look that crept across his face, he saw a look of complete satisfaction upon Ima's.

Ima took one hand and tossed back her long hair, which had covered long gold loop earrings, now swinging to a rhythm he couldn't hear but was certain was seductive. Humming an off-key melody, she sashayed over toward where Leotis stood rooted by his desk.

He quickly looked away. He shook his head, remembering how it'd been only minutes ago when she appeared on his porch. She'd been uninvited, and her boldness had surprised and paralyzed him.

With the sunlight framing her beautiful face and causing the normal specks of brown to appear darker in her green eyes, she'd removed any chance of him not allowing her to enter his house. Her perfume rivaled the fragrance from the roses spread about his yard, making him want to inhale continuously, as though the scent caused orgasms. She had on a formfitting red- and white-striped sundress, wearing it as if it had been designed solely for her, and her painted toenails peeked out of sandals of the same color and pattern.

"Thank you for allowing me to use your bathroom," Ima purred. "I guess if Sister Betty had been home when I passed through this neighborhood, I could've used hers."

The way she'd spoken the lie had a sobering effect. She'd done it easily, and he wasn't certain if she hadn't convinced herself. "Are you certain you knocked hard enough or rang her doorbell?" He wavered between calling her a liar outright and getting her to admit it on her own.

"Look at me, Reverend." Ima took a step back so she could present him with all she'd brought to work him over with. "I'm too small to knock but so hard or press persistently on a doorbell." She stopped to lift a leg, holding it in midair to fix a sandal strap that needed no fixing. As if the sunlight had followed her inside, its rays filtered through Leotis's living room window. A seductive halo formed around Ima's mango body-buttered leg. She turned her ankle so he could get a good glimpse. She'd been around long enough to know a leg man when she saw one, and she'd bet all she had that he was definitely one. Slowly lowering her leg, she continued with mock remorse. "I guess upon second thought, though,

Sister Betty is old. Perhaps she don't hear as well anymore and I should've knocked harder."

Ima didn't wait for Leotis to respond. She went directly into the second act of her self-directed play. "Please, again, accept my apology for barging in. I should've known better than to bother a man in the midst of doing the Lord's work."

"It's not like we haven't had this discussion." Her lie having a sobering effect or not hadn't stopped Leotis from sweating. His heart pounded. He cleared his throat, losing count of how many times he'd done so since she'd raised and lowered her leg. "Neither of us would want to give anyone or the other the wrong impression." He then quickly folded his arms and nodded toward the door. "I think you'd better go —"

Ima's eyes lit up as she interrupted Leotis, asking playfully, "Says who?"

While Leotis and Ima played a game of kitty and mouse in heat, a few doors away, Sharvon arrived home. She walked inside the kitchen, greeting Sister Betty and tossing her briefcase onto one of the counter chairs before heading straight for the refrigerator. She poured a glass of lemonade, drinking it in one gulp.

"You must be exhausted working these nine- and ten-hour days, running back and forth between your office and home," Sister Betty told her. "How much longer will you need to do that? It's been almost a month and a half nonstop."

"You worry too much," Sharvon replied between gulps from a second glass. Licking her lips and turning the glass in her hand, she said, "I tell you, this is so good. It's like precious liquid gold. But I can't stay. I've got to go out again."

"Again?"

"Yes, I caught a cab home. My car broke down over by the Anderson Library."

"Are you okay?"

"I'm tired, but other than that, I'm fine." Sharvon rinsed out her glass and set it on the counter before reaching for the telephone on the wall. "I've got to call another cab to take me back."

Sister Betty walked over to Sharvon and gently took the telephone from her hand. There was a noticeable twinkle in her eyes, and a playful grin appeared. "It don't make sense spending all that hard-earned money on no cab to go so far."

"It's not like I can't afford it." Sharvon laughed. "I'm almost filthy rich since you won't allow me to pay rent. And that reminds me." Sharvon placed her arms around Sister Betty's small shoulders. "I'm going to need you to deposit those checks I gave you toward the telephone bills and all the dry cleaning you keep picking up for me and paying for."

"You'll have plenty of time to repay me when you hit the really big time with your new partnership." Sister Betty slipped out of Sharvon's grasp and headed toward the living room. She arrived just in time to answer the phone, which had rung just once.

"Hello."

"Sister Betty, I need your help!"

Sister Betty placed the telephone closer to her ear. Leotis was whispering, and she could only imagine why. "Why are you whispering in your own home? What's the matter?"

"Sister Betty, it's about Ima, and I don't know what to do."

"What about her?"

"I know she's gone through a lot with her former fiancé hurting her, and she's probably just seeking attention, but she can't be popping up on my doorstep anytime she pleases."

"I tried to tell you those Hellraisers gonna land you in hell if you don't stand your ground —"

"You just hold on, Leotis. I'm coming over there right now!"

"Sharvon," Sister Betty snapped, "why are you in my conversation?"

"I'm sorry, Cousin Betty. I picked up the phone the same time you did. Besides, *our* pastor needs help with that trollop, and I am an attorney. I can help!"

Leotis spoke up quickly. "That's all right, Miss Sharvon!"

But Leotis wasn't quick enough, and neither was Sister Betty. Sharvon had slammed down the phone and was practically out the front door before either of them could say another word.

Sister Betty snatched a spare bottle of blessed oil off the fireplace mantel and raced out the door.

A few minutes later Sharvon stood in Leotis's living room, her hand on one hip and her finger pointed in Ima's face. "This man of God does not want you stepping on and off his property or inside his home anytime you feel like!"

Sister Betty heard Sharvon's voice booming through Leotis's open door as soon as she stepped onto his front porch. No sooner had she come inside his living room than she saw Armageddon in full swing. Sharvon was still dressed in a nice pair of blue fitted slacks, a white short-sleeved blouse, and See by Chloé three-hundred-dollar, five-inch white sandals. Nothing she wore was a match for Ima's hooker-work gear. Despite his call for help, Ima's man-getting halter top held Leotis's eyes imprisoned. It didn't look like he was trying to escape.

"If he didn't want me stopping by when I'm in the neighborhood, then he could've said so," Ima lied to Sharvon. "The cat ain't got his tongue."

Oh yes, that cat does have that tongue, Sister Betty thought as she looked over at Leotis. O*r he would've said something during the three minutes that I've been standing here.*

"Well, I'm here now as his attorney, and I'm telling you to back off, before I get a restraining order on your trifling behind."

"Who are you calling a *trifling behind*?" Ima's huge bosom seemed to swell, threatening to break loose and breast slap Sharvon. Her green eyes became the color of moss as she stepped forward, placing both hands on her hips, but nowhere near where Sharvon could reach out and snatch her by her halter. Words shot out of her mouth, aiming with accuracy at Sharvon. "I work hard for what I have!"

Using the space Ima had left between them, Sharvon took several steps in Ima's direction, stopping within a couple of inches. "And I'm certain your *back* must be killing you from it." Sharvon, who was only slightly taller than Ima at five foot eight to Ima's five-six, then took a few steps back, leaving her anger still in Ima's space. "Spend time with a chiropractor and stay away from my client! I am not telling you again."

During the time the two young women traded barbs, Sister Betty had moved quickly to the other side of the room. She stood by Leotis, who remained by the telephone. She leaned in. "You're a man of God, son," she whispered loudly in his ear. She thought it was the only way of getting him out of the she-devil's trance.

He jumped just a little, which told Sister Betty she'd surprised him. Still whispering loudly, she snapped, "You letting this go on and from the way you drooling, I'd say you was enjoying it a bit too much."

It took Leotis a few minutes to finally move from his comfortable buzzard perch. He began talking in his bass-like preaching voice, trying to sound in charge. "I'm trying to be as delicate as I can, and it doesn't seem to work. So from this point on, I will act as I should. I'm not a best friend. I'm a man of God who will be available only for spiritual matters, unless it's a matter of the utmost urgency. Is that clear, ladies?"

"Yes, Reverend Leotis Tom," Ima purred. She shot a quick glance toward Sharvon. "You can call off your legal buzzard."

"Sharvon does not handle any of my legal affairs!" The words had flown out of his mouth a full two seconds before his brain had a chance to choose them wisely. The pained and embarrassed look on Sharvon's face made him feel as though he'd stabbed someone who'd wanted only to help. *Lord, help me.*

Sharvon didn't say a word — not to Sister Betty or to Leotis — and never looked in Ima's direction. She held her head high, losing count of how many times he'd tossed her feelings aside in Ima's presence. She turned and slowly walked out the front door, leaving behind any thoughts of or plans for saving Leotis from himself for him in her love life.

No sooner had Sharvon walked out the door than Ima looked at Sister Betty. With her back now to Leotis, Ima winked and quickly extended her left hand. She wiggled her vacant ring finger before giving her a thumbs-up and a wide grin. Quickly dropping the facade, she turned around. Her eyes appeared watery as she looked at him.

Sister Betty glared at Ima's back. She knew Ima had just given her an "I won" gesture. But Sister Betty had a look, too. She peered past Ima and gave Leotis a look that said, "You've lost big-time."

During the days after Leotis put his foot down, shaming Sharvon and surrendering his willpower to Ima to continue her shameless pursuit, Sharvon was away on a case consultation in Spartanburg, South Carolina. All that week, whenever possible, she'd call home. Each time Sister Betty tried to bring up Leotis's name, no matter the context, the conversation between them was always the same, and tonight wasn't any different.

Sister Betty began their conversation by speaking so fast, it was hard to tell if she was speaking English or in tongues. "Sharvon, I wish you'd been here last Friday night," she gushed. "Chile, the service was hot. The young adult choir almost came out of their robes when they sang 'He's Able.' And you know Bea and Sasha almost beat each other down to the floor, trying to outshout one another."

Sharvon's reply was quick and a bit out of character, yet she left no doubt that she wasn't interested. "Well, you know Mother

Sasha and Bea should just go ahead and sign up for a WWE wrestling match and get it over with," she told Sister Betty. Sharvon then began laughing, almost to the point where she seemed to lose her breath.

She's trying so hard, Sister Betty thought. *I wish she would just forgive Leotis so she could get back to her old self.*

"Hmmm, so, Cousin Betty, how is the wedding planning coming along? You don't have a lot of time, because fall is just around the corner."

"Freddie and I are still trying to decide on a few honeymoon details, but you and I can discuss the wedding later in person." At this moment neither the wedding nor the honeymoon was something she wanted to discuss. She really wanted Sharvon to get over her anger with Leotis and not let Ima get the upper hand. Sharvon wouldn't have to date Leotis if she didn't want to; she just needed to make sure he didn't let Ima dig her claws into his oughta-be-sanctified soul.

Sister Betty inhaled, silently prayed for wisdom. This was her younger second cousin, the only daughter of her closest first cousin, Belle. From the time Sharvon came to visit after burying Belle over in Belton, South Carolina, six months ago, Sister Betty had stepped up to the plate, trying to become as close to Sharvon as she was certain Belle would've wanted.

Taking a deep breath, Sister Betty continued. "Reverend Tom preached so hard that before the congregation knew it, he'd gone deep into the Word of God and taken us up before the throne of grace."

"Well, some of those preaching *the Word* so high and mighty are the very ones that's living the lowest!" Sharvon spoke quickly, stepping all over Sister Betty's praises of Leotis. "Right now there is nothing that man can do to make me believe that he's all of what he preaches."

"Oh, Sharvon, you've got to forget about Ima. She don't mean nothing to Leotis. I know it. He's just trying to save a soul the best way he knows how."

"No, he's not!" Sharvon shot back. "He's trying to save his ass the best way he knows how!"

Sister Betty was shocked, not only at Sharvon's attitude but also at her language. The word *ass* as it was used in the Bible meant "mule." Although at that moment, Sharvon definitely was acting as stubborn as a mule. Sister Betty was certain that a mule was the farthest thing from Sharvon's mind.

A few minutes later Freddie arrived just as

Sister Betty hung up from her telephone call with Sharvon. Before he could give her a peck on the cheek, missing her face by inches, she began pacing back and forth.

Sister Betty began reciting chapter and verse to Freddie. Sharvon's words had stung and were trapped in her ears, and in her heart, and needed releasing.

"Honey Bee, are you sure you heard her correctly?"

Sister Betty twisted her lips, as if he'd said something disgusting to hurt her feelings. "I have good hearing, Freddie. I know what she said. I'm telling you that Sharvon tore Leotis's Christian reputation apart, as though he'd never done a good thing for nobody! She cussed, too!"

"Honey Bee, I'm sorry this whole mess has upset you." Freddie sat on the sofa, and with nothing else coming to mind that would immediately calm her, he pulled from under his arm a packet of brochures he'd been holding. "I am hoping that perhaps we can finalize our honeymoon plans. I need to put down a deposit as soon as possible since I couldn't get the money back from the cruise we missed."

They had decided months ago, when they'd begun making plans, that they wanted to spend their honeymoon in places where neither of them had ever been. They'd settled on Mexico and Jamaica. They'd gotten as far as deciding that it would not be Dunn's River Falls, because they were too old to climb slippery rocks, plus neither would wear a bathing suit in public.

When he'd fallen ill almost nine months ago and the wedding had been postponed, they had to start anew with their planning. Although Sister Betty seemed preoccupied with everything that was happening with Sharvon, Leotis, and Ima, earlier that day Freddie had gone ahead with the planning. He'd added Cozumel to their itinerary. All he needed now was for her to say, "Okay, honey. That's perfect." But she didn't seem interested enough to even ask about the brochures now lying plainly in his hands. She also didn't seem to notice the sad face that'd replaced the one of concern a moment ago.

CHAPTER 9

Several days after Ima's visit to Leotis's house, Ima left her sparsely furnished apartment in a poorer area of Pelzer. It was the only area she could afford at that moment, and she was truly happy that the reverend had never offered to drive her home, although that was what she'd wanted. She was sure she could handle the awkward situation if things went her way. Feeling the need to clear her head, she decided that instead of driving, she'd walk the ten blocks to visit Sasha. She stepped off the elevator just in time to find Sasha returning to her apartment from emptying the trash in the incinerator.

Between the elevator and the four doors separating it from Sasha's apartment, Ima declared, "I'm marrying Reverend Leotis Tom."

"Get real," Sasha replied as they entered her apartment. "I'd rather believe a chicken has an udder and cows have feathers."

"Oh, you'd better believe it," Ima bragged. "I'm gonna become a first lady."

"And just how will this miracle happen?" Sasha sucked her teeth hard enough for her dentures to slip. She used her tiny tongue to push them back into place before she began chiding Ima. "First of all," Sasha said, "what do you know about being the first lady of a church? You've only come close to being a first lady by way of a dumb engagement to a married preacher."

"Whatever!"

"No, it's not *whatever*," Sasha snapped. "It's whenever. It's whenever you get one of those ridiculous ideas in your head about a man, you always come up with the short end of the condom."

"Say what you wanna," Ima said, pointing her finger in Sasha's face. "I have a plan, and when I'm done, that man will see me as nothing but first-class first lady material!" Ima quickly turned on her heels and left Sasha's apartment. With no time or desire to wait on the elevator, she raced through the exit door instead and took the steps down.

That afternoon Ima went shopping in downtown Anderson. She managed to max out several of her credit cards by shopping in expensive boutiques. When she finished, she called Leotis. She decided not to leave a message when his answering machine at home answered. Instead, she called the cell phone number on the business card he'd given her when they first met.

"This is Reverend Leotis Tom speaking. How may I help you?"

The deep Isaac Hayes sound of his bass voice coming through the cell phone gripped Ima as though it'd lassoed her entire being. She'd fallen for other men from time to time, but she'd never swooned at the sound of a voice, not even Barry White's, whose sexy music she kept on repeat.

"Hello, Reverend," Ima said softly. "I hope I haven't disturbed you, but I feel so awkward from how things went the other day. I'm not certain what to do."

"You don't have to do anything, Ima. I believe I made myself clear to you and Sharvon."

At the mention of Sharvon's name, Ima clenched the cell phone hard enough for it to crack. Somehow she maintained her composure, because she had other things to consider.

"I know you feel that it was settled, but I

don't. And just to show you that I mean no harm and would really like for us to be friends, I have an offer."

"That's not necessary," Leotis said with a questioning tone. The way the conversation was going, he wasn't sure if Ima was setting him up for something confrontational or if his semi-harsh words had finally gotten through to her. "I'm going to accept your apology at face value," he told her. "I need to return to Pelzer, and the traffic in downtown Anderson is bumper to bumper right now."

As soon as Ima heard the words *downtown Anderson,* she took it as a sign that her plan was ordained. Perhaps God was showing her favor, but she'd just have to work a little harder to get this man.

"I know what you mean about this traffic," Ima replied. "I'm stuck in it myself, as we speak. I'm about ready to just pull over and wait for the rush hour to die down, or whatever is that's causing the delay to go away."

"Oddly enough," Leotis said, chuckling, "I thought about doing the same." Leotis looked at his reflection in his rearview mirror. He had a big grin on his face, and there was no one responsible for it at that moment but Ima. He wasn't sure if that was a good thing or not.

"I've got an idea," she told him.

"Should that make me nervous?" Leotis teased.

Ima sensed him weakening. "Probably, but not today," she sighed. "I'm sure you're probably hungry, and like me, you're not a fan of fast food. Why don't you see if you can make your way over to Le Posh, and if you can, then the late lunch is on me."

"Now, that's sorta ritzy," Leotis teased. "I know the place well. In fact, it's where I usually bring my out-of-town clergy to dine, and it's only a couple of blocks away from Sharvon's law office, too."

At the mention of Sharvon's name again, Ima tuned him out. "So it's a date, then?"

Leotis tried several times to say no, but each time he spoke to Ima, it went from "Today is not a good time" to "I'm about ten blocks away. I'll meet you there."

Ima hung up her cell phone and laid it beside her on the car seat. She removed the pearl-trimmed sunglasses she wore and glanced toward the Anderson skyline. The weather couldn't have been better, and it seemed to cooperate with her quickly thought-up plan. She'd picked a beautiful sunny day to suggest eating at Le Posh Restaurant.

She'd chosen the high-class restaurant not only for its location in the historic part of Anderson but also with another purpose in mind.

First ladies from megachurches in Pelzer, Belton, Piedmont, and Williamston, South Carolina, dined at Le Posh. Although some of their husbands weren't particularly handsome, the men had enough fame and fortune to offset their lack of good looks, so their wives brought them along as arm candy. In the winter the women shamelessly showed off their latest first lady attire of floor-length mink coats. In the warmer weather, they wore two- or three-tiered hats designed to impress, and their manicured hands sported expensive diamonds and other jewelry that rivaled the sun's shine. Along with the silent fashion show were whispered conversations coming from various cliques seated around the room as the women planned events or caught up on the latest gossip.

Then there were the other first ladies, anointed and a gift to their husbands and their churches. Ima wasn't interested in those women.

Ima parked outside the restaurant and waited there for Leotis. She could've gone inside and waited for him, but then that wouldn't have suited her purpose. She hadn't planned beyond getting Leotis to see her as someone appropriate to be on his arm and in his life. She'd already ruled out always acting like a vixen or tossing out sexual innuendos. They weren't having the desired effect, and she didn't want to go around showing Leotis her legs to get his attention. She would if she had to, but she wanted to try something different first. If what she wore got the right reaction from those she considered the stuck-up first ladies and their equally pious husbands, then she believed Leotis's doubts about her would vanish.

Twenty minutes passed. Ima soon tired of waiting inside her hot car for Leotis to arrive. She'd have preferred to enter the place on his arm, but she figured the heavy traffic still had him running late. Within a few minutes after entering Le Posh, Ima strutted slowly behind the maître d' as he led her to a white linen table for two at a window, where she could watch what was happening outside as well as enjoy the cool air inside. Immediately, her eyes fell upon one of the women. The woman, coffee-colored and stout, was the first lady at the Resurrection COGIC out of Belton. Ima scanned her more thoroughly than any

X-ray machine could. She wasn't surprised to see that the woman sat with others of her ilk and, like them, looked as though she'd just finished a photo shoot. Ima also recognized the first lady's husband. He was a renowned bishop who'd made millions off his incredible ministry, parlaying it into everything from books to films to conferences and numerous television appearances.

Ima nodded out of respect and admiration toward the first lady, just in time for the woman to quickly look away. Ima was stunned and embarrassed, praying no one had seen what she perceived as a slight. "That's okay," Ima muttered. "One day you'll come to me and ask if I can get your husband an audience with mine. Leotis Tom is on his way. You can believe that!"

But there was still the matter of that particular first lady being able to afford Le Posh. Ima, on the other hand, couldn't afford one thing that was on the menu. Even the outfit she'd purchased had needed special authorization from her credit card company before the boutique would ring up the sale. She'd chosen to wear the expensive, modest, gold-colored two-piece dress with its knee-length hemline, its hand-stitched, embroidered bodice jacket, and its modest matching veiled and wide-brimmed hat. And so she hesitated when the waiter asked if she'd like a glass of water. According to her plan, if things worked out, it was Leotis who'd offer to pay for lunch and she'd let him.

"Excuse me, madam. I would like to *again* offer you Le Posh complimentary water with lemon while you await the arrival of your guest."

It was the third time the snobbish man with perfectly aligned freckles across his rosy-colored cheeks and plastered auburn hair had approached her table. He was dressed in black and white and had a red sash, and he had interrupted her mental tirade. He'd kept offering her something "complimentary," as though, despite what she wore, he knew she was broke.

"No thank you," she told him again. And so she balled her fist and let the smile stay plastered upon her face, as she'd done for the past thirty minutes, waiting on Leotis, who had yet to show.

After another ten minutes of idle waiting and shooing away the annoying waiter, Ima's anger reached its peak. Now she didn't care if the entire restaurant heard what she was about to lay on Leotis. She quickly opened her purse to pull out her cell phone, only to remember that she'd left it on the front seat of her car after speaking to him earlier.

That late afternoon, when Ima returned to Pelzer and went directly to Sasha's, she was in a foul mood. Earlier, she'd raced from the restaurant past all the first ladies that she'd wanted to impress, like a thief trying to run out on paying her bill. She'd gotten into her car and discovered that Leotis hadn't left any messages on her cell phone to explain why he hadn't shown up.

Again inside Sasha's apartment, Ima continued the conversation from earlier that morning. Ima paced back and forth in Sasha's living room, throwing magazines and plucking the fake leaves off Sasha's potted plants. She even began ranting about paying someone to put roots on Leotis. In the meantime, Sasha kept trying to calm her and delay another insanity hearing for one of her family members.

"Putting roots on somebody, Ima? Really? You done lost your ever-loving mind!" Sasha ranted. "Why in the world would you want a man who obviously don't want you in the first place?" Having chased, caught, and lost almost all her male pursuits, with the exception of the one she married, and having quickly become a widow by choice,

Sasha knew a thing or two about unrequited love.

But Ima hadn't come there to discuss her plans for snatching up Leotis through roots or otherwise and then to give up so easily. She figured Sasha had been a member of his church long enough to give her some advice, perhaps tell her something she'd overlooked.

"I didn't come over here to hear a lecture," Ima told her.

"Well, that's too bad, because you're about to get one." Sasha then pointed to one of the small framed pictures hanging on her living room wall. "I know desperation when I see and hear it, and your desperation is loud and clear, Ima. You're jealous of your sister Zipporah. She's as pretty as you, *and* she can sing and you can't. She's married to a successful record label executive, and you ain't married to nobody and can't keep a man. She's got a child, and your baby-having eggs is approaching their expiration date —"

Ima didn't need or want to rehash her mother, Areal's past decision to give her younger sister, Zipporah, away at birth, even if her aunt Sasha's comparison had some truth to it.

"As usual, you don't know what you're

talking about." Ima snatched the picture from the wall and laid it facedown on the coffee table. "I didn't even know I had a sister until a few years ago. I could've had June Bug, or Chandler, as he's called now, if I'd wanted him when we were teenagers." Ima's voice trailed off as she added, "I can sing if I want to, but I don't. She ain't got nothing that I want. Let her live her life, like she did all the years we didn't know about each other. . . ."

Sasha said nothing. She shook her head as she took the picture off the table and returned it to its place on the wall before sitting again.

Ima pretended she'd not noticed what her aunt did, and continued talking. "I'm falling for this man, and I aim to have him. He ain't no different than all the others I've run across in church."

"I think you're wrong, Ima." Sasha leaned forward, pointing her finger in Ima's face. "Reverend Leotis Tom is different, and that's why you want him."

"You don't know what you're talking about." Ima pushed away her aunt's accusing finger. "He's got a pulse, an imagination, and a desire to be with a woman. He's just not as bold as some of those I've dealt with before."

Sasha shook her head. "Let it go, Ima. I've been telling you for as long as I can remember that them churchmen that done felt you up and molested you when you was younger because you blossomed early, they done got their just rewards from the Lord, or they will get them. You can't just keep on cheapening yourself because those low-down demons lowered your worth."

"Leotis is supposed to want me," Ima said sharply. She'd deliberately sidestepped her aunt's history reminder. She didn't need to hear it; after all, she'd lived it. "I can tell he wants to get to know me better every time we share the same space. He couldn't keep his eyes off me, not even if he were quoting scripture."

"So did those other men, including your recent fiancé, Reverend Lyon Lipps."

"Leotis is different!"

Sasha rose slowly. Her eyes widened. "Well, suh," she said softly, "I believe I know what it is now. I see why he's different," she said before she sat again.

"Well, it's about time." Ima began to smile, thinking she and Sasha were now in agreement.

"He's different because either you think another woman wants him or he may be interested in another woman." Sasha began biting her lip but not her words. "And if that ain't the reason, then my pastor is different in your eyes because he's not trying to feel up all over you, like almost every man since you was in elementary school. If he don't try something unchristian-like, then you don't get to judge and punish him, because, like I told you before, you've never believed God was ever really on your side and would!"

"Well," Ima said, "Maybe God is, or maybe God ain't. But I believe I've heard it said that God helps them that help themselves." Her eyes swept over Sasha, blinking and determined. "I'm just helping myself to what I want and deserve."

"And you think you want and deserve Reverend Tom?"

"Yes, I do!"

"Does he have anything to say about it?"

Ima placed her hands on her hips and turned her ankles from side to side, first one and then the other. "Not if I keep showing him the total package."

"You are back to that again. Ima, you are totally out of control," Sasha barked. "You fixing to get yourself hurt, messing in uncharted territory."

Ima waved Sasha's words away with a flip of her hand. She smiled and spun around, checking out her reflection in the large scallop-edged gold-framed mirror on Sasha's living room wall. "I'm a grown woman, or can't you accept that?"

"Shuddup! You're acting like a spoiled child. And I know what I'm talking about when I tell you Leotis is uncharted territory. He's a holier-than-thou man who I normally wouldn't want anywhere near one of my kin. He's probably up to his eyeballs with unfulfilled seed, too, and there's been plenty of young women in church who's tried to get some of that seed for womb planting. So what makes you think you gonna arrive in town and within a month or two change or snatch him? Like I said before, you are out of control."

Determined to show she was still in control, Ima ran her fingers across her latest get-a-man outfit, which she'd changed into before coming there. It was a see-through, green-laced, strapless one-piece pantsuit. She also wore a pair of five-inch white heels that accentuated her perfectly shaped size six feet. The neon green–painted toenails were the final come-hither to any male with a foot fetish. She'd already decided he was a leg man, but she wasn't certain if Leotis was into feet or not. She intended to find out that very day.

Ima turned and, again, looked into the large scallop-edged, gold-framed mirror. She smiled and then released the white pearl hair clip she used to keep her hair from falling fully onto her shoulders. Turning from side to side, she smiled again, running her fingers through her hair.

Sasha didn't like that Ima ignored what she knew was the truth. She thought she'd try harder to convince her by using plain old common sense. "Okay, why don't you just give yourself a little more time to think things over? Leotis ain't going nowhere, and I don't see him chasing after no one in particular," Sasha pleaded, "Besides, you just got over the heartache of messing with that other so-called man of God, Reverend Lyon Lipps. Don't dip your heart back into the love shredder."

"Hmmm," Ima whispered, ignoring Sasha's alleged wisdom. "If this outfit don't catch him, then he's either dead in spirit or stuck in the closet." She then winked at her reflection before turning around to face Sasha with an almost maniacal smile. "Look up the word *perfection* and you'll see a picture of me in this outfit right next to the word."

"Whatever." Sasha still wasn't giving up. She pointed her cane in Ima's direction and then hit the floor hard with it to make sure she had her attention. "I see you ain't gonna listen, and since you're determined to get hurt again, I'm gonna help cushion your fall. Pay attention, because I don't have a lot of time to spend on your wishful and dumb thinking."

"And for the last time," Ima yelled, "it's not dumb!"

Ima took a step forward. She ran both hands along her hourglass-shaped body and tossed her hair to the side. Smiling again, she whispered, "Don't forget you and me are kin." Ima twirled back around to face the wall mirror before she continued. "And although I might be a bit younger and more experienced, Aunt Sasha, it's still your scandalously vicious blood that's running through my veins."

Sasha's eyes became so large, they made her glasses appear like two dots covering her pupils. She became temporarily stunned by Ima's remarks. And yet she couldn't and wouldn't argue with the vanity of Ima's reasoning. With her addled mind racing at warp speed, tripping and falling over all the downright sinful and often scandalous works of her past, she shook her head and sighed. "Well, okay then," Sasha said, surrendering, as she came nearer to Ima. "I'll give you some intimate details I know and have heard about the man."

Sasha stopped and began shaking her head again. "Listen, I ain't got a lot of time, because I need to get back to planning Sister Betty's wedding reception before Bea, the sherilla, messes up the plans she don't know I've changed. But I'm gonna do what I can to help you to achieve this foolishness. But don't come crying to me when you mess up. You might have my scandalous DNA, but even with all your arrests and shenanigans, you still ain't had as much experience as me." Sasha looked Ima up and down before walking around her and stopping in front of her. Looking in her eyes, she declared, "You're an addle-brained something, but I'll work with what you have."

Ima and Sasha gave one another an air kiss before retreating into Sasha's kitchen. Over several cups of iced tea, they would make hellish plans that would snatch Leotis from the hands of bachelorhood.

"Folks in Pelzer been downing me all my life," Ima told her aunt. "And if I become the first lady of the church, that'll be cherry-sweet revenge."

The next day, over in the other part of town,

Sister Betty was still praying for wisdom as she confronted Sharvon, unknowingly much the way Sasha had dealt with Ima.

Sharvon was off for the entire week after finalizing a big case. Sister Betty had been using the time to badger her relentlessly into forgiving what she called Leotis's unintended slight. "He doesn't have the experience of gently letting a woman down who's chasing him so openly and shamelessly," she'd explained. "Normally, he doesn't place himself in a position to deal with something like that. I'm sure he'd have kicked Ima quickly to the curb if he knew how to do it without hurting her feelings."

But Sharvon was too full of anger. Her disappointment had caused her to lose sleep, because she had refused to accept any of Sister Betty's reasoning. Instead, over the past few days she'd avoided Sister Betty and the occasional visit from Freddie by retreating to her bedroom.

But now, at this moment, Sharvon stood in the doorway of Sister Betty's bedroom, looking as though she had the weight of the world upon her small shoulders. She still wore the clothes she'd worn the day before: a cream-colored tailored pantsuit and a purple cotton blouse that had many wrinkles and looked more like crushed velvet. Her hair was disheveled. "I've messed around like an idiot and fallen in love with that dumber-than-a rock preacher man," she moaned.

Sister Betty knew it hadn't been easy for Sharvon to walk into her bedroom and blurt out her feelings of disappointment about Leotis. Sister Betty stood and took Sharvon by the hand, leading her back to the bed. They sat on its edge. For several moments Sister Betty cradled the young woman's head, rocking her as though she were a young child. Sharvon, a woman filled with enough confidence and wisdom to solve complicated legal cases, began weeping like a lost soul.

Like Ima, Sharvon had finally come to realize that she had feelings for Leotis that went beyond friendship. This morning it took Sister Betty's words of prayer, more words of encouragement, and a few soft kisses upon Sharvon's forehead. Sister Betty believed Belle would've done that same thing for her daughter, had she lived. Somehow it all came together, and Sharvon calmed down enough to sit quietly for several moments without finally giving in to weeping. She did not say a word aloud but mouthed the words "Thank you" before she finally rose and left the room.

The next sound Sister Betty heard was the water running in the bathroom inside Sharvon's bedroom. She continued sitting on the side of her bed, with her arms now lifted in prayer. She thanked God for the small breakthrough. And she began wondering after Sharvon left the room if she would have been as effective a mother in calming her own baby boy if he had lived. She smiled a little, because she always arrived at the same conclusion. She must have some mother wit. After all, how often had she calmed Leotis or advised him in some matter or the other?

Sharvon had showered and gone into the kitchen. It wasn't quite noon yet, but since they'd not had breakfast, she began preparing two small meals for herself and Sister Betty. It wasn't long before the smell of bacon, eggs, and home-fried potatoes brought Sister Betty into the kitchen. After Sharvon had left the bedroom, Sister Betty had dozed off for a short time and had slept longer than she normally would.

Neither said a word about the sad shape Sharvon was in earlier. After eating, they turned on the local gospel music station on the kitchen radio. Humming and singing, which neither could do very well, they moved about in the kitchen, wiping countertops, filling the dishwasher, discussing what to cook for dinner. They then sat down at the kitchen table and chatted about Sharvon's heavy caseload, the drizzling rain outside, all sorts of things that really didn't matter, avoiding what Sister Betty believed was truly still on Sharvon's mind.

Yet some things needed saying quickly. Sharvon unknowingly opened the door to the conversation by saying, "Until the other week I had been thinking about offering more pro bono work to the church."

"Pro bone? What's that?"

"Pro bono," Sharvon said, correcting her. "It means offering a service for free."

"I see." Sister Betty smiled slightly before adding, "So what's changed?"

Sharvon ran her fingers through her hair and leaned in. She made the move suddenly, as though there were others in the kitchen who would hear what she was about to say. "I know you may not approve, and you've explained Leotis's awkward way of handling things the other week, but . . ."

Now it was time for Sister Betty to lean in, too. She clasped her hands, appearing to hunger for more. "But?"

"I still have feelings for Leotis that I shouldn't have, and obviously, he's not interested. If I offer to perform pro bono work for the church, I want it to be just for the church, with no ulterior motives. Right now the way I feel about him, I probably should just stay away until those feelings leave."

Nothing Sharvon had revealed was a real surprise to Sister Betty. And as much as she wanted to give advice about romance, she was new to it and uncertain as to what to add. So she gave Sharvon her usual advice when something needed addressing. "Why don't you just pray on it and see what God says about it?"

"Is that your answer for everything?" Sharvon smiled. "Well, I guess if that advice is good enough for you, and I see how well it's worked, perhaps I should give God a chance to straighten me out." She stood and walked around to Sister Betty's side of the table and gave her a pat on the shoulder. "You are one amazing woman. The church, Freddie, and this community, they're all fortunate to have you." She then kissed her on the forehead. "I know I am."

Sister Betty stood and continued humming and buzzing around the kitchen. She felt uplifted and proud of the way she'd handled Sharvon's misery earlier. She'd barely put the last pot away, after Sharvon went to her room to gather her laundry for the wash, when suddenly she caught a cramp in her knees. She reached out to hold on to the counter. *This ain't no time for my arthritis to be kicking up, Lord, and I'm not thinking that it's you, 'cause I don't feel crippled by it. Gotta be this damp weather.* The constant sound of raindrops hitting her windows always calmed her. She was just about to go to her room to sit and read her Bible when the kitchen phone rang.

"Hello."

"Praise the Lord, Sister Betty. I know it's barely past noon, and I hope I didn't interrupt your usual noonday prayer."

It was Leotis, and when he mentioned her noonday prayer, it caused Sister Betty to shudder. Too much had been happening. She couldn't remember the last time during that week that she'd had her noonday prayer at noontime. *Sweet Jesus, please forgive me.*

"I'm doing just fine, son," Sister Betty said softly. "I'm surprised to hear from you. I thought you and Freddie would be over in Anderson, bringing prison ministry forth today."

"No. I had trouble with the Civic again while stuck in traffic yesterday. I'm using the Tahoe today, and I haven't seen or spoken with Trustee Noel."

"Oh. I'm sorry. My days and mind seem

to be jumping all over the place lately."

She needed to reclaim her tranquility. In that same moment she made her mind up that when she finally did have that day's late noonday prayer, she would be untethered from problems not directly connected to her. She believed her pastor was a man of God, and she figured that by now God would have troubled enough to make him see that nothing good would come of messing around with Ima.

"What can I do for you?" she added.

"I don't know how to come out and say it without sounding a bit foolish. But as usual, when I'm bothered, I need to chat with my spiritual mother."

"Did you speak to God first?"

"Yes, Sister Betty, I did."

"And . . ."

"He's led me to talk to you."

Before Sister Betty could form a reply, a sharp pain raced from one kneecap to the other. It felt as though a hot poker had been plunged into them. She dropped her head. "What is it?" Her eyes swept around her kitchen, as though they were under the control of a higher power, before landing upon the travel brochures Freddie had left. It was definitely a sign that whatever Leotis needed didn't matter. She needed to look through them before Freddie made a final decision without her regarding their honeymoon. Feeling that she now had an excuse to cut short their conversation, she said quickly, "I'm sorta busy. Are you certain this can't wait for a better time?"

"Please, Sister Betty. I wouldn't put this on you if there were any other way." Leotis's reply was cloaked in desperation. He began to make a choking sound. It wasn't clear if he was choking on something or was about to cry. "She's here at the church."

"She who?"

"Ima," Leotis whispered. "She asked me out to lunch yesterday, and I told her I'd meet her at Le Posh. But when my car started acting up and I called a tow truck, I completely forgot about calling Ima to cancel the plans. I'm in my dressing room, outside my study, and she's down the hall with Mother Pray Onn and some of the choir members."

He stopped and took a breath before he continued. His voice turned apologetic. "It's my fault. I don't know what possessed me to open the choir rehearsal room door, but I did. She looked directly at me and winked, as though nothing had gone wrong yesterday. Then she said in front of the entire choir that she had need of my counseling and she'd come to my office directly when the choir took a break. I should've told her to schedule an appointment, but I didn't, because I was feeling guilty about not showing or calling, and now I don't know what to do. She's still a soul, and I don't wanna jeopardize it."

Sister Betty was about to respond and ask what it was about Ima that'd turned him into a man-child or a punk when she heard the sound of a phone being placed back on its base. Since she could also hear Leotis breathing, she figured it had to be Sharvon. *Oh, Lord, Sharvon's been listening the entire time again.*

Ima had stepped inside Leotis's study only moments ago, when he'd not answered her knock. Accidentally looking at the LCD on his multibuttoned conference phone, she discovered that the button labeled PASTOR read "in use." Ima, in addition to being gorgeous, was also a snoop without a conscience. She saw an opportunity to listen in, and so she did.

After hearing Sister Betty's voice on the other end, a noise in the outer hallway startled her. When the footsteps came dangerously close to entering Leotis's study, she carefully replaced the phone on its base. The last thing she wanted was for someone to catch her inside the study and on the phone; she was also hoping Leotis wouldn't discover she'd been listening to his conversation. Because she'd been alarmed by the noise in his hallway, she wasn't able to hear everything that was said. Whatever it was, it involved Sister Betty, which meant it could involve Sharvon. *I'm nipping this in the bud right now.*

Sister Betty suddenly felt crowded in her own home. The feeling overwhelmed her once she hung up her telephone. She'd grown tired of listening to Leotis sound desperate and pathetic about a bad situation he'd brought upon himself. She was also certain that Sharvon had listened in on her private telephone call, again while Leotis was asking for help. "As soon as she steps into your office, call that heifer a cab or give her a permission slip to ride with Sasha on the Access-a-Ride van," Sister Betty had barked into the telephone a few moments ago. "You're a grown man, and one who God has chosen to lead His sheep. Now, act like it."

Still determined to finally and firmly confront Sharvon about respect for another's privacy, Sister Betty walked down the hallway toward Sharvon's bedroom. As she passed a hallway window, she saw Sharvon outside. It'd stopped raining, and Sharvon was chatting with the next-door neighbor, Missionary Patience. Although Sister Betty couldn't hear the conversation, just watching Sharvon and Patience laughing and exchanging high fives was enough to convince her that perhaps she'd been mistaken. Maybe there was something wrong with the phone. "Lord, thank you for not letting me make a fool out of myself and pile more trouble onto Sharvon's heavy load."

Singing, Sister Betty turned to walk back up the hallway. She stopped only long enough to pick up the brochures so she could add her vision to her honeymoon plans. Somehow it made her feel better just holding on to the stack of brochures and knowing that by the time Freddie came over later that evening, as he often did, she'd have a decision to give him. *Freddie's been looking poorly lately. I'm probably worrying him to death by dawdling around here. I'm to be Mrs. Freddie Noel in less than a couple of months, and so I might as well start doing my share of the heavy decision making.*

By the time Leotis reentered his study, Ima had already made herself at home and was thumbing through one of the many study

Bibles lying out on his desk.

"I wasn't sure if you'd forgotten I said earlier that I wanted to see you or not," she lied, "but you were taking so long, so I took matters into my own hands and decided to look through God's book to see if I could find help." She held up the study Bible. "I found this CD in the back of it. *Sacred Love Songs.* It sounds like something I'd be interested in listening to. I hope you don't mind if I take it home." Ima, with the CD still in her hand, walked over and stopped within inches of Leotis. "I hope I'm not being too presumptuous."

"It's definitely presumptuous," Leotis said, "but I'm certainly not going to hold it against you, especially given how things turned out yesterday. . . ."

"Really," Ima purred, taking several steps toward him, "I'm the one that should apologize. Something came up, and I wasn't able to get to the restaurant. The battery on my cell phone died, and I couldn't call you. I hope you didn't have to wait around too long before you realized something must have come up."

Leotis folded his hands and looked about his office for somewhere to place his eyes besides upon Ima. He was certain she'd lied again, and without so much as any sign of remorse. Whatever guilt he felt about yesterday, she'd just erased. Sister Betty's words of advice echoed in his head. *Call that heifer a cab!*

"If Mother Pray Onn is ready to leave, then I suppose you should leave to. I'm really rather busy, and perhaps next time you can do as most do around here and make an appointment."

Ima gave no indication that his words had had any effect on her. "Well, she has already left to meet up with Bea. I didn't go with her, because I really needed to talk with you and I didn't want her around when I did."

Leotis stood his ground. He didn't retreat, and neither did Ima. With the *Sacred Love Songs* CD still in her hand, Ima tossed her long hair to one side and quickly began reading the liner notes, as if she intended on doing so the entire time.

"Hmm. This Reverend T. D. Jakes is a very popular preacher. I've heard of him, but this is the first time I've read or heard anything by him." Ima pursed her lips as though she were about to pout. "Did you also know that King Solomon tried playing hard to get?" She smiled, waiting to see if the mention of King Solomon piqued his interest. His face was blank, and so she couldn't tell. She teased him further. "While I was waiting on you, I did a little reading and discovered that the king was full of tricks and romance."

That time Leotis did retreat. He retreated to his desk. "This is something that is discussed in our couples' therapy or within the women's groups, along with the CD in your hand. It is improper for me to go into something so obviously of a sexual and personal nature without one or two of the deaconesses or someone from the single women's ministry present."

"But Solomon was so wise. I haven't read the entire book, but it doesn't appear that he needed to *call* upon anyone. He just handled the situation."

"I'm not King Solomon. I don't play tricks, but I am going to make that call."

"Which call would that be?" Ima wasn't about to take no for an answer. A man saying no to her was as foreign as her speaking Martian. It just didn't happen on planet Ima. "I truly would like to discuss my problem, and since Aunt Sasha has already left and it doesn't appear as if you are needed around here . . ." Ima stopped and smiled. "Perhaps you can drive me home."

He could feel an invisible Sister Betty perched upon his shoulder. She was poking him with a hot iron, repeating her order.

Call that heifer a cab!

"I'm going to call you a cab," Leotis blurted. "I can't take you home. I've already made plans."

"Can't you change them or be a little late?" Ima's childlike mannerisms took over, and with a mischievous grin on her face, she twisted and turned in one spot. "I can make it worth your while."

"Excuse me?" Leotis's hands flew up to his ears, as though to ward off her implicit offer of a dalliance.

"I meant I would give you gas money," Ima replied quickly. Her eyes began darting about the room. She hoped the lie covered her obvious innuendo.

"Gas money is *not* the problem. However . . ." Leotis stopped speaking and pulled his hands away from his ears, clasping them together as though to pray or to ward off Ima, should she decide to rush at him. He spoke slowly, praying he sounded more authoritative doing so. "Some time ago, I truly thought I'd made things clear."

"Well, yes, sir, you did." Ima's green eyes danced, turning the color of daiquiri ice, as she clutched the CD to her bosom. "You said that neither me nor what's-her-name . . ."

"Sharvon . . ."

"Yes, Sharvon," she replied. "We shouldn't approach you unless it was about a very urgent spiritual matter."

"And I meant exactly that." Leotis could almost hear his own heart beating as Ima began to wiggle like a small puppy trying to throw water off its back. It wasn't hard for him to imagine that because he'd begun staring at the short, formfitting, lime-green one-piece dress that fitted her like a second skin. He could also tell that the top was a soft cotton material, and her huge breasts peeked through, looking like two mountains lying on their backs.

He gulped and prayed there was as much conviction in his next words, because he'd convinced nothing below his belt. "I cannot take you home. Like I just told you, I will call you a cab. Inside your home, alone, is not a place to discuss spiritual matters at all."

"Only if you say so," Ima remarked. She tilted her head a little and allowed her long hair to fall to one side of her head. She now felt more in control each time she saw the veins popping on his forehead and his neck, and she could only imagine where else veins were throbbing. She walked toward him, stopping only long enough to plant two quick kisses upon his surprised face and a longer one upon his lips. "You see," Ima said, "I'm not about to let the sun go down with us being upset with one another. That's not biblical." Ima's smile grew wide and knowing as she slowly walked out the door.

No sooner had Ima walked out of his office than Leotis sat and his head fell forward onto his desk. He was out of his league and into dangerous territory. His rapidly beating heart began exposing the lie he'd told his head; he'd tried believing that it was okay if more than one woman sought him. He also knew he'd not fought hard enough to stop Ima from kissing him, nor did he want to. "Lord, please help me." He hadn't kissed a woman in so long. He'd done his best, or so he believed, to remain chaste until the one God had sent arrived.

But Ima had awoken something in him. But truth be told, so had Sharvon. He rose and looked around his office. This was the room where he was supposed to spend time alone with God and prepare to feed the sheep. Instead, he now wondered if a kiss from Sharvon would compare to Ima's. Sharvon was at least ten years younger than Ima, of that he was certain, but would age matter if she were to make him feel like Ima just did? So many women inside the church and without had approached him, and he'd survived with his spiritual man intact. Now torn between two women, it was as though he'd spoken providence when he laughed about having to choose like King Solomon.

Whether Ima meant to or not — and he was certain she had — her touch had quickened him, as though he'd been reborn. It only made him want to explore more and see if a deeper relationship with Sharvon was possible.

Leotis sat down again. He read scriptures and he prayed, but he did not repent.

CHAPTER 10

Freddie's face turned red with anger as he began pounding on Sister Betty's kitchen countertop. Whether he meant to do it or not, he had managed to break two expensive crystal flower vases. His foot kicked aside the shattered glass strewn among the red roses, which Sister Betty had plucked earlier that day from her garden. "Lord, help me! I can't take this."

"Freddie, honey, please calm down. Remember your high blood pressure and what the doctor said about you taking it easy."

He'd been pacing around Sister Betty's kitchen for the past few moments, building up an emotional and lethal combination of anger and disappointment. And he believed he had a good reason. No sooner had he come over for a visit than she began what had become her normal habit for the past month or so. Except today he wasn't in the mood. Today she hadn't even bothered to

163

meet him at the door with a quick peck on his cheek. She hadn't offered him a hot meal, something to drink. There was no concern for how his day had gone. Instead, by the time they'd gone from the side door, down the hallway, and into the kitchen, she'd filled him in, almost in alphabetical order, about the latest soap opera drama of people he'd come to call church nuts. He'd never raised his voice to her before with such venom, but Sister Betty had kicked him to the back of her priority pile without an apology or a notice.

Sister Betty's hands remained inside her apron pockets, but her eyes, wild with surprise, darted about the kitchen. Her head rolled from side to side, as though she were trying to spot the invisible demon that'd somehow invaded her home. *Oh, Lord, he's lost his mind. Father God, I rebuke this deranged and angry demon in your Holy name.*

She didn't care about the expensive vases or the colorful flowers she'd tended so carefully. She was, however, concerned about the man she'd given her heart to. This kind and unassumingly quiet and usually shy man she'd planned to marry was lumbering about her kitchen, obviously out of his mind. Finally pulling a hand from one of her apron pockets, she laid it on her head. It was as though she was trying to remember if there'd ever been a sign, aside from the threats to Bea and Sasha, that showed he was capable of becoming so angry and potentially violent.

"This mess has gone on too long," Freddie scolded, his eyes now narrowing and appearing menacing. "I've never wanted to do anything but love you as Christ loved the church." He began pacing and slapping his hands together. "That's what a man is supposed to do when he takes a woman as his bride." He pivoted and pointed at Sister Betty. "But your meddling instead of praying has taken over everything. I come over here wanting to discuss our wedding and the honeymoon. But the first thing I hafta hear about is what the doggone drama of the day is between Leotis and Ima. And if it ain't between him and Ima, then it's some craziness between him and Sharvon!"

He was now past caring and dismissed her shaken appearance. He walked over to where she stood cringing and leaning against the dishwasher, apparently for support. "I know I've never challenged you on anything, Betty. Perhaps that's why you felt it was okay to just push me to the side while you interfere with a grown man who's all tangled up betwixt two grown women." He bared his teeth like a dog about to gnaw on a bone before adding, "So I'm sure you can understand now why I'm wondering where my place in your life is once we say . . ." He stopped talking. His head dropped. Now speaking barely above a whisper, he added, "That is, *if* we ever say 'I do.' "

He said nothing more; he didn't look back as he again kicked at the broken glass. Shards of glass spread out, making tinkling sounds. He stomped out of the kitchen with his heart shattered much the same as those two crystal vases.

Sister Betty couldn't move at all, not even when she heard the thundering sound of a door slamming shut.

Sister Betty hadn't ever cried as much as she'd done over the past few minutes, ever since Freddie left. She sat shivering in the darkness of her living room, a darkness that rivaled the pitch blackness of the night sky and the dread that flooded over her.

She was tired all throughout her body. Using her hands for support, she tried to rise up off the sofa. She couldn't. Falling back against it, she began to weep again. She'd had no rebuttal to his fears and accusations. Yet how could she have said no to Leotis.

He was more than her pastor; he was her spiritual son. After all, she'd known Leotis longer than she had Freddie.

Leotis was her second chance to experience what it was like to be a mother, since she'd lost her only child. When it began with Ima, she'd convinced herself that he needed her to lean upon as much as she needed him when troubled.

She'd also been convinced that having Freddie in her life would lessen that dependence. And now she'd unintentionally driven him away. "Father God, I've never felt so low and so lost," she prayed softly. "I've never felt so out of touch with you and your purpose for me. Didn't you send Freddie to me?"

A chill raced through her body as she faced another possibility. "Am I doing this only because I don't want to grow older alone?"

"Cousin Betty, are you okay?"

Sister Betty's body shook and quickly stiffened. Leaning forward, she strained to see who stood in her living room doorway, although she'd already recognized Sharvon's voice.

Sister Betty's voice quivered as she fought to regain control. She'd never heard Sharvon come home. "I'm fine, Sharvon." As she fell back against the sofa cushion, she turned her head away from her. "I just need a moment of some 'me and the Lord' time."

"I promise you that I'm not trying to interfere or question you." Sharvon's promises were empty, because she'd arrived home about fifteen minutes ago. It was obvious that they'd not heard her as she crept past the kitchen, catching the last moments of their argument.

Despite what Sister Betty had just said, Sharvon walked farther into the living room. She went directly to the end table by the sofa to turn on the lamp. What she clearly saw then was a figure of a woman bearing no resemblance to the strong and rooted-in-God super saint she knew and loved.

Without saying a word, Sharvon pushed aside one of the sofa's back cushions and sat beside Sister Betty. She reached over, grasped her shoulders, embracing her without any resistance. Whatever questions Sharvon had could wait for the moment. The sobbing sounds now coming from Sister Betty had silenced her. All Sharvon could do was rock her in her arms like a baby. Yet knowing that she'd heard Freddie mention her name during that argument still caused Sharvon to wonder what she'd done to make him so angry.

Mentally and physically drained from the fight minutes ago with Sister Betty, Freddie had reached the end of her block. He began walking slowly, holding his head as he did. Crossing the street to go home, he stepped off the curb and right in the path of Leotis's car. The loud blast from the car's horn caused him to jump back onto the curb.

Although it was unusually dark that night, the car's bright headlights lit up Freddie's horrified face. Leotis stuck his head out the car window and yelled, "Trustee Noel, I'm sorry. I almost hit you. I never saw you. Are you okay?"

Freddie, still stunned, looked toward Leotis for a moment. A scowl quickly replaced his look of panic, and then, without saying a word, he began walking away.

Leotis jumped out of his car, leaving it where it'd come to a stop a few feet from the curb. He walked up behind Freddie, whose walk suddenly seemed to speed up. "Trustee Noel, what's wrong?"

Freddie's words were harsh but direct as he spewed them over his shoulder without stopping. "Leave me the hell alone, Reverend."

Leotis's face morphed. His eyes began

squinting, and his mouth fell open. He'd never seen this type of behavior from the trustee, and it was unsettling. He quickly regained his composure. "Wait one moment," he commanded before he began walking after Freddie again. "You need to tell me what the problem is. You don't just speak to a man of God like that and walk away." Despite his anger, he suddenly remembered he'd left his unlocked car parked on the corner. He turned around. Aiming the car's remote, he locked the car doors. Leotis turned around just in time to see Freddie stumbling. *Lord, not again,* he thought.

Freddie had begun to stagger. He knew he wasn't drunk, yet he was certain he appeared that way. As much as he wanted to get away from Leotis, Sister Betty, and the world at that moment, he could only stop and rest against the front gate of a nearby house.

"He couldn't have meant it the way you took it," Sharvon told Sister Betty. She'd spent several minutes using the same soft and convincing voice that'd won over most juries, hoping it'd work with her cousin. "Every couple, so I hear, argues as their big day grows near. So tonight it was about

170

honeymoon planning. It'll probably be about something just as silly next time."

She'd listened to her cousin weep to the point of near exhaustion as she told her what'd happened between her and Freddie. "Just give him a couple of days to calm down," Sharvon said. "It's probably just a case of the pre-wedding jitters." She took a deep breath, hoping she'd sounded convincing. "Even though this is yours and Freddie's first wedding, it will be the second time you two have tried to get to the altar. He probably feels responsible because he fell ill, and for not having the wedding when you first planned. I'm sure he just doesn't know how to handle it."

There was some validity to what Sharvon had said. It was true that the first wedding date had been postponed due to Freddie's health, but Sister Betty hadn't been fully forthcoming when she told Sharvon about the argument. It wasn't in her nature or character to divulge everything, and she'd left a lot out, mentioning only that they'd disagreed about the honeymoon. She hadn't wanted to tell Sharvon how she believed she'd come up short as his fiancée. She'd not even mentioned to Sharvon Freddie's anger over the way Leotis had mishandled the situation between Ima and himself.

Instead, when Sharvon mentioned she'd clearly heard her name called out, Sister Betty had shaken her head, so as to deny it without saying so. *Lord, please help me. I know a half-truth is still a whole lie.*

She rose and walked into the kitchen, hoping Sharvon would stay behind, and she'd not have to answer more questions. Instead, Sharvon followed her. Words of explanation still hadn't come to mind, and of course, Sister Betty wanted to find a way, again, not to respond to any questions.

While Sister Betty piddled around in her kitchen, trying to avoid Sharvon's questions, down the block Leotis had his hands full trying to understand Freddie.

Leotis had reached out to Freddie, catching him before his body hit the pavement.

"Get ya h-hands off me," Freddie stuttered. He tried wiggling out of Leotis's grasp but couldn't.

Despite the disrespect he felt from the way Freddie had spoken to him moments ago, Leotis, being stronger, placed an arm under the skinny man, leading him back to his car. Once they reached it, he almost had to fold Freddie in half to get him inside the car.

Leotis climbed inside the car, and when he looked toward the passenger seat, where he'd deposited Freddie moments ago, he saw that Freddie had pulled his body into a fetal position. He looked uncomfortable. Leotis adjusted his rearview mirror, saying, "I'm taking you to the hospital immediately."

But before starting the engine, he glanced over at Freddie a second time. That time what he saw made him wince. Although the inside of the car was unlit, he could see that Freddie's face had taken on a jaundiced pallor, with a grayish color mixed in. "I haven't said anything, but you haven't looked that well to me in several weeks." He caught himself. The last thing he needed to do was to criticize Freddie or make him feel as bad as he looked.

"No hospital," Freddie blurted. "Take me home."

"You need to see a doctor!" Leotis had begun easing the car into reverse to turn it around and head to the hospital.

Like a jack-in-the-box, Freddie's body sprang forward. "I need to go home."

If he can unfold himself like that, then he's serious about not going to the hospital. Although conflicted, Leotis gave in. "Whatever you say." There was definitely something wrong with Freddie. He could think of only one person who could make Freddie

173

do what was best for him. "I know what to do."

Leotis completed the U-turn. He began driving back up the block, toward Sister Betty's.

As ill as Freddie felt at that moment, he was suddenly aware that Leotis meant to take him to the last place he wanted to go. "No!" Freddie yelled with strength he didn't know he still had. "Not to her house. Please, just take me home."

There was something foreign about the trustee's voice. It contained a combination of anger and sadness, which told Leotis that no matter what was wrong, Sister Betty was the last person Freddie wanted to know about it or to see.

While Leotis was down the block, grappling with his conscience and with Freddie, Sister Betty was grappling, too. She was trying to find a way to keep a persistent Sharvon from learning what part she'd played in the argument between her and Freddie.

"I've got to accept it," Sister Betty told Sharvon. They'd gone from room to room, with Sister Betty fiddling around, moving things that didn't need moving. Each time Sharvon tried to get her to discuss how she figured in the argument, Sister Betty would

Check Out Receipt

Rosedale Branch
410-887-0512
www.bcpl.info

Wednesday, May 5, 2021 3:12:56 PM
20294

Item: 31183194888548
Title: The handmaid's tale
Call no.: Graphic Novel ATW
Due: 05/26/2021

Item: 31183166869732
Title: Sister Betty says I do
Call no.: Large Type Fiction GOR
Due: 05/26/2021

Total items: 2

You just saved $54.94 by using your
library today.

Extended loan fees permanently suspended for all
 material checked out with youth library cards

begin adjusting lights, which would remain unlit once they left the room. Still determined not to answer Sharvon's questions, she told her, "You've got to understand. Freddie didn't just argue with me as he did weeks ago with Bea and Sasha. Tonight he frightened me." Throwing up her hands, she declared, "He doesn't want to go through with this, and that's all there is to it."

Suddenly Sister Betty stopped. She spun around, facing Sharvon, nearly stepping on her feet. Her voice became strong and defiant. "I've lived all these years by myself, and I don't need a man."

"You don't?"

"No, I've got Jesus."

To Sharvon's way of thinking, they'd played follow the leader long enough. Sharvon removed one of her pearl earrings, as though she were getting ready to fight. Instead, she reached for the cordless phone. "I'm calling Leotis. I don't want to call him, but you're making me nervous."

Sister Betty needed to do something to stop her, but all she could say was, "Put the phone down. Don't call him!"

Sharvon ignored Sister Betty's pleas to put down the phone. She quickly dialed Leotis's home phone. After several rings her call went directly to his voice mail.

175

"Leotis," Sharvon began, "I believe you might want to stop by the house and check up on *your* Sister Betty. She's in a bad way, and I believe it has something to do with Freddie."

Sharvon didn't bother to turn around after hanging up the phone. She could feel a shift in the room. Without saying another word or looking back, Sharvon left the room, muttering, "I still don't want to see him when he gets here."

A short time ago, Leotis had taken Freddie to his home, as the old man had requested. No sooner had he returned and entered his own home than he heard his phone ringing. Before he could reach it, his answering machine intercepted the call. He was about to interrupt the recording when he heard Sharvon's voice leaving a message: "I believe you might want to stop by the house and check up on *your* Sister Betty. She's in a bad way, and I believe it has something to do with Freddie."

Leotis let the machine continue while he plopped down on his living room recliner. His head fell forward, and he held it for a few moments in the palms of his hands. *Lord, please help me. I'm glad I didn't answer that phone. What could I have said to Shar-*

von? What can I say to Sister Betty?

Because he'd raced through the door moments ago, trying to get to the ringing telephone in time, he'd not bothered to turn on the living room light. And as he knelt beside the chair, he still made no move to turn on the light. It didn't matter. He felt that there wasn't enough light in the world beyond Jesus Christ to bring him out of the darkness he'd just fallen into.

A frown appeared upon his young face, making him suddenly look much older than his thirtysomething years. He didn't clasp his hands together in prayer. Instead, he lifted his hands, with his open palms stretched high. Leotis began to pray. "I'm humbled before you, Lord, in repentance. Whatever I've done or said that was displeasing in your sight, please forgive me."

Leotis's plea for God's grace and mercy was for a good reason. Earlier he had done as Freddie insisted and had not taken him to the hospital or to Sister Betty's. Instead, he'd taken Freddie home, and because he'd insisted on knowing from where Freddie's anger stemmed and why Freddie had directed it toward him, he'd learned much more than he'd wanted.

Leotis followed him inside. They barely entered Freddie's home before Freddie collapsed on his bed. Leotis had entered the house only to make sure Freddie would be all right if he was left alone. But Freddie wasn't all right, and the way he suddenly began perspiring in his air-conditioned home caused Leotis to stay put. His need for an explanation fell away as he watched Freddie grab for a pill bottle. Freddie hadn't asked for water and didn't seem to need any as he quickly swallowed a pill.

"Freddie," Leotis said slowly and with compassion. "You're perspiring, and you really look like you should see a doctor . . . not tomorrow, but tonight."

Freddie didn't respond, and no sooner had he set the pill bottle down upon the nightstand than Leotis grabbed it. He had seen a lot of illness, had visited many of the sick from his church, and had served as a hospital chaplain, and in his heart he knew this was no ordinary illness. A look of sadness blanketed his face as soon as he read the label.

Leotis's hand began shaking. "Thalomid," he murmured. "How long have you been taking Thalomid?"

Freddie had turned his head toward the opposite wall, away from his bed, and said nothing.

Leotis placed the pill bottle back upon the nightstand. "Trustee Noel, I'm here as your

178

pastor and your friend." He went to the side of Freddie's bed and gently turned him over so he could look him in the eye. "I promise unless you tell me to, I won't say anything to anyone." He sighed. "I know Thalomid is a chemo pill."

Freddie's eyes swelled with tears, but he still refused to speak. There was no need.

At that very moment the light from a lamp on the nightstand framed Freddie's pain-filled face — and made many things clear in Leotis's mind. "When did you learn you had cancer?"

Leotis leaned in closer. He'd recoiled as he faced Freddie before peering closer, looking at him as though for the first time. And it'd felt that way because he noticed that much of the patch of spiked silver hair the man had always pulled on when nervous was missing. And for how long, he wasn't certain. And yet he did not ask the question, not fully expecting Freddie to confide such a private and delicate matter in him. And then there was still the matter of how he figured into Freddie's anger.

But that didn't matter at that moment, and he pressed on. Before him lay someone he considered a friend, a soul he'd pastored, and a man who was supposed to marry the woman he loved like his own mother. And so he'd told the trustee, "You can't face this alone, and I'm not about to leave you."

179

It took less time than Leotis thought it would, but within minutes Freddie finally came around, and without divulging much detail, he shared his predicament. He told Leotis that he'd been feeling poorly for months. He didn't know when he became ill the first time that it'd been cancer. He'd also gone to see doctors for quite some time, complaining about the pains in his back and his side, but he hadn't shared those aches with his Betty, fearing she'd think less of him.

After a few tests he'd seen a pulmonologist, because it'd been determined that what he had was just a respiratory problem. It'd taken several CAT scans and MRI scans to finally find what looked like old rib injuries. Then a biopsy was done before they found the real problem, and by then it was too late. Upon the recommendation of one of the oncologists, he was accepted as a participant in a multiple myeloma trial at Anderson General. It was away from Pelzer, so he could keep his affairs private, and hopefully, he would be one of the ones who benefited from a newly reformulated drug, Thalomid. The downside was that he needed to postpone the wedding date they'd set last year. He hadn't liked misleading Sister Betty, making her think it was just pneumonia that'd had him hospitalized, but he'd done it.

Leotis's muscular arms suddenly felt

weak, and they twitched, causing him to break loose from the burden of Freddie's news. Looking around the darkened room, he glanced at the wall clock's lit panel. He didn't know how long he'd been thinking and praying. However long it'd been, he now felt completely exhausted. He'd gotten more information from Freddie, aside from his illness, after a gentle badgering. Freddie had told him what'd sent him reeling earlier. He'd said that when Sister Betty met him at her door earlier that evening, he'd wanted just a little attention after an afternoon at the doctor's in Anderson.

"I know she doesn't really know that I've been seeing an oncologist, and maybe I shouldn't have kept it from her, but that shouldn't have mattered. Things were supposed to continue like they did before I got sick. I figured she'd offer me something to eat and I'd pick at my plate and say I was too excited to eat. That's the excuse I came up with. And I figured I'd somehow just steer her around to discussing our wedding. Me marrying her kept me hoping and believing I'd make it."

He then hung his head at that and made a wheezing sound. "Well, this is new," he said. "I don't usually start wheezing in front of folks. I thought I had it more under control."

"Can I get you a glass of water?" Leotis asked.

"No," Freddie said harshly. "Just let me finish saying what I got to say."

Leotis kept quiet, not moving away or trying to find a seat. He stood, ready to take whatever Freddie would put upon him. And Freddie did just that. He went on to complain about how Sister Betty had dismissed the obvious tired state he was in, that she'd begun immediately telling him about her concerns.

"She didn't talk to me," Freddie told him. "All she did was talk at me. She dove right in and started complaining about the way them gals, Sharvon and Ima, have been acting. She even had the nerve to mention how she'd heard that I'd missed a few of the prison ministry visits, and to say that I never told her." Freddie's voice regained its strength as he blurted, "Tell her what and when? Somebody had to tell her about me missing some prison ministry. That is as much a part of me as she was supposed to be! And she didn't even bother to insist on an explanation. Do you believe that? She didn't care enough to ask."

Leotis knew better than to respond, and he didn't.

"And then there's you and your part in this mess."

Leotis knew it would come out somehow; at

that moment he'd have settled for a calmer time.

Freddie, even in his temporary weakened state, didn't hold back his anger toward Leotis. He angrily rebuked him. "A grown man that can't handle his own affairs felt quite comfortable in putting your burden on a woman who's been like a mother to you."

And because Leotis had indeed thrown himself in the middle of Sister Betty and Freddie's lives with such nonsense, he realized, there was now a price to pay.

Leotis walked over toward his living room window and looked at Sister Betty's house. Only a few yards separated his and Sister Betty's homes. Now he wondered if keeping his promise to Freddie would forge a separation between him and the woman Sister Betty, whom he loved like a mother, a separation that couldn't be measured or forgiven.

He pressed his face to the window both for the coolness of the windowpane and a glance at a star or two that might appear in the night sky. Just as he started to turn away from the window, the headlights of a car entering Sister Betty's driveway caught his attention. The floodlight on the side of the house came on, triggered by someone exiting the car. It was Sharvon, and she was alone, and that was when it occurred to him that there were no lights on inside Sister Betty's home. He looked at his watch and wondered aloud, "It's not even eleven o'clock. Why is she not with Sharvon if there's no lights on inside? What if she's sick, too?"

With fear of the unknown urging him, he started for his front door. And that was when arrows of condemnation pierced his spirit. He'd almost put his hand on the doorknob when his promise to Freddie rushed into his mind. He took a step back. He'd now have to keep Freddie's serious and life-threatening illness a secret from Sister Betty.

He was more certain now than before that Sharvon's message on his answering machine had been a cry for help for Sister Betty. And after all he'd put them through, there was nothing he could do. The promise he'd made to Freddie had made him a prisoner to and a participant in a lie.

He pressed his back against the door. He was unable to move, because he knew that one of the biggest lies was the one he'd told himself, and it was about him being able to control the situation with Ima and Sharvon without ultimately damaging his ministry or his church.

He ran his fingers through his hair as a distraction. It wouldn't work, because the truth was that there were many women in and outside of the seminary and the church that had come on to him. But he'd always found a reason or two not to entertain the idea of pursuing any relationship, and none of the reasons had anything to do with how the women looked or their ages. That was one truth he could claim. His truth was rooted in his belief that he'd been set aside to do God's work, and though it wasn't so for many other preachers, for him, marriage or a relationship would've been outside of God's assignment.

And then Sharvon had entered the picture, and he'd become comfortable with going to a dinner or a movie or just chatting, without needing to take it further. He'd loved the idea that she was as dedicated to her career as he was to his ministry.

And now, as he pressed his back against the door, he could see Ima's long legs, unblemished, perfectly shaped, and honey complexioned. He felt a quickening in his manhood, and at that moment he was certain that, as Sister Betty had forewarned, Satan had sent Ima to disrupt him and awaken his desires. He felt carnality unlike anything he'd felt in years, the lustful feelings he'd kept under control through years of prayer and his dedication to what he believed was God's will that he remain celibate. Yes, he'd lied, and it was a lie seeded in his needs as a man, and yet one that would certainly doom his ministry if he didn't do something about it.

CHAPTER 11

It'd been two days since Sister Betty and Freddie had argued. Sister Betty had sulked around the house, pretending she was fine. Every time Sharvon approached the subject of marriage, Sister Betty would end the conversation quickly. On one occasion she said, "He and I are both too settled in our ways. God is probably trying to show us that we should probably forget about marriage." But in her heart Sister Betty knew better. God had never used the word *probably* in anything He'd ever communicated. She'd never seen the word *probably* written in the Bible, either.

"So are you telling me that it's not a problem if the two of you end things? You'll just continue attending the same church, having the same friends, giving each other a hello and a good-bye every now and again?"

"Leave it alone, Sharvon," Sister Betty insisted.

But today was the third day since the argument, and on this third day Sister Betty's spirit still remained wounded. Her spirit had sunk so low, it felt as though she trampled on her heart with every step she took. She rose and, as was her habit, got down on her knees to chat with God before starting her day.

She told God this humid morning what she had yesterday and the day before: about how unhappy she was. "Why did you let me glimpse happiness if you weren't gonna let me keep it?" She also went on to let God know that she was repentant for getting off track. "I'm sorry I haven't visited the sick or helped out at the church's food bank," she whispered. But she still needed to say what she would always start to tell God but then would stop.

This morning she finally confessed her willingness to interfere in Leotis's affairs and declared that she would've done so even if he'd not come to her. "Lord, I just don't like Ima. I never have," she admitted. "How could I pray to you with such ill feelings in my heart? Did you decide to teach me a lesson? Did I sidestep what you might've been trying to do with Ima where Leotis was concerned? Is that why he hasn't come by to see about me since Sharvon left him that message? Lord, I've messed up badly." She kept itemizing all her shortcomings, as though God hadn't created her or didn't know her.

By the time she finished praying, her knees had stiffened, yet she refused to budge from the spot beside her bed until she felt God would let her back into His good graces. "Father God, I know you say we have new mercies and grace daily, but, Lord, I need a little more. I need your guidance. I'm not giving another bit of advice, making a move toward Freddie or Leotis, or interfering with anyone's business unless I hear it from you. And I've got to know that it's you. I'm gonna fast because I wanna feel it deep down in my . . . sha-na-na," she prayed, whispering in tongues.

While Sister Betty spent time at home, on her knees, in Pelzer, Leotis was miles away. He had pulled up to the front parking area of Anderson General Hospital. He carried inside with him a small carry-on suitcase with a change of clothes for Freddie.

The other night, after Leotis discovered Freddie's secret about having cancer, the situation had taken a turn for the worse. Since that night, every time he thought about it, Leotis had no doubt that God was involved.

It'd started almost immediately after he watched Sharvon arrive home late without Sister Betty in tow. It'd bothered him that he wasn't able to go see about Sister Betty without betraying his word to Freddie, and he'd become just as concerned about leaving Freddie alone. It'd begun to rain that night, and on other occasions the patter of the rain would've calmed him, even helped him to sleep. Not that night. He had remained fully awake and had gotten out of his bed.

At first, he'd thought about walking around the corner to Freddie's home, but it was raining. He decided it made more sense to drive the short distance. After he arrived there, it took a lot of pounding on the door, peeking through Freddie's windows, and discovering him lying on the floor before Leotis broke the glass to the side door and entered. At first there was no response from Freddie, and he had no choice but to call an ambulance.

Since the night of Freddie's admission to the hospital, Leotis had already had the glass replaced in the door. He'd also taken some of Freddie's clothes back to his own house in case Freddie should need them. He'd done it all before he went to the hospital yesterday to see about Freddie. During that visit, he'd learned that Freddie would be discharged today.

Leotis stepped off the second-floor elevator. A sudden whiff of the sterile alcohol smell almost overpowered him. *I will never get used to this odor,* he thought. He shifted the small suitcase from one hand to the other before heading directly for the nurses' station. A young, small-framed nurse sat behind the counter, chatting with another nurse, who appeared a bit older. The freckles on her smooth brown skin seemed to widen when she looked in his direction and smiled. Leotis met her smile with one of his own as soon as he approached.

"Hello. I'm back again," he announced. He hoped he looked and acted more rested than he had the day before. He set the suitcase down beside him. "Is the *unwilling* patient ready?" He put emphasis on the word *unwilling* to show that he appreciated her attending to such a difficult and hard-to-please old man. Freddie's behavior was quite contrary when they admitted him. It'd taken a threat to bring the prayer team to the hospital to get him to do as the doctor had suggested.

"Yes, Pastor," she answered abruptly. Her smile then faded like melting peanut butter.

"Thank God he is ready."

"Is there something wrong?" Leotis placed his free hand under his chin, waiting for an answer. He was very surprised by her manner. Yesterday they'd stood together, going over the medical chart outside of Freddie's room. She'd mentioned how she was happy that a single and obviously alone man like Freddie had him on record as his pastor and had also given written permission for the hospital to discuss his care with him. In between giving him details, this same nurse had seemed radiant, telling him that she'd heard him preach when the choir from her home church, Mount Kneel Down, attended an anniversary service.

"You'd better believe there's something wrong." She darted her large caramel-brown eyes toward Freddie's room. "And you got here not a moment too soon."

Leotis's blinking eyes then followed hers, landing on the sight of Bea. Bea stood looming in Freddie's hospital room doorway. She had both hands on her wide hips, a sneer on her face, and her legs were spread wide in defiance.

Earlier, Sasha and Bea had gone to Anderson General Hospital to see one of their not-too-close friends and neighbors, the former beauty queen and congresswoman

Cheyenne Bigelow. The acid-tongued senior, who never took back anything she said, a result of her time as a politician, was a longtime friend of Sister Betty's. Although she lived in the same seniors' complex as Bea and Sasha, she'd never wanted anything to do with either them or their insane bickering. Because she was presently in the hospital and was confined to a bed, for the moment, she hadn't changed her mind.

Bea and Sasha had barely gotten in her hospital room when she came to from taking a nap. Even in her senior years, Cheyenne still turned heads with her good looks and long white hair pulled back into a ponytail that hung to her waist. And although Bea and Sasha had told her they just wanted to check up on her, they'd lied. They were there just to see how bad she looked without access to her beauty aids. Cheyenne's good looks and closeness to Sister Betty had always irked Bea and Sasha. The plan was that Bea would take a quick picture with the cell phone she had recently bought and didn't know how to use.

"We'll just take the cell phone to the drugstore and get them to develop the pictures," was Sasha's contribution to the dumb idea.

Things hadn't gone as planned with their

visit. Cheyenne had threatened to heal quickly and then kill them. They'd been ready to leave, but then they'd discovered Freddie was there, too. Sasha had become enraged, thinking he wasn't sick but was once again trying to avoid getting married. She'd left Bea there to interrogate Freddie while she went to terrorize Sister Betty.

"Hope you're prayed up," the nurse remarked. "That's an extra-strength demon standing over there." The nurse walked away, shaking her head.

Leotis hung his head. He remained in that position for a moment, no one knowing whether he was calling on God or cursing the Devil.

But at the same time, things weren't going much better for Sharvon back in Pelzer.

Sharvon stood with one earring in her hand and the other dangling from one ear. She had a folded magazine in her hand as she stood on Sister Betty's front porch. She waved it like she was swatting at an annoying fly. The only annoying thing standing on the steps was Sasha, who, despite Sharvon's warning for her to leave, insisted upon seeing Sister Betty.

Sasha kept hopping up and down on the steps, sidestepping Sharvon's swats with the magazine. "You listen up, Sharvon," Sasha warned. "I got something to discuss with Sister Betty. It's important."

"She doesn't want company, Mother Pray Onn. She's trying to rest."

"She can rest after we see to it that she gets married," Sasha told her.

Once the word *marriage* flew out of Sasha's mouth, Sharvon's aim became more direct. She almost decapitated Sasha's bun with one of her swats. Unless Sasha shot her with a gun, she wasn't getting inside to see Sister Betty.

At the same time Sharvon was trying to remove one pesky Sasha, back at the hospital, Leotis was trying to remove another pest, Bea.

In just a few steps she made it to where he'd planted his feet on the hospital hall floor. He knew she was beyond angry when she didn't try to straighten the lopsided blond Afro wig she wore. She looked like the underside of an over-ripe, burnt ear of corn.

"Why I got to find out that one of our trustees is in the hospital by mistake?" Bea didn't care that she was addressing her pastor. She pushed out her chest, as though it gave her more authority or straightened her spine.

Leotis sidestepped Bea's question and threw out one of his. "What are you doing in Trustee Noel's room?" He folded his arms, nearly brushing against Bea's ample bosom, which she'd not moved out of the way.

Bea finally relented and told Leotis that she and Sasha had arrived earlier to pay Cheyenne Bigelow a visit. "Cheyenne wasn't up to company," Bea said, giving Leotis her revised version. "Me and Sasha was about to leave" — she pointed toward the trustee's hospital room — "and that's when we happened to see Trustee Noel sitting on the edge of that bed in there."

"So where is Mother Pray Onn?" Leotis looked past Bea in case he'd missed Sasha. "I don't see her."

Bea sighed and placed her hands on her hips before leaning in. "That's because she ain't here."

"Where is she?" Leotis then looked down the hallway and back at the nurses' station to see if she was there. The only person he saw was the nurse he'd just spoken with who then sucked her teeth and looked away. "What is it that you're not telling me, Mother Blister?"

"The only thing I haven't told you is that

196

Trustee Noel done locked his self in the bathroom and that Sasha left to take the Access-a-Ride back to Pelzer."

"Back to Pelzer?"

"Yep," Bea said, smiling. "She's gone back to see if she can cheer up Sister Betty. We know she must be feeling something terrible. Here it is yet again that the man she's supposed to marry done gone and supposedly got himself sick."

At the mention of Sister Betty's name, Leotis felt his jaw tighten and a headache coming on.

Bea took a step back and looked her pastor up and down before she took a deep breath. "Are you okay, Reverend Tom? You look like they need to put you in one of these hospital rooms. Maybe I need to get you a doctor."

"Is that you, Reverend Tom?" Freddie called out from inside his room. His voice sounded strong, almost Herculean, compared to the other night. "Is that wildebeest, Bea, gone?"

Before Leotis could answer, Freddie came out of his room dressed in nothing but his hospital gown, which he wore open in the back, exposing his yellowed and wrinkled butt cheeks. Once he saw Bea, he fled back inside his room.

197

"Who are you calling a wildebeest?" Bea shot back. She swung her body around, and before Leotis could holler, "Mother, don't," Bea raced back inside Freddie's room.

Freddie hadn't gone back inside his room because he was afraid of Bea. He'd gone back inside to find a weapon. "I don't care if they keep me another week," Freddie yelled. "I warned her what I'd do if she tried messing in my affairs again."

Just as Bea rushed inside his room, she ran straight into Freddie, who was holding a half-empty bedpan. They both fell to the floor. Each time Freddie tried to get up off the floor, he'd fall back into the puddle of urine. Bea's wig had fallen off, and she began screaming as the urine smell rushed into her nostrils.

Now they both had a reason to be pissed. Bea and Freddie finally got up off the floor and fell onto the bed. They then began throwing air punches, neither really wanting their hands to touch the other, but feeling the need to beat each other down.

It took two big-boned nurses, several laughing orderlies, and one Leotis, all locking hands, to pull Bea and Freddie apart.

A short time later, after he was asked to leave the hospital, Leotis was inside his car, and he kept jerking the steering wheel, causing the car to swerve like a drunken maniac, as he mumbled under his breath, saying something about kicking the Devil's behind. He also kept one eye on Freddie.

The old man was back into his old fetal position, still fussing. "They ain't gonna be satisfied until I end up in jail, right alongside them I be trying to help." He uncoiled himself and threw a nasty look at Bea in the backseat before he returned to his folded position. "Old crones just won't mind their business." He then mumbled something that couldn't be said in polite company, in church, or to anyone under the age of twenty-one. But at least he had changed into the clean clothes that Leotis had brought.

Bea, on the other hand, had the car lit up. The weather had turned very humid and the rain had stopped, and Leotis had all the windows rolled down and the sunroof top completely open. Keeping the windows rolled up and the air-conditioning running wasn't an option.

"Mother Blister," Leotis said for the third time since she'd insisted he drop her home. She couldn't put on the wig, which still smelled of urine, and she wasn't about to be seen bald-headed, she'd told him. "I really wish you had accepted the offer of a couple of hospital gowns and had changed your clothes."

"So what is it that you keep trying to say, Pastor?" Bea wanted to pinch her nose to keep the smell of urine from entering it. "Ain't nothing wrong with my clothes that can't be washed out in the laundry. I believe you playing favorites, anyhow." She turned and quickly stuck her bald head out the open backseat window, hoping, humidity or not, that some fresh air hit her face, before pointing to where Freddie sat and adding, "Why he gets to sit up front in this here fancy car? It ain't like he's still sick. If he was, then they should've kept his old . . . blah-blah-blah . . ."

With the way Bea behaved, there was no doubt that Leotis would drop her at her apartment before he took Freddie home.

He pulled up in front of Bea's building and was opening the car door so he could hurry her out when he saw Sasha stepping off the Access-a-Ride bus. She had her cane and Bible in one hand and was swinging her white pillbox hat in the other. No sooner had she hit the curb than she began hop-scotching all over the cement walkway that divided the two buildings. Her mouth was twisted, and she had fire in her eyes. "Thank

God the trustee stayed in the car," he murmured.

He glanced at Bea, who was holding her head in her hands. He wasn't about to tell her that the way she clasped her head would only bring more attention to her baldness. He prayed silently, *Lord, please don't let her see Mother Pray Onn. Amen.*

Despite Bea trying to use her hands to cover her baldness, Leotis yanked one of her hands away from her head. "C'mon. We need to hurry," he told her.

"What the ham and cheese? Are you crazy, Pastor?" Bea hissed as she looked around to see if what he'd done was drawing attention to her baldness.

Leotis didn't answer; instead, he began urging Bea along by pulling her elbow toward the front door of her building.

Bea quickly dropped her free hand away from her head. She tried pushing her pastor away, struggling to keep a dignified bald-headed appearance.

However, Leotis resisted Bea's attempt at freedom. The last thing he wanted was a confrontation with Sasha, and he was certain she was mad about something. When wasn't she? Despite the odor rising off Bea's clothes and her trying to pinch him, Leotis still wouldn't turn her loose. When they got to her building, he almost shoved her through the door.

"Bea . . . Pastor, hold up!"

He didn't have to turn around. He could almost imagine the fire coming out of Sasha's mouth. The only thing he could do was pretend he hadn't heard her. "I've got to get the trustee home," he told Bea before he spun around and began trotting toward his car, but Sasha beat him there.

"Somebody better tell me something." She looked over toward Bea, who hadn't gone inside, despite her need to keep her bald head out of view. Sasha didn't say a word about Bea's nude scalp. Instead, using her pillbox hat like a flag, she began waving at Bea so that she'd come over.

Bea's curiosity trumped her pride, and she rushed back to the car. As soon as she got within inches of Sasha, Bea quickly snatched Sasha's pillbox hat and slapped it down on her own head.

Sasha didn't care about the hat, and without realizing that Freddie sat within earshot in the front seat of Leotis's car — not that she would care if she knew — she began her tirade. "There ain't gonna be a wedding, Bea!"

"Say wha—"

Sasha cut Bea off with a wave of her cane.

"That's right," she snapped before turning to face Leotis. "How could you let something like this happen?"

No matter what Leotis could say, he knew it would do nothing to convince Bea and Sasha to calm down.

Even having upon them the eyes of all those in the crowd that'd begun to form didn't stop Bea and Sasha from causing a scene. Instead, the two old women tag teamed Leotis, peppering him with questions and accusations.

"Bea and me done gone out of our way to give them two undeserving somethings a classy wedding reception. And the way the trustee's been acting and threatening folks, we know there's nothing physically wrong with that son of a gun!"

"That's right," Bea added. "And him hiding out in some hospital room ain't gonna stop nothing, 'cause you best believe there's gonna be a wedding. That coward ain't gonna get away with playing with Sister Betty's emotions!"

"Or ours!" Sasha added.

Bea continued. "There's gonna be a wedding, even if we have to hold it at his funeral, because I'm gonna kill him if he's wasted our time." Bea stopped and nodded toward Sasha. "Sasha and me done put

203

aside our differences and come up with one of them things called a business plan."

Leotis buried his face in his hands. He needed to do something with his hands before he set aside praying with them and began throwing punches.

"Sure did," Sasha agreed, ignoring whatever her pastor thought he was doing. "It was my idea first. I stopped putting up with she-rilla's crazy plans, and I let her throw in with me."

"Quit lying!" Bea hissed. She filed away Sasha's insult for payback at a later day. She put a hand on one hip and spoke directly to Leotis, ignoring Sasha altogether. "We planning on starting our B.S. event-planning service, and doggone it, when folks see what a good job we done with our first wedding reception, we gonna do like them young folks always saying —"

"That's right," Sasha proclaimed. "We's getting paid!"

They held their heads high, gave a high five, and then, without waiting for a reply from the gape-mouthed reverend, they walked away. Sasha, using her cane, and Bea, with that pillbox hat on her bald head, waded through the onlookers, not caring who pointed and laughed.

Getting on the elevator to their apartments, Bea and Sasha didn't even say another unkind word to each other. They knew that if what Sasha had heard from Sharvon was true, then they had their work cut out for them. But they were two old women on a budget. They'd already put down a hundred-dollar down payment at Porky's El Diablo Soul Food Shanty. It was the place they'd decided was within their budget to give the couple the wedding reception that'd launch their latest sure-to-fail moneymaking scheme. Neither had planned to tell Leotis or many others about it until they mailed the invitations, but they were also determined not to lose their hundred-dollar investment.

But there was one loser there already. Freddie had overheard everything. Before he heard Sasha say so, he'd already figured out that Sister Betty might want out of the marriage. He wanted to have enough time to figure things out so he could win her back. Freddie hadn't counted on her giving up without a fight, and he especially hadn't figured she would tell Sasha or anyone else she'd thrown in the towel before she told him.

Dark circles began forming around his eyes as he reached for the hair sprig, now long gone along, as were his appetite and much of his strength, sapped by taking the chemo pills. "She could've told me first," he murmured as his lips began fluttering from anger. He looked up toward the roof of the car, as though he'd expected to see God hanging from it. "Why'd you give her to me if you was gonna take me out of here? Couldn't you have let me have her love for just a little while?" Freddie stopped praying aloud as soon as he heard Leotis's hand on the car door. *I ain't never had love. It looks like I never will.*

Before Sasha's unwelcome visit a short time ago, Sister Betty had every intention of praying and fasting from six o'clock in the morning until six o'clock in the evening. She was going to fast until she received a breakthrough to God. Yet now Sister Betty sat on the edge of her bed, still dressed in her nightgown, with her hands under her chin. She kept thumbing her chin and throwing dirty looks around the room. She was murmuring and fussing one minute and then asking God the same questions she'd been asking Him since Sasha fled from her porch. "Why, Lord? Can I get a smidgen of peace? I have done promised to give up Freddie until and unless you say different, so why I am still tormented?"

Sharvon soon came into the room with her long hair all out of place. There were several rips in the tight, formfitting beige jeans she wore, and two buttons were missing from the top of her blouse. "I'm so sorry, Cousin Betty," she said softly. "I'm a guest in your home, and as an attorney, I knew better." Sharvon walked over to where Sister Betty remained seated, and sat down on the bed next to her. She placed an arm around Sister Betty's shoulders before laying her head upon it. "I hope you'll forgive me."

Sister Betty lifted Sharvon's chin and kissed her gently on the cheek. "Don't worry, Sharvon," Sister Betty told her. "I'm just glad you didn't get hurt when you tripped down the steps and fell into my rosebush."

"But I was trying to hurt that old hen," Sharvon reminded her. "I wanted to take that magazine and push it where the sun won't shine!"

"Sharvon, you've been in Pelzer long enough to know that Sasha has that effect on everyone."

Sharvon smiled at Sister Betty and rose from the bed. "Yes, I know. I just hope none of your neighbors were looking. I don't want to embarrass you." Sharvon began laughing. "But you should've seen that old biddy get out of the way. She was quicker than I imagined. She got the message, though."

"What makes you think that?" Sister Betty laughed slightly. "Sasha could hear something twenty-four hours a day and seven days a week, and she still wouldn't get the message." Sister Betty stood and stretched. "Well, I guess there's no sense in just lying around. I'd better get started on picking out something to wear to service tomorrow. It's the third Sunday, and I think it's the trustees' board that is in charge."

No sooner had she mentioned the word *trustee* than her smile vanished from her face and a tear took its place in the corner of an eye. Sister Betty reached out behind her. She found the mattress and fell back onto it. Pulling the covers over her, she turned away from Sharvon.

Sharvon now felt completely helpless. At this moment she didn't have the nerve or the heart to admit to Sister Betty that in her anger at Sasha's stubbornness, she'd blurted that there'd probably be no wedding. Instead, she quietly backed out the door. She went to her room to give Sister Betty her space and to change from her battle clothes.

While she changed and brushed her hair,

208

Sharvon began trying to figure out a way to help her cousin. She wasn't out of step to the ways of the world, but her experience was limited. She had dated and was open to more dating, but her focus had always been career oriented, until she had let her guard down with Leotis and had allowed Ima to turn her green with jealousy.

Pinning her hair back, she continued imagining how she could've made things better for Sister Betty. Sharvon began thinking how if this were a court of law, and her cousin's fate were in the hands of a jury and not left to God, she would argue her cousin's case before it. She'd produce evidence that Sister Betty had been a long-time member of God's army and, for the most part, had served with good standing. She'd tell the jury to look at the way the woman had set herself aside for many years and had never looked for love or companionship in her advanced years, but once finding it, she'd believed God had sent the man Freddie Noel her way.

Sharvon would go on to convince the jury that it was the bond Sister Betty had with Leotis that'd caused her to take her eyes off the marriage prize. She'd convince the jury to sentence Sister Betty, along with Freddie, as her codefendant, to a life of nothing but marital bliss and service to the Lord.

Sharvon's thoughts faded once she finished dressing. She then went to the kitchen to make the most of her first full Saturday off in quite some time. She was about to put together what she'd need to cook for their dinner, believing Sister Betty wasn't up to it, when she realized she needed something from the garden. She went to the garden, and on her knees, she gathered several fresh herbs. Just as she was standing up, the sound of a car door closing caught her attention.

Sharvon watched Leotis retrieve a small suitcase from the trunk of his Tahoe. She also saw Freddie exit the passenger side of the SUV and walk slowly around to its front. Even though there was some distance between the houses, she could see that there were dark circles around Freddie's eyes. The circles made his lemony complexion look like the skin of a leopard. He'd never been a handsome man by any standard, but at that moment Sharvon was truly shocked that he looked worse than the last time she'd seen him. He looked almost emaciated, and that was saying something for a man who was naturally skinny.

What is wrong with Freddie? Why is he with Leotis? Sharvon lifted the pail in her hands as she stood and looked back at the door she'd left ajar. She really hadn't expected Sister Betty to be standing there, but nothing normal had happened all day. When she didn't see her, she turned back around to discover the two men were no longer there.

"Something's not right," Sharvon muttered. And then it occurred to her that whatever the reason Leotis had been avoiding her cousin, it must have something to do with Freddie. She was disappointed, because she'd already blamed it on Ima keeping Leotis occupied. "This is ridiculous!"

Sharvon didn't bother to take the pail filled with herbs back inside. She left it right where she dropped it in the garden and headed straight for Leotis's house. She didn't care that she trespassed through the neighbor's yard that separated the two homes. The determined look upon her face even cut short the barking from the neighbor's dog, Felony. The normally aggressive mutt sped away, whimpering.

CHAPTER 12

After Sasha had blurted out the bad news about Sister Betty calling off the wedding, Freddie seemed to deteriorate physically and mentally right before Leotis's eyes. Leotis had a hard time convincing Freddie to stay with him. "Now the whole church will know," Freddie explained, hanging his head.

"Just lie down and relax," Leotis told Freddie after leading him directly from the car inside the house and into a spare bedroom. "You need to get back your strength." Leotis threw back the bedcover while Freddie waited, slumped in a recliner off in the corner. "I've got the prescription the doctor gave for your blood pressure. He also wants your pressure taken when you wake in the mornings, and to make sure you take the Thalomid about the same time every night."

Leotis went over to Freddie and led him

to the bed. "This room is smaller than my others, but it has the best sunlight." He pointed toward a door off to the left of the bedroom. "You've got a bathroom with a shower. I'll pick up a shower seat to put inside when I pick up your prescription."

Freddie's weakness had traveled throughout his body, and even his tongue felt too weak to speak. His strength that day seemed to have come and gone with the least exertion. He nodded at Leotis and mouthed, "Thank you."

"Go ahead and lie down," Leotis told him. "Later you can change into some pajamas or whatever you wear." He walked over to one of the dressers and opened the top drawer. He pulled out a small Bible. Placing the Bible on the nightstand, he looked at Freddie, expecting him to protest about what he was certain must've seemed like treating him like a baby.

"Thank you, Pastor. Thank you." Freddie had caught Leotis by surprise when he spoke.

"God is able," Leotis replied. "You'll get through this."

"If you say so," Freddie replied before shifting his body so that Leotis couldn't see his face. "Not sure I want to."

Leotis saw in real time Freddie's depression settling in. At that moment, as he closed the door to the bedroom, he could've truly laid his hands upon Sasha and wired her big mouth shut.

Leotis decided that while Freddie rested, he would run to the nearby drugstore. He'd fill the prescription and pick up the shower seat. He grabbed his car keys and house keys to leave, opened the door, and came face-to-face with Sharvon. She had her hand out, reaching for the doorbell.

"I hope you weren't going anywhere, because we need to talk, and I mean right now!" She came across as harsh. At that moment she cared less if he was a pastor or not, especially since, to her way of thinking, he hadn't acted like one. "I need to come inside, unless you want me to speak my mind right here at your front door."

"You've got the wrong idea, as well as a lot of nerve." Leotis's eyes seemed to turn darker with anger, but he didn't budge. He stood there as if he were an immovable object facing down another immovable object, one that he objected to, as it was up in his face in a disrespectful manner. "This is not the time," he snapped as thoughts of Bea and Sasha's shenanigans came to mind. "Trust me when I say this." He leaned in with his brow furrowed, his lips clenched tight. "It's been one of those days, so I know for certain the Devil is testing me. You need to back down, because I'm not certain I'd pass that test."

While Leotis and Sharvon went toe-to-toe at his front door, Sister Betty got up to wash her tear-streaked face. She was passing by the window in the hallway when she saw Sharvon standing in Leotis's doorway. She then remembered that she still hadn't heard from him since Sharvon left a message several days ago. It wasn't like him to stay away, and she became angry.

Lately, anger had become an emotion that seemed readily available. She concluded that somehow he'd abandoned her. Even though she had protested and hadn't wanted Sharvon to call him, since Sharvon had, he should've come running. After all, it was her running to help him that'd caused so much strife between her and Freddie.

Glaring in Leotis's direction, she mumbled, "I hope Sharvon is letting him have it!" Sister Betty quickly dropped her head, clasping her hands. "Oh, Lord, please forgive me. Anger is overtaking me, and I'm still so brokenhearted."

Sister Betty turned away from the window and continued down the hallway toward her living room. She sat on the sofa, whispering, "I need a word, Lord." She reached for her Bible and began thumbing through it.

Finally arriving at what she believed God had intended just for her, she began reading. "Psalm twenty-seven, fourteen," she whispered. "Wait on the Lord. Be of good courage, and He shall strengthen thine heart. Wait, I say, on the Lord."

Sister Betty reread the passage several times before allowing her head and her mind to rest against the back of her sofa. "Thank you, Jesus," she kept repeating. "Lord, I've been with you long enough to have known better. I'm to come to your Word whenever I become weak." She sighed as she smoothed her housecoat. "You did say this was a journey from the cradle to the grave."

This time she decided to rest totally upon God's Word and His promises. She didn't know if what she'd read meant Freddie would return to her, but she believed that no matter how it turned out, she'd wait. And if she waited, God would strengthen her broken heart. With the Bible still in her lap, she unconsciously began turning the engagement ring on her finger. In no time the sleep that'd evaded her last night and the nights before overtook her. She began snoring softly, and a smile appeared upon her face.

Inside Leotis's spare bedroom Freddie had finally found the strength to sit up. He was used to his own bed and bedroom, so even in his tired state he couldn't find rest at Leotis's home. As he sat there, he listened for a while but didn't hear a sound throughout the house. He also called out Leotis's name but got no response. Freddie then remembered Leotis mentioning he was going to get the prescription filled, and so he figured perhaps that was where he'd gone.

With nothing to do and unable to sleep, Freddie reached for the television remote on the nightstand. Instead, his hand landed upon the Bible Leotis had placed there earlier. He hadn't meant to trade the remote for the Bible. He was too angry with himself, Sister Betty, and yes, even with God at that moment. Yet he picked up the Bible, and without resisting, he began turning the pages.

As he turned the pages, he began complaining. "I'm mad, Lord. You want me to love you, but you don't wanna let me have nobody to love me."

Freddie began turning the pages faster.

"I can rest in your Word, but I'm still a

217

man. At my age, I'm not trying to be a lover, but I do wanna rest in my Betty's bed." Freddie's eyes began to water.

He began turning the pages fast enough to rip them, but they didn't tear.

"Why must I wait? Ain't it enough I got this cancer riding my body? This multiple myeloma ain't curable," Freddie said bitterly. "I'm accepting I gotta leave here someday." And then he added, pleading, "But, Lord, can't I have Betty? I don't care if she never fixes me a meal or stays put in everybody's business. Lord, I'm tired, but I still wanna love her."

Freddie's tears began blurring his vision. He didn't realize he'd stopped turning the pages of the Bible until he began wiping away his tears with the sleeve of his shirt. The Bible passage became sharper with each swipe.

He began reading aloud. "Isaiah forty, the thirty-first verse. But they that wait upon the Lord shall renew their strength. They shall mount up with wings as eagles. They shall run, and not be weary, and they shall walk, and not faint."

Freddie reread the passage before laying the Bible beside him on the bed. As was his habit, he reached for the sprig of hair, which was gone. His baldness didn't bother him now. It occurred to him that it must not bother Betty, either. "Perhaps that's why she's not said anything."

He looked toward the bedroom window. From the window he could see past the house next door and through her living room and hallway window curtains. He then lay back against the pillow and began rereading the passage of scripture again. He did not finish the third reading before sleep overtook him.

Leotis couldn't keep Sharvon from trying to wake the neighborhood. Her mouth was in overdrive, and she made loud accusations about his character and his abandoning Sister Betty for the trustee. He finally closed his front door and headed for his car to escape any possible embarrassment. There was no escaping. Sharvon rushed around the car and jumped in on the passenger side to continue blasting him.

Before he had buckled his seat belt, Sharvon started in on him. "Ever since I came to Pelzer, my cousin has been at your beck and call," she said as he tried to steer the car out of his driveway without having an accident. "Where is your loyalty? She's been like a mama to you, so what's Freddie to you? Oh, don't tell me," she hissed, almost

219

spitting from anger. "Is he now the father you didn't have?"

Leotis didn't say a word as he drove. In his present state of mind, he knew whatever came out, he couldn't easily take back. His hands clenched the steering wheel tightly until he felt either his wrists or the steering wheel would break. He had a sermon to preach tomorrow, and all he'd done that day was transport home a delusional and crotchety church mother who smelled like an outhouse and deliver a very sick but cranky old trustee to his house. He still hadn't done what he really wanted to do. He glanced over at Sharvon, whose mouth was still in gear, and wished he had delivered a punch to Sasha's rabid mouth. And he was also ready to add Sharvon to that mix.

"And now because of you and your selfishness," Sharvon told him, "because you can't handle a skank named Ima that's trying to get you to the altar or the bed, or vice versa, you've caused Freddie to break off the wedding to my cousin. You'd better be glad I'm almost saved, or I'd really tell you what I think!"

Leotis quickly hung a mental RESERVE sign at the altar, along with removing his invisible turned-around collar, before he slammed on the car's brakes. "What does

Ima have to do with any of this?"

"I say she does." Sharvon turned around in her seat to face him, ignoring the blasting car horns from the other cars, which finally drove around them, but not without calling out a few unkind words as they did.

"Well, you've been wrong about things since you showed up on my doorstep," he said loudly. "She doesn't play any part in my life." Yet even as the lie leapt from his tongue, images of the fiery, long-legged, and worldly woman crossed his mind. It didn't matter that he'd not seen or heard from her in the days since she tried brazenly to seduce him in his pastor's study with kisses.

However, Ima and Sharvon had something in common. Each knew how to quickly work his nerves, while at the same time making him want to hold and kiss them, making him feel more deeply than he'd ever felt about a woman before.

He quickly dismissed the thoughts of the flesh and then turned to face Sharvon, who was still lambasting him. "Just so you know," he argued, "I've been busy, too. And if I've befriended Trustee Noel, it's because he's —" Leotis stopped and exhaled. He'd almost betrayed Freddie by telling Sharvon the truth. Yet he knew he'd better say something, because she'd already shown she wasn't backing down. "He's been in the hospital for the last couple of days. And before you ask why he was there, I can't tell you, because it's his business. But I can tell you that he's now heartbroken that Sister Betty just called off the wedding without telling him."

"What are you talking about?" Sharvon leaned over the armrest. "*He* broke up with her." She paused, taking a breath before adding, "I told you that he didn't actually say the wedding was off, but he hasn't reached out since they argued, so she believes he's changed his mind."

"Well, that's not how it went down according to Mother Pray Onn."

Sharvon looked at Leotis. She leaned back with her arms folded, asking, "What's she got to do with it?"

Leotis became so heated again, he could've activated the car's air-conditioning. "She's got everything to do with it. She's the one who ran her big mouth to Bea, and that's how the trustee first heard the news."

Sharvon turned back around in her seat, unfolding her arms and placing a hand across her heart. She fell back against the car seat. "Oh, damn."

As they continued driving, Sharvon confided to Leotis what she'd told Sasha earlier that day. "It just flew out of my mouth," she said. "I am too ashamed to tell Cousin Betty."

"Wow," he said slowly. "That's what happened."

A short time later they returned from the drugstore, and Leotis asked Sharvon if she'd like to come inside and perhaps talk to Freddie. "Perhaps if you told him it was a misunderstanding about what Sasha said, it would help him."

"Maybe later, but not at this moment," she told Leotis. "I need to get inside and check up on Cousin Betty. Whether I set it off with Mother Pray Onn or not," Sharvon confided, "there was already trouble brewing in paradise with the two of them."

"Well, nevertheless, I'm praying things will get better," Leotis replied. And as an afterthought, he added, "I know as far as Mother Pray Onn and Blister are concerned, they intend on giving Sister Betty and Trustee Freddie a wedding reception, whether they're together or not, and whether they want them to or not."

Sharvon had already put her hand on the car's latch to open her door. Yanking her hand back, she tilted her head and asked, "What are you talking about?"

"I'm telling you that they told me earlier

that they're determined to use this wedding as a way of showcasing their event-planning skills. They are under the delusion that if they do a good job with the wedding reception, they'll get, as they put it, paid. So in their minds it doesn't matter if the wedding is called off. You'd better believe they'll be up to some immature craziness to interfere."

"We've got to put an end to this."

"Oh no," Leotis said, throwing his hands up. "I've got enough on my plate."

"You're not going to help me?"

Leotis lowered his hands, asking, "Are you going to help me get back in Sister Betty's good graces while the trustee spends time recuperating at my home?"

"We'll see what happens when you come over," Sharvon replied before she left to see about Sister Betty.

Leotis sat in his car and watched Sharvon walk away. Again, guilt hijacked his thoughts. He had allowed her to share what she believed was the reason things had gotten to a bad end for Sister Betty and Freddie. And yet he couldn't confide in her the seriousness of Freddie's condition. But, on the other hand, he was grateful that she hadn't pressed him as to when he'd come by to see about Sister Betty.

Once he walked inside the house, he went

into the spare bedroom and found Freddie just waking up from a nap and seemingly in a completely different mood. He laid the medicine on the nightstand and took the shower seat into the bathroom.

"I'm glad you were able to nap while I was gone," Leotis told him. "You should feel a little better."

"I truly do," Freddie told him. "I'm not saying that I'm ready to perform cartwheels, but I believe God's got this. I feel so good, I'm gonna try to make it to service tomorrow morning."

CHAPTER 13

Much to Leotis's surprise, Freddie woke up earlier than expected this Sunday morning.

"I'd still like to go to the eight o'clock service with you, that is, if you don't mind," Freddie announced.

"Certainly," Leotis replied. "I'm only preaching the one service this morning."

"Why is that?"

"Because the trustees' board is in charge of the eleven o'clock service this Sunday, and they've asked one of the associate ministers to bring the Word."

"I've got to get myself together. I forgot this was the trustees' day, and I'm one of them." Freddie gave a weak smile. "I might as well get started. I don't want to be the one making you late this morning."

No sooner had Freddie gone back to his bedroom to get ready than Leotis went to his bedroom and called Sharvon on her cell phone. He didn't want to take a chance on

Sister Betty answering the phone. Not yet, anyway.

"Trustee Freddie just told me he's coming to the eight o'clock service with me this morning," Leotis told Sharvon once she answered.

"Well, good morning to you, too," Sharvon replied, letting him know that he'd not started off the conversation properly. "I'm surprised he's feeling well enough, since he just got released from the hospital."

"I don't have a lot of time," he responded, ignoring her slight rebuke. "He's actually acting like he's not been sick at all. Anyhow, I just wanted to let you know, in case Sister Betty was planning on coming to the first service."

"Really?" Sharvon replied. "That's funny."

"It doesn't sound funny to me."

"I meant that it is funny because Cousin Betty's been up for a while. She's in the kitchen, just humming and praising God."

"Well, that's a good thing, isn't it?"

"I guess it is, since the two of them was in the valley of misery yesterday. She hasn't said anything about going to church yet. If she does, I'll try and steer her toward the second service, even if I have to go with her."

The conversation went on for another

minute. Leotis threw in a remark about how Sharvon's busy work schedule was not an excuse for not coming to church, to which she did not respond one way or the other. They also concluded that it'd be a good thing if the couple stayed apart for the time being, and away from Bea and Sasha in particular.

The weather outside this Sunday morning was hot, though the usual perspiration-inducing humidity was absent. But at Crossing Over Sanctuary's eight o'clock service, there was heat and sweat to spare.

Despite all the distractions that past week, and especially yesterday, Leotis was determined to preach. He had donned one of his old robes, a blue, white, and gold short-sleeved one that he didn't mind getting dirty.

He tossed his handkerchief in the air, throwing his head from side to side while hollering, "Thank ya, Jesus," preaching as though the apostle Paul whispered every word in his ear. The night before he was so consumed by guilt, he'd been unable to study his Bible. "Y'all just don't know!" he told the congregation as he brought the sermon to an end. "The enemy will always be at his job."

"Say that, Pastor," came a response from someone in the congregation. "Satan's a sneaky sumpthin'."

"There's a reason God wants us to watch as well as pray. The Devil can come at you in all sorts of ways." He paused and wiped his brow while shaking his head in the direction of the organist, who'd just begun playing a run of staccato notes designed to set the congregation to shouting. "But I'm going to leave that alone," he said as he laughed a little. "We still have another service at eleven o'clock, and we haven't had the altar call yet. But one day I'm going to preach in depth about watching and praying and the consequences when one doesn't."

Leotis stepped down from the pulpit and went to stand in the middle of the floor. As he stood there with his arms opened wide, a pastor's aide member removed his robe and wiped his brow. Then Leotis asked, "Are there any who are in need of prayer? God is not slacking in His promise to forgive your scarlet sins and make you whole again. I won't stand here in judgment this morning. I stand here with the agape love of the Lord."

"I'm in need of love," a soft feminine voice called out. All heads turned in the direction

the voice had come from, which was somewhere in the back of the sanctuary. The
person to which it belonged was hidden
among the many who'd attended this morning. "I need some of that agape love you
have."

A sudden movement from Freddie caught
Leotis's attention. With one hand in his lap,
Freddie had begun waving one finger back
and forth, like it was on fire. He then
quickly began mouthing, "No, no."

But Freddie's warning came too late. By
the time Leotis's attention turned back to
the rest of the congregation, there was a
short line of folks headed his way. Bobbing
and weaving down the center aisle was Ima.
Two ushers, one on each side of her, were
both supporting her by her arms and fanning her at the same time. Another usher
was trying to help Mother Pray Onn, but
she kept using the tip of her cane to push
the usher away.

"Sweet Jesus," called out a woman with a
huge pink hat shaped like a tree stump. She
was seated near Leotis. "He's soon to
come!"

"Sho'nuff," chimed in the woman who sat
next to her, whose girth took up two seats.
"I know Jesus is in the saving business if
that heifer's tossing in her sin-filled towel."

Other unkind remarks echoed about the sanctuary, as though none had heard the sermon that morning. And even those who normally sneaked out before the prayer and benediction stayed put.

There was nothing Leotis could say or do. He had preached on forgiveness, on watching and praying with fervor, and had offered God's agape love, which meant a love for all was plentiful. But now, standing there with his arms outstretched, beholding the sight of Ima and Sasha pushing toward him, all he wanted was to fold his arms and, with his peace of mind still intact, go home.

Ima was attending church that morning battle ready. She'd come with her long hair bouncing and behaving, determined to get Leotis's and the congregation's attention. After getting all Leotis's history she could from Sasha, especially bits about him being rather narrow-minded, and putting it together with what she definitely knew about men, she didn't just *come* to church that morning. Lady Ima arrived there a very different woman.

Shooing away the ushers, Ima walked the last few feet toward Leotis. She wore a neon purple, short-sleeved cotton dress with a jacket that modestly covered her large bosom. Although the outfit had looked plain

231

on the store's mannequin, Ima had filled it out in all the right places and had made it still look church classy. Besides wearing a pearl necklace and pearl earrings to accessorize her dress, she'd settled for matching three-inch, open-toed heels, instead of the normal five-inch heels, and had white polished toenails peeking through. The dress's hem hit just below the kneecap but could easily rise to show where many men had gone before when she sat.

Mother Pray Onn, dressed in her usual white, two-piece mothers' board outfit and tight bun, walked a few steps behind Ima. She looked like she was trying to hide from Leotis, but she needed to be close enough to hear and see Ima perform.

Lord, you take the wheel, Leotis thought as he beckoned Ima to cover the final few feet between them.

Leotis made no effort to acknowledge her presence any differently than he would that of others needing prayer. "My daughter," he told her as his adjutant, who'd been standing by, poured a little blessed oil into the palms of his hands. Closing his eyes, he began placing his hands on her head, saying, "I want you to give over to God all the concerns you've brought to this altar." He opened one eye slightly and saw Ima peeking, too. He quickly closed his eyes again and continued.

Leotis prayed aloud for Ima's salvation and silently for his own. Despite what he had told Sharvon and had even admitted to God, Ima could still get to him, even at God's altar.

Ima swayed a little, silently accepted all that he'd asked God to do for her, and inwardly presented her own petition. *Lord, I truly can change. I'd make a fabulous first lady.*

While Leotis went to his study to change after the service so that he and Freddie could return home, Freddie met with a few of the other trustees. He needed to ask them to put a hold on the surprise they'd been planning for his wedding. He hadn't figured out how to tell them why, and after praying and reading the scriptures the other night, he wasn't sure if he should.

"Glad to see you back in the service this morning," Elder Batty told Freddie, while others added their welcomes, as well. "Things have been rather quiet since the last time we spoke."

Freddie knew the elder was fishing around to see if there were any hard feelings. He imagined the man was still embarrassed after the way Bea had behaved badly at

Sister Betty's home and at the hospital.

"Everything is just fine, Elder Batty." Freddie could feel tiredness spreading through his body, and he wanted to continue with business. He found a seat.

One by one the trustees brought him up to date on all the outstanding business, but they never mentioned the surprise they were working on for Freddie's wedding. If they had any thought that he looked bad that morning, they kept it to themselves, perhaps thinking it was a result of whatever had caused him to pass out weeks ago in the fellowship hall.

While Leotis was still in his study, preparing to return home, and Freddie was concluding his meeting with the other trustees, Ima and Mother Pray Onn were sitting outside in Ima's car. Ima wanted to know what her aunt thought about her approach to winning over Leotis.

"You don't think this purple number is a little too understated?" Ima removed the jacket. She folded it before flinging it into the backseat. "I still want him to see what a real blessing looks like, one he could have if he ever stops acting a fool."

At first Sasha didn't answer. She was looking away, toward one of the church's three parking lots. She turned around and smiled at Ima. "I don't think it's too understated, but you might want to keep reminding him of what he could lose if he don't loosen up a bit."

"Why do you say that?"

"Because if you don't," Sasha said before pointing her finger at one of the parking lots, "she will."

Sharvon helped Sister Betty from her car. Sharvon had said she wanted to attend service that day, but she had also done everything to make sure they wouldn't make the same service as Leotis and Freddie.

Although they were attending the eleven o'clock service, Sharvon had wanted to get there early enough to park on the street rather than in one of the church's parking lots. "I don't know where the church gets these slow folks from. They either can't find you a parking space or they don't know how to direct the others to get out of the lot."

"It's probably because the first service let out late, Sharvon. Don't get so upset. We still have time, and you want your mind clear so you can receive the Lord's Word."

"I'm okay," Sharvon told her. "I'm just happy to finally have the time to attend church with you."

Sister Betty was happy to attend the service but a bit sad because she still hadn't heard from Leotis. She'd already decided not to confront Freddie, should he approach her. It was in God's hand, and she'd made up her mind that that was where she should leave it.

"Ain't no way I'm leaving now," Ima hissed. "I thought you told me that Sharvon worked on weekends and didn't come to church?"

"I said she's been working on the weekends and hadn't been to church in a while," Sasha replied. "You need to pay more attention."

But once Ima saw Sharvon walking toward the church with Sister Betty beside her, Ima's green eyes blazed. She watched Sharvon walk like a runway model, with her hair sweeping over her shoulders in long curls and her all-white dress making her look more like a bride than Ima ever could. Ima's eyes darted about the car, like she was looking for something to throw. "She's gonna get told today, I'm gonna be the first lady," she declared to Sasha.

A few minutes later it was Sasha's turn to become livid. She'd asked Ima to drive her home first before going back inside the church. She had left food baking in the oven and needed to get back and see about it. But Ima didn't care about that.

"Let your building burn down," Ima told her. "I am not driving you home first. I'm going back inside that church."

Sasha tried reasoning with her. "I don't have no reservation to take the church bus. You can't just hop on any bus going to the Promised Land development."

None of Sasha's arguments worked. Ima was on her way back inside the church while Sasha threatened to testify falsely against the bus driver if he didn't make room for her on that bus. The old bus driver, with his fatty stomach supporting the steering wheel, announced that he had one more passenger. Once the others realized it was Sasha, a few got off to give her room. Some hoped she'd give them the real deal on why Ima had asked for prayer and to join the church.

Driving home, Leotis fended off a tired Freddie's need to discuss Ima's sudden desire for prayer in morning service.

"I'm not pretending to be her judge and jury. I certainly do believe that God can save anyone," Freddie said. "But this is Ima Hell-raiser."

"God's got a use for us all." Leotis wanted that comment to end the discussion. However, nothing he'd said so far deterred the trustee from offering his opinions.

"Oh, I know that God can clean up anyone. I mean, look what He's done in my life."

"Well, then," Leotis said quickly, hoping this was the last of their conversation about Ima, "He can do it for Ima, too."

"What you need to do is pray that He can do it for you." Freddie's stare met that of Leotis, who had just swerved the car to keep from hitting a running squirrel.

"I'll tell you what, Trustee," Leotis said with authority. "You don't talk about Ima, and I won't mention my Sister Betty." He drummed his fingers on the steering wheel and began speaking to the rhythm he kept. "However, I must go and see about her. I know she's wondering why I haven't. And I've promised not to discuss you with her, even if she brings up your name. I won't even mention her name to you, either."

"You can discuss my Honey Bee all you want."

Leotis's jaw dropped. "What are you talking about? What's happened?"

"God's got this," Freddie said, smiling. "I've nothing to lose now. I'm throwing it all into God's hands. I've no time to let the Devil get a toehold on my remaining days."

"Does Sister Betty know about your sudden change of heart and plans?"

"If she don't know," Freddie said with a tired smile, "she will. She's a praying woman. God can and will show her what's up with our wedding plans, just like He did me. Either way, I'm not giving up on having that ole gal in my life some kinda way." Freddie stopped smiling, and his look became one of concern. "You, on the other hand, need to follow your own sermon."

"Which one?"

"The one you just preached this morning. You need to be the one doing all that watching and praying. What God was saying through you might have been more for you than for the rest of us."

What Freddie had just said dropped like a rock into Leotis's spirit, and for the rest of the way he said nothing more.

It'd taken Ima a while to calm down. Each time she'd started to reenter the church, she'd stopped and thought, *Don't I like a good challenge? What's Sharvon got on me? I light that man's fire. She can only douse the flames with her do-good ideas.* Ima had finally concluded that confronting Sharvon wasn't a good idea. It would not leave a good impression on either Leotis or the congregation, which she hoped to win over. *Let that woman have her dreams. They'll only be nightmares if she goes too far.* Concluding she had the upper hand and better looks, Ima got back inside her car and drove away.

The first person Sister Betty and Sharvon ran into as they entered the sanctuary for the eleven o'clock service was Bea. Sharvon immediately walked away, after telling Sister Betty that she needed to speak with someone she recognized before the service began. "You just tell the usher that we need two seats," she told Sister Betty before she walked away. "I'll be back in a few minutes."

Bea and Sasha had arranged to go to separate services that morning. They figured if Sister Betty and Trustee Freddie came to church separately, then either Bea or Sasha could keep an eye on them. If they came together, then the two women could put away any plans of getting them back together. Either way, Bea and Sasha already had their event-planning debut set in stone, and Sister Betty and Freddie would be a part of it.

"You're looking well rested this morning," Bea told Sister Betty.

"Why wouldn't I?"

"Well, we haven't chatted since that little misunderstanding at your home, when Trustee Freddie —" Bea stopped and looked around the sanctuary before she whispered, "When the trustee was staying in your bedroom, naked."

Sister Betty shifted her Bible to the other hand, straightened the small, white, mesh-material, beanie-shaped hat upon her head, then leaned in as she, too, whispered to Bea. "Viagra."

Bea jumped back so fast, the arch in her back almost straightened. "Harrumph!" Bea said before she turned and scurried away.

An usher escorted Sister Betty to one of the pews near the front of the sanctuary. She found Sharvon already seated there and chatting with one of the deacons. It didn't take long for one of the associate ministers chosen to give the sermon to get started, and he brought the service to a close much quicker than Leotis would've liked, had he still been there.

Although the service had ended some time ago, Sister Betty had insisted on hanging around and greeting some people she hadn't seen in a while. Sharvon almost had to drag her from the church so they could go home.

"Even though Leotis didn't preach the eleven o'clock service," Sister Betty told

Sharvon as they drove back home, "I figured he'd at least be in his study or close by."

Sister Betty had been throwing hints and asking about Leotis for the past ten minutes, ever since she discovered Leotis had left the church after the eight o'clock service, but she had managed to do this without ever mentioning Freddie.

Sharvon needed to fashion a reply that wasn't a total lie. "I really don't know what to tell you."

"Well," Sister Betty said as she fiddled with the car's air-conditioning knob and turned down the radio, "you never did mention why you were standing in his doorway yesterday."

"You saw me?" Sharvon hadn't meant to respond in a way that could bring about more questions. In fact, she hadn't thought at all about the possibility of her cousin seeing her and Leotis on his front porch. Since they'd left in his car almost immediately, she had just assumed that no one had seen them. "It wasn't much of anything," Sharvon lied. "I, too, had wondered why he hadn't been by the house, and he apologized about it." Sharvon's face lit up as she spoke, because even if she was making it up as she went along, she was going to milk that apology for all it was worth.

"That's very sweet of him," Sister Betty replied. "I just wanted to tell him that I'm thinking about taking a short vacation. Perhaps I'll go to Myrtle Beach, read the Word, and spend some time with the Lord."

"Where's this coming from? I've never heard you mention Myrtle Beach before."

"I've never been there." Sister Betty turned to look out the window again. "There's so many things I've never done before that I'd like to experience."

Sharvon said nothing more. One of the many things Sister Betty had failed to mention was a trip down the aisle. She quickly sped up. Somehow after she took her cousin home, she was going to talk with Leotis. The sooner the old couple realized that what they'd had was just a misunderstanding, the quicker they could get back to making those wedding plans. And if she and Leotis couldn't come up with something, she knew who could.

CHAPTER 14

The Tuesday afternoon following that Sunday's morning service, Ima visited Sasha's apartment. She went there to discuss the act she'd put on at the church. Since it'd been Sasha's idea in the first place; Ima's ego needed stroking. After all, she thought she'd put on quite a show, throwing herself upon the church's altar while doing the same to Leotis's libido.

It turned out that Ima would need to listen to Sasha rant about the pot roast that'd burned because she'd taken the church bus home.

Ima shot back in her seat at the kitchen table. She'd listened to enough. "I'll take you to dinner, and you can order all the damn pot roast you want!"

"I want no profanity in my home!" Sasha slammed down the pot she'd just taken off the stove. "Respect my home, where the good Lord abides."

"I see," Ima replied as she stood and towered over her aunt. "When we discuss me tempting Leotis in front of God's altar and congregation, making Leotis propose to me, and me becoming the first lady, that's okay with the good Lord, who resides in your home?"

"I have my standards," Sasha said stubbornly, looking up and almost bumping Ima on the chin with her bun. "You can always walk or drive them ten blocks back to your own low-rent apartment and stay hidden from anyone trying to deliver a certified letter, like you've been doing ever since you came back here. In that place you can do all the cussing you want, but in my home . . . my standards."

"You don't have standards, Aunt Sasha. And I ain't afraid of no pieces of paper, certified or otherwise. You're having delusions."

"Whatever I have," Sasha said adamantly, "it still resides in my home."

Suddenly the two women stepped back and burst into laughter. They hugged and did a quick two-step before going into Sasha's living room.

"How long have we been going at one another like this?" Sasha teased.

"Since the day I could walk, talk, and

learn to shut up and stay out of your business." Ima's eyes twinkled. "You know I love you like any true Hellraiser would."

Sasha's lips began to curl. "I know you put me out of your car and onto that slow-behind church bus, and then you told me that you'd changed your mind about going inside the church and taking Sharvon down a peg or two."

"Like I said . . ." Ima laughed, as though she'd not heard Sasha mention Sharvon's name. "I love you like a true Hellraiser. Now, let's discuss part two of the plan."

However, Sasha insisted that Ima first eat before getting down to business. After serving the burnt pot roast she had saved from that past Sunday just for Ima, Sasha watched her niece pretend to enjoy what she was certain tasted like crow.

Back at Sister Betty's house, Sister Betty rose, her knees stiff after having a long noonday prayer. Grabbing her Bible from its place on the table, she read a few scriptures, placing scallop-edged purple bookmarks between the pages she felt needed revisiting. Sharvon was back on her hectic schedule for the week, so for the most part, Sister Betty stayed home alone.

The one thing that brightened her day was

news that Leotis was stopping by later that afternoon. Hearing the front doorbell, she smoothed her apron and went to answer the door.

She flung the door open wide. "Well, look who's finally come to see about me," she told him. The wide smile on her face betrayed the annoyance she feigned.

A short time later, over homemade chicken noodle soup and tuna sandwiches, they ran out of church business to discuss. It was she who finally mentioned Freddie by name.

"I understand some of the men," she began, while putting away the dishes, "including Freddie, are preparing for a fall concert to raise monies for the prison ministry. How is he doing with it? I hope he's taking better care of himself. He has high blood pressure, you know." Without waiting to see if what she'd said made Leotis uncomfortable, she patted him on his shoulder. Then she quickly added with a sigh, "I know that you already know that he and I haven't seen each other or spoken much to one another in the past few weeks."

She left the conversation open for him to jump right in and fill in the blanks.

Leotis didn't answer right away. Instead, he placed his fingers together, forming a steeple. He thought about what he and Sharvon had discussed the past Sunday evening. Neither of them had figured out a way to ease the old couple back together. Sharvon still feared Sister Betty would be livid if she discovered that it was she, Sharvon, who had caused Sasha to head off in the wrong direction, one which sent Freddie off the rails and to the wrong conclusion.

"Well, I'm still waiting for the final proposal," Leotis finally said. "Elder Batty is working with the trustee on getting permission from the prison to hold a concert there."

"But that's not leaving too much time," she told him. "It's already the middle of August. Both of them and the entire men's team should've had that done months ago. Why are you men so hardheaded?"

Leotis laughed and nodded. "I'm afraid I don't have an answer. Perhaps God just made us that way." He said nothing more for a moment and simply looked at his watch, something he'd been doing for the past few minutes. "But maybe at the next prayer and testimony meeting, I can mention it again and put some fire under them," he mused, breaking his silence. "By the way, folks have been asking why you haven't been to prayer meeting in a while. I guess that's partially my fault. I haven't really been able to take you."

"It's not your fault. If I'd really wanted to go, I wouldn't have waited on you. But since you say folks have been commenting, next time tell them I've been praying at home," she said slowly. "I'm just trying to spend time alone with the good Lord." She would've said more, but she saw he was still checking his watch, without really appearing to listen. Looking at her wall clock, she asked, "Am I keeping you from something?" That time she didn't try to hide her disappointment.

"Of course you aren't." Leotis forced a laugh. "You know I'm a healthy eater, except when it comes to your baking, but I can't cook. I need to pick up something before I head off to a meeting. A man can't live on soup and sandwiches, you know."

Sister Betty still wouldn't smile. She might not have seen him in a while, but she knew her pastor. Something wasn't right. But she'd told God that she would not interfere in anyone's business, unless God wanted her to. She didn't feel a pain in her knees or anything akin to a spirit telling her to butt in, and so she would not.

"It's nearly two thirty," he announced. Leotis stood up, his way of indicating that he was about to leave.

Sister Betty was about to say something, but her telephone rang. "I don't know who this could be." She looked at it and raised her brow. "But the number does look familiar."

"You'll probably need to get that," Leotis told her. "I'll let myself out. But like the Terminator, I'll be back," he said in his deep voice. He then laughed and headed through her foyer toward the front door. Leotis knew who was calling, and it'd happened just in time. "Your idea better work, Sharvon," he whispered.

It'd been Sharvon's idea to get more involved when neither she nor Leotis could come up with a plan to get her cousin Betty and Freddie back together, or at least on speaking terms. Since there wasn't much time, Sharvon had called on the only gun-toting, preaching ex-convict deacon in her family — Sister Betty's first cousin and Sharvon's second cousin, Deacon Thurgood Pillar. Thurgood, a skinny man who had worn a hardened and greasy forties-style conk for most of his life and had the worst sense of style since Adam wore fig leaves, had become the go-to man for all things romantic and spiritual.

Thurgood and his wife, Delilah, were

experts when it came to elderly love. The two were always happy and were known to make their bedsprings surrender. They had remarried after forty years of estrangement. It'd taken the sudden death of their son Jessie's wife to make them see how foolish they'd been to part in the first place. They'd parlayed their experiences into a successful counseling career.

"You have a blessed day," Sister Betty called out to Leotis before she heard her front door shut, and picked up her telephone.

"Hello. Praise God."

"Hey, gal," a male voice said, laughing. "It's your New York City slicker cousin, Thurgood. I'm calling to check up on you. Me and Dee Dee been getting things together for your big day next month. Ain't been no easy task getting you married. I'm prouder than an old rooster with an extra comb to walk you down that aisle."

Sister Betty heard Delilah, her cousin Thurgood's beautiful Lena Horne look-alike, acid-tongued deaconess wife, whom he always lovingly called Dee Dee, chime in. "That's right. We seniors in love gotta stick together. As your matron of honor, chile, I can't wait to put you in the hands of a good stylist. You gonna look much better than anything bought from Beyoncé's House of Deréon. Not quite certain how it's pronounced." Delilah took a breath and added, "Whatever the name is of the gal married to that rapper, the one using two letters from the alphabet for his name. You know the gal I'm talking about."

As happy as Sister Betty was to hear from a couple who were the same age as she and Freddie, Thurgood and Delilah were the last ones she'd expected to call. And she certainly didn't want to talk about Freddie or tell them that there might not be a wedding.

"This is such a surprise," Sister Betty said, meaning every word. "I hadn't expected to hear from you two this soon, since you seem to travel so much."

"Ain't that the truth," Delilah remarked. "You know me and my Thurgood still traveling around the country, giving safe-sex and relationship seminars to seniors."

"That's right," Thurgood added. "Whole lot of old folks getting HIV and AIDs, instead of getting the regular stuff, like high blood pressure and dementia."

"Oh, stop it," Delilah snapped. "Your cousin Betty fixing to get married. You and I know she ain't raised nothing but praise to the Lord, and not her legs. She don't need to be hearing about no STDs and such."

"Yeah," Thurgood replied. "You're right, Dee Dee. But I don't know too much about the man she's marrying. If he's like most, then she still needs to know what's happening, because I'm sure he ain't heard from everyone he's touched."

"We're here in Greenville, getting ready to hold a seminar this weekend," Delilah said.

"That's right," Thurgood added. "We weren't supposed to get in till this Thursday, but it was cheaper to fly in a day or so early."

"So," Delilah said, "you know there ain't no way in this world that we're this close to you and don't drop by. Ain't that right, Thurgood?"

Sister Betty slowly sat, with the phone still attached to her ear. As they always did, Thurgood and Delilah had started a conversation with her, only to end up talking to each other. All she could do was listen as they talked about her and wait until they talked to her.

Leotis was almost fifteen minutes late in picking up Freddie from his latest oncology visit. He'd learned last week that Freddie's participation in the cancer trial would soon end and Freddie would not need a stem cell transplant. Freddie had gone through all the testing and had fared much better than some of the other participants, who would need donors. He'd already endured a two-day procedure involving harvesting stem cells from his own blood, which would be available should he ever need them. After getting the news, Leotis and Freddie had been overjoyed as they sat at the kitchen table, praising God that day that Freddie would not need a stem cell transplant, after all.

"Looks like you're beginning to get your old color back," Leotis told him as they pulled out of the hospital's parking lot.

"That's right," Freddie said. "The folks at the hospital told me that it shouldn't take long before I won't look like I've been sleeping on and off in an Easy-Bake Oven." He reached up and tapped the top of his head. "Don't know when this little peach fuzz I got will grow out, but I don't think I'm gonna be mad if I don't get that one-piece I've been pulling on for years. But I said I'd leave all this up to the Lord, and that's what I'm gonna do."

"Just claim your healing, Trustee. God has the final say, because all man can do, whether it's cancer or something just as bad, is give a diagnosis. God's in charge of the prognosis."

"Amen," Freddie replied. "Amen."

As they neared Leotis's house, Freddie decided to share some other news with Leotis. "Reverend Tom," Freddie began. "I'm so grateful for all the hospitality you've given me over these past weeks, but I think it's time I get back to my own home. I sorta miss it, and I don't want to keep on intruding."

"You are no bother," Leotis said. "I've enjoyed your company."

"I gotta tell you something else, too," Freddie said as he began laughing. "I had an ulterior motive or two."

"Well, those motives must be a hoot. I haven't seen you laughing the way you are now in quite some time."

"Don't know if you will think it's funny, but I stayed partially so I could be closer to my Honey Bee. Around the corner would've been too far away, should the Lord give me a sign to see her."

"I'm glad that you are still waiting on the Lord and haven't completely written her off." Leotis smiled. "And what's your other motive or motives?"

"I had hoped that Ima or that big mouth, Sasha, would come around." Freddie laughed harder. "I'm still waiting on God to ease my heart on them two. But so far every time I think about them, my fists ball up." Freddie's tone then turned serious. "And I definitely wanted to block whatever sexy pitch Ima threw your way."

"That's okay," Leotis replied. "I haven't seen or heard from her since she came to the altar and asked to join the church."

"Maybe it's because new members' class won't begin again for a few weeks. Don't be surprised if that she-devil don't try to follow through with joining the church *and* having you two joined together. Hope you getting my drift."

Leotis knew that what Freddie had said was possible. Ima wasn't off his mind, just out of sight. Even lately, having a couple of dinners with Sharvon hadn't completely taken Ima out of the picture. Although his thoughts of comparing a kiss from Sharvon to ones from Ima had increased, he knew that if Freddie saw the two women as a problem, then others might, too, and that truly was a big problem.

Once they arrived back at Leotis's house, Freddie quickly decided he wanted to go home that very same day. They gathered his things together, and no sooner had they headed out the door than they saw Sister Betty coming out of her house. She had her arms filled with several small boxes. They watched her stumble slightly when she looked over and saw them. Leotis also saw the look of relief on Freddie's face when she didn't fall.

Not waiting for the apparently stubborn pair to acknowledge each other, Leotis called out to her. "Good afternoon again, Sister Betty."

Sister Betty heard Leotis, but her eyes remained on Freddie. "I guess it's either I don't see you much at all or it's more than once in the same day," she teased without smiling. She realized she'd just revised what Leotis had said, but it was the best she could do at that moment.

Leotis leaned over to take one of the duffel bags from the trustee. "Aren't you going to at least acknowledge that she's standing there?"

"I didn't hear her say nothing to me, and I don't wanna be too pushy. I didn't leave a good impression the last time I hollered at her."

It didn't appear that Freddie would speak to her, after all. Rather than risk further embarrassment, Sister Betty dropped the boxes into her garbage can and quickly walked around to the other side of her house.

Leotis shook his head and shoved one of the duffel bags into the backseat of his car. He looked at Freddie, who had remained standing and had watched Sister Betty turn and walk away. Shutting the door to the backseat brought Freddie out of his trance.

"Well, coward," he told Freddie, "that was one opportunity you quickly tossed away."

"So how did it go?" Sharvon's call had caught Leotis just as he was returning from taking Freddie home. "I got your text."

"Can we talk in person?" Sharvon asked.

"I hadn't expected that he'd want to go home right away," Leotis told Sharvon when she arrived at his house moments later. "At least if he were still here, there'd be an easier way for them to run into each other."

"Well, perhaps it was time," Sharvon said. "I have never seen anyone stay away from his own home for this long because he was heartbroken or had high blood pressure."

"Everyone reacts to situations differently."

"I know," she told him. "But if having high blood pressure is going to make me lose my hair and to cause my complexion and skin to look like the back of an elephant's behind, then I might wanna reconsider this heavy caseload I'm overseeing."

Leotis listened carefully as Sharvon laid

out her observations. She'd seen just about everything that would normally make someone question whether Freddie's behavior was all due to high blood pressure. She didn't mention that she thought otherwise, and he had to keep his word and not tell her the truth about Freddie.

"And now that my second cousin Thurgood and his wife, Delilah, are going to stay nearby for a few days," she told him, "perhaps they can counsel Cousin Betty and put her mind at ease until things calm down and she and Freddie get their act together."

Leotis quickly removed a smile that'd begun to spread across his face before he asked, "I just remembered something. Aren't they the elderly sex therapists?"

"That's one of the descriptions you might label them with. But they are a bit over the top with their presentations. However, according to them, they're saved, sanctified, and Holy Ghost filled, and they believe they're on a mission from God."

"That seems to run in your family," Leotis told her, smiling before adding a wink.

"Whatever," Sharvon replied, pretending to be offended. "They're very serious about senior citizens getting the right information regarding their sexuality. Seniors are losing their husbands and wives all the time. When they eventually jump back into the dating game, they're now sleeping with everyone that the other person has slept with. These days, men are taking Viagra and other sex stimulants, thinking they have permission to sleep around. Most don't realize or care that sex can kill you and your partner."

"So I guess you told them Sister Betty might not want to have that type of conversation since you unintentionally implied to Mother Pray Onn that the wedding wasn't happening." Shaking his head, Leotis added, "If you haven't, then that's the conversation you need to have with them quickly."

"Not quite." Sharvon took a deep breath and began twirling strands of hair that'd fallen over her shoulder as her eyes darted between Leotis and a huge picture of the Crucifixion hanging on his wall. "They were so excited about the upcoming wedding and how happy they were to be involved in the counseling, I couldn't get another word in edgewise."

"Sharvon, let go of the excuses and get in touch with your cousins."

"I know you're right, but rather than over the telephone, I want to sit down with Thurgood and Delilah. And I will before they see Cousin Betty in person."

"Well, you better hope they don't speak to

her about wild honeymoon bedroom antics before you speak to them."

"Why would you think that could happen?"

"I'm guessing that it might've been their phone call that Sister Betty took when I was leaving."

"If it was them, they probably called just to let Cousin Betty know that they were in town. They won't say anything to her over the telephone about sexual matters, so I've got time to explain the messy situation I created. As far as I know, they don't arrive here in Pelzer until Thursday morning. In the meantime, I promise you I am going through with it and will tell Cousin Betty that in my frustration I foolishly mouthed off to Sasha that the wedding was off. That way Thurgood and Delilah may not need to get involved. You can take my word for it."

Chapter 15

Sister Betty had completed her current daily prayer ritual of trying to prod the Lord into having pity on her. Sharvon had come in late last night and had gone straight to bed, and it'd meant that Sister Betty had had no one to talk to.

Around the corner, Freddie had gotten up and done the same. Both had piddled around their homes since the day before, doing mundane chores, trying to avoid thinking about each other.

Although Freddie had a car, he still didn't feel confident enough to drive it any long distances. So he decided he'd just take a walk around the area, exercising, as the doctor had suggested, not too far but far enough to make it worth his while. The thought crossed his mind that he might run into Sister Betty, but then he knew she rarely walked anywhere. With the warm sun kissing the top of his bald head and a walking cane in his hand in case the weakness came, he walked out of his front yard.

"I might as well go out of my way and do something different. If I walk up the block this way," he muttered while pointing with his cane, "then I won't even pass by my Honey Bee's or Leotis's homes." With his cane dangling from his wrist until he felt a need to use it, Freddie began his walk in the opposite direction.

"Well, Lord," Sister Betty whispered, adjusting the wide brim of her straw hat, which she wore to keep the sun out of her eyes. "I'm depending upon you to touch these old rickety knees. I haven't walked a block or two in quite a spell." She closed her door and slowly headed out her front yard. As soon as she looked toward Leotis's house, she saw his car was gone. She remembered Leotis had told her yesterday that today he was going to the Promised Land development to meet with some of the store owners.

"No sense in taking a chance. Freddie showed me yesterday that he's still mad at me. He didn't even act like he seen me," she murmured. She felt the signs of sorrowfulness and immediately straightened her shoulders and held her head high. *If I walk the other way, then I won't even pass his house.* Sister Betty closed her front gate and began slowly walking in the opposite direction of Freddie's house.

Freddie hadn't walked too far before he became winded. By the time he reached the corner, he needed to lean on both a mailbox and his cane for support. He began panting from shortness of breath as he tried to determine if he could make it back home if he turned around.

It took Sister Betty a moment to realize that she wasn't missing Freddie so much as to imagine it was him leaning on a mailbox. She recognized his dark blue pants and the sky-blue shirt hanging off his bony frame.

No sooner had Sister Betty begun to pick up her pace than the sound of a car's horn and someone calling out her name stopped her. She turned to see a silver Mercedes, one she didn't recognize. Thinking perhaps she was wrong about hearing her name, and seeing that Freddie hadn't moved off the mailbox, she continued on.

"Betty," a female's voice called out. "Wait up."

The silver Mercedes had driven a few feet ahead of Sister Betty and then had begun driving in reverse. Ahead, she could see

Freddie beginning to move away from the mailbox. She didn't have much time to observe much else, because when the car's window rolled completely down, she saw long blond hair and then Delilah's face appear.

"I told Thurgood that was you," Delilah squealed. "We were on our way to your house and made a wrong turn."

Sister Betty tried to smile but couldn't. At that moment all her attention was on Freddie. He had moved completely away from the mailbox and was now trying to walk using a cane.

"What's wrong, Betty?" Delilah's eyes followed where Betty looked. "Get in and let us take you back so you won't have to walk."

Sister Betty walked quickly to the car and jumped into the backseat, her behind slapping the leather seat with a thud. She hadn't known she could move that fast. Her eyes met Thurgood's. He didn't have a chance to say hello before she ordered, "Quick, Thurgood. That's Freddie on up ahead. He ain't looking too good. Hurry up and catch up to him."

Thurgood rolled up on Freddie and dashed out of the car to help him. Freddie jerked away and began to sway.

"It's me, Thurgood Pillar." As Thurgood

pulled Freddie toward the car, Freddie resisted more.

And then within seconds it appeared Freddie regained enough strength to throw a punch in Thurgood's direction.

By the time Sister Betty and Delilah made it to within a few feet of the mailbox, Thurgood was standing with his feet spread apart, his fists in the air, about to knock some recognition into Freddie.

Sister Betty shouted, "Thurgood, don't you dare lay a hand on him!"

It took a few minutes for everyone to calm down, and several more before Freddie could be convinced to go to Sister Betty's. In a measured tone Sister Betty had told him, "You can come back home, where I can tend to whatever is wrong with you, or I gonna let my cousin Thurgood finish what he was about to start." She'd hoped Freddie would see some humor in her warning.

Freddie paid no attention to Sister Betty's threats. However, the essence of Delilah's fragrant come-hither perfume was suddenly like catnip. He didn't try pretending that he didn't want to get in the car. He even closed the car door himself, albeit before Sister Betty could get in all the way, causing her hat to fall off.

"Freddie," Delilah cooed, "I'd have never

recognized you. It's a good thing we came upon Betty, 'cause we might've driven by thinking you were probably putting mail in that mailbox."

"Yeah," Thurgood added, "today God was with you in more ways than one." Thurgood began laughing. "I was about to lay your butt out New York style."

Freddie didn't laugh, but he did respond. "I think you must've forgotten I'm from New York, too."

"I'm glad you men are feeling well enough to fight," Sister Betty snapped. "Y'all are men of God and are all up in this car, talking like you're getting ready for a pay-per-view."

"Honey Bee, it's what men do," Freddie told her quickly. He covered his mouth and coughed. He felt he should have covered it before he spoke, but now it was too late. He certainly hadn't meant to call her by her pet name.

Delilah looked over at Thurgood, who was about to turn into Sister Betty's driveway. "Did you hear what he called Betty?"

"I'm not deaf, Dee Dee."

"Don't you mean Dee Dee *honey*?"

"Since when have I ever called you Dee Dee honey?"

Thurgood turned off the ignition and

shifted in his seat to face Freddie before he said with a sneer, "Thanks a lot, playa. Now I'm gonna have to hear about how sweet you are to Betty all the way back to New York and probably a lot longer after that."

"It should've come naturally," Delilah said, pulling down the sun visor, sliding back its cover to reveal a mirror. She bared her teeth, checking them for any stains from the soft pink lipstick she wore. Seeing that everything, including her hair, was flawless, Delilah turned in her seat to face Thurgood and started in. "You know what, Thurgood," she began. "You can get rid of your conked hair and wear just two colors — instead of looking like you searched for the rainbow inside a box of Crayola — and you can stand before thousands of men and tell them what they should and shouldn't do when it comes to courting and sexing, but you can't give me a reason why you don't call me honey?"

"Keep running that mouth, Dee Dee," he told her. "I'm sure one will come to me."

That's what's different today. Thurgood ain't wearing that greasy conk, Sister Betty thought as she peered over and caught sight of Thurgood in his rearview mirror. *Well, suh, he is looking coordinated. Delilah done cleaned him up real good.*

Sister Betty leaned back and gently tapped Freddie on his hand. Narrowing her eyes and nodding her head, she indicated that they should get out of the car. At the rate Thurgood and Delilah were going at it, she was certain they wouldn't notice. She'd wait until they got inside the house to remind him that when Thurgood and Delilah finished talking to each other, they would remember that they'd been talking to them.

In the past, whenever Freddie and Sister Betty arrived at her home, Freddie had always led the way. He'd take her key, open the door, and then wait for her to enter. He was the kind and caring gentleman. Now he stood at the bottom of her steps, waiting for her to walk past and enter her house. As tired as he felt at that moment, and despite the fact that he just wanted to hurry and sit, he still didn't presume that it was okay for him to act like the old Freddie.

Sister Betty wanted to push him ahead of her so he'd enter the house first, but she didn't. She hurried past Freddie when she saw him hesitate. "Come on inside," she told him gently. "They should realize we're not in the car in a few minutes."

Feeling kidnapped, Freddie used his cane as little as possible when he did as she asked, but not without looking back at

Thurgood and Delilah, who were still going at each other in the car. "Well, I guess it's good to know that some things haven't changed." He smiled, but not too broadly.

Freddie followed Sister Betty into the kitchen and waited for her to tell him when and where to sit. It was as though he had forgotten the steps to their love dance and now relied on her for choreography.

"I'm not too happy putting you through this inconvenience." Freddie looked around for somewhere to lay his cane.

Sister Betty gently took the metal cane from his hand. She hung it by its handle on the back of the chair. Standing behind him, she noticed what looked like baby-fine hair growing on his scalp. She also saw his color didn't look quite as dark as she thought it had before. But there was no doubting the tiredness, and she wondered if he'd been overdoing it by trying to keep up with Leotis. "Freddie," she said as she walked over to a cabinet for a glass, "I don't want to hound you or get all up in your business."

"What is it, Sister Betty?"

He'd called her Sister Betty, and to her, it didn't sound right. She'd been surprised when he first called her by her pet name, but he hadn't called her Sister Betty since they became engaged. That reminder caused her to look at the engagement ring still shining bright on her small ring finger. She wondered if he was trying to get up the nerve to ask her to return it.

"You were about to say something?" Freddie turned around and saw her fingering the engagement ring. *Lord, please don't let her take my ring off.*

Outside, in the Mercedes, Thurgood and Delilah sat quietly for a moment before Thurgood spoke first.

"Do you think we've given them enough time to be alone?" Thurgood reached over and kissed Delilah on the cheek. "I don't know why you didn't stay in the acting game long enough to win an Oscar. Gal, you were on fire a while ago."

"We both should take a bow," Delilah agreed. "Calling that poor Freddie a playa was mean."

"Hey, it takes one to know one. I wasn't being mean to him. I was just giving him a possibility."

"So what do you think we should do next, Thurgood? Your cousin Betty still ain't acting like a bride-to-be filled with certainty. I know this is their first time, but those two were acting like they'd just met sitting back there."

"I picked up that same vibe. Except for the idle threats Freddie was throwing about when I tried to get him inside the car, there wasn't an ounce of communication between them."

"Well, we can't expect them to have the special communication skills we have. Besides, the man's been under the weather, and he looks like it's more than just some high blood pressure. He's skinny like a nail."

"You can't go by that, Dee Dee. Look at me. I'm thin, too."

"Yeah, Thurgood," Delilah said, allowing her tongue to sweep over her lips. "You're well proportioned, and your beige and brown leisure suit makes a difference."

"Yes, I definitely still got it."

Delilah didn't want Thurgood wandering off the thought track, so she quickly added, "But I gotta tell you —"

Thurgood laughed. "Go ahead and tell me with your fine self, Dee Dee. What you got to tell me? About now I'm feeling like a rocket about to shoot off on the Fourth of July."

Delilah sighed and shook her head. "Sharvon only wanted us to get together for dinner and discuss the wedding and such. But it looks like we gotta test them a bit more before we decide if they gonna need some

of our special sexual communication counseling for late bloomers or we gotta go
Christian gangster on their stubborn butts."

"You mean do a little more role playing?"

"Yes."

"Well, let's get to it," Thurgood said
before he got out of the car and walked
around to open the door for her. "It's show-
time."

"In which one of these rooms in this big
ole mansion are you two hiding?" Thurgood
called out as he and Delilah entered Sister
Betty's home.

"We're in the kitchen, Thurgood." Sister
Betty peeked out of the kitchen and waved
at them as they walked down her hallway.
"We're in here enjoying something cold to
drink. Can I get the two of you something?"

Thurgood and Delilah entered and sat at
the kitchen table. Each of them had deliberately grabbed an empty chair that separated
Sister Betty and Freddie. Thurgood apologized to Sister Betty for making an unan-
nounced visit. "We might not have planned
it that way, but think what might have happened if we didn't come along." He then
motioned to Freddie, who sat stiff as a stone
and was just as helpless as he was when he
was leaning on that mailbox.

"Tell me something," Delilah said in

between tiny sips of lemonade. "Have you two written your wedding vows yet?"

The surprised looks that sprang up on Sister Betty's and Freddie's faces didn't go unnoticed.

"You two look like we done walked in on you naked," Thurgood teased.

"Don't be embarrassed," Delilah said softly. "Me and Thurgood didn't write ours until the night before. We'd completely forgotten about it."

"Well, that's not necessary," Sister Betty said and then glanced over at Freddie, who looked like he was shrinking from fear.

"Of course it's necessary," Thurgood replied and then turned to Freddie. "Don't you think so, my cousin-to-be?"

Freddie remained speechless.

"Obviously, they haven't done it, so we might as well share what we did," Delilah said as she pulled two sheets of paper out of her purse. The papers were well read and the type was smudged, but she smiled as she handed one sheet to Thurgood. "Suppose me and Thurgood show you how we did it when we got remarried?"

Feeling trapped and with nothing else to do, Sister Betty and Freddie nodded. They then leaned back in their seats, prepared to watch *The Thurgood and Delilah Show.*

"We didn't just read our vows," Thurgood announced as he stood. "We acted them out."

Delilah rose from her seat. She and Thurgood stood together with paper in hand and began to show them how it'd gone at their wedding.

Thurgood waved one hand about Delilah's body, as though he had a magic wand. "I, Thurgood, will always love you, Delilah, because you are like a prince's daughter. Your feet in sandals are so beautiful. Your graceful legs are like jewels. The hands of a skilled worker must have shaped them. Your navel is like a round bowl that always has mixed wine in it. Your waist is like a mound of wheat that is surrounded by lilies."

Thurgood stopped to see if what he was saying was having an impact. As soon as he saw that Freddie's mouth was agape, he grinned, turned back to face a smiling Delilah, and continued with his eyes and hands sweeping across her chest. "Your two breasts are lovely. They are like two young antelopes. Your neck is smooth and beautiful, like a beige tower. And I will forever see you this way and hold your essence in my heart."

"Don't you two say nothing yet," Thurgood told them quickly. "It's my Dee Dee's turn now."

Delilah smiled and adjusted the paper she held. Looking up at Thurgood, she threw back her hair and, with one hand on curvy hips any thirty-year-old woman would covet, began. "Thurgood, I will never forget the time when God brought you back into my life." Her smile grew. "I went down to a grove of nut trees. I wanted to look at the new plants growing in the valley. I wanted to find out whether the vines had budded. I wanted to see if the pomegranate trees had bloomed. Before I realized it, I was among the royal chariots of your firmness."

Sister Betty looked at Freddie, who seemed to be hanging on to every word Delilah said. He didn't appear to understand what she was saying, but his glazed-over eyes didn't try to hide his appreciation. "I imagine when you two get finished reminiscing and serenading, you'll remember you was talking to us."

"Oh my." Delilah blushed. "All this time and Thurgood and me still act like newlyweds."

"That's right," Thurgood said. "Take a good look at me and my Dee Dee."

"Why?" Sister Betty leaned back in her chair to obstruct Freddie's wanton gaze.

"This will be you and Freddie once y'all

are hitched." Thurgood let out a chuckle. "Any blind person can see you two got that Thurgood and Dee Dee potential." Without any resistance from Freddie, Thurgood pushed Freddie's seat closer to Sister Betty. "Now, that's better. I ain't expecting Freddie to set off no sparks right away, but one look at him tells me his fuse been lit."

Thurgood and Delilah took turns encouraging Sister Betty and Freddie. They repeated their story of estrangement, mentioning that Thurgood had gone to prison and Delilah had fled to Hollywood, and describing how God had brought them back together. Delilah's eyes became bleary when she told them how she'd delayed telling Thurgood that she'd placed their son, Jessie, then a two-year-old, in foster care. They told their story slowly, as though anticipating questions from the couple. However, neither Sister Betty nor Freddie asked questions, nor did they move their chairs away from each other.

After a few more glasses of lemonade, Thurgood and Delilah prepared to leave.

"Well, we have taken up enough of your time," Thurgood said as he kissed Sister Betty on her cheek. He then looked at Freddie. "You looking much better than earlier, but if you want, I can drop you off at your house."

"Thank you, Thurgood," Freddie replied. "Just let me gather my things." He rose and took his cane off the back of his chair. For the first time since he'd sat down in her kitchen Freddie smiled at Sister Betty. "Thank you, Betty," he told her. "I'm praying —"

"Praying what?" Sister Betty asked. The hope in her voice lingered.

But as though the words were caught in his throat, Freddie headed toward the front door, taking the unspoken words with him.

"I'm right behind you, Freddie," Thurgood said before turning to Sister Betty. "We are gonna be here until Sunday. We might not see you again to go out for dinner, because after our last seminar on Saturday night, we'll probably need to rest up so we don't miss our early morning flight." Then he added, "Of course, our plans are always subject to change."

Delilah came over to Thurgood, tapping him on his arm. "Why don't you swing back around here and pick me up after you drop Freddie off?" she told him. "I just thought of a lovely idea for their wedding, and I want to run it past Betty first."

"That's not a problem, Dee Dee. You just take your time. I got an idea I want to discuss with Freddie, if he don't mind. But it just might take a little more time than it would if I just dropped him around the corner."

Sister Betty heard the sound of Thurgood's car engine as he backed out of her driveway. She gathered the glasses, almost dropping them as she placed them on the counter. She could feel Delilah's eyes watching her every move. It didn't take but a few minutes to remove the napkins and reset her table. The way Delilah's eyes burned into her back made the whole process seem like an eternity.

"So what are you going to do?" Delilah finally asked. "Clear the entire kitchen and mop the floors before we sit and chat? Before you start protesting, I'm telling you that Thurgood and I can tell something's wrong."

"I really don't want to talk about it, Delilah. I've left it in God's hands."

"Oh, ain't that about nothing," Delilah said as she maneuvered a chair to block Sister Betty from leaving her kitchen. "Do you think God is going to come down here and fix your mess? He has His people to do that for Him. You, above all, should know that, especially the way you keep butting in folks' business and saying the Lord sent you."

Delilah's words brought Sister Betty's mind to a halt. She'd promised God that she wouldn't involve anyone in her troubles with Freddie. She'd kept her word so far, because she hadn't discussed whether there'd be a wedding with anyone, not even Freddie.

"Delilah, are you telling me that God has sent you?"

"I'm telling you that you need to stop aggravating God about things that He's already promised you. I'm telling you that you need to understand that whatever God's got in store for you, the Devil wants to cancel."

"I know that, Delilah." She did know it, and especially when it came to other people. How often had she given that same encouragement to someone when they'd begun to lose hope or become impatient? "I've been reading the Word, fasting, and praying."

"That's wonderful," Delilah remarked. "And yet you haven't believed what God has promised you. Luke, the eighteenth chapter and first verse, tells us that we should always pray and never become discouraged."

"I have faith. . . ."

"Sure you have faith," Delilah said as she pulled the chair away so Sister Betty could pass and sit opposite her. "You have super-saint faith that you will receive everlasting life. You have faith that Jesus went to the cross. You even have faith that God will supply all your needs. Yet because you've reached three score and something, you don't believe God can finally give you a husband, and that even with all the crazy drama that sometimes come with a relationship, that you won't ever know what to do to make it work. You're acting like all this is nothing but a dream. My goodness, Betty, I'd hate to see how your faith would react if God told you like He told Sarah that you were going to have a child."

Sister Betty burst into tears.

They hadn't been inside Freddie's home but ten minutes, and all during that time Thurgood had done nothing but scold him. Freddie wanted to toss Thurgood out the door.

"You need to pray and cancel this shameful pity party you've been holding," Thurgood said.

"You don't know nothing about what I've been doing since your cousin canceled the wedding without saying a word to me first!"

The words were finally out there, and there was nothing Freddie could do to take them back. All he could do was wait for a look of shock to appear on Thurgood's face.

But the shocked look never came. Thurgood placed his hand on Freddie's shoulder, telling him, "Well, it's about time you said something. Sharvon finally phoned us last night and said what'd gone down and that it was her fault. She hadn't meant to tell old blabbermouth Sasha that your wedding was off."

Freddie didn't need to express his anger in words. The furrowed brow, the turned-down mouth, and the clenched bony fists said it all. "I don't care what Sharvon finally told you. I'm sure Betty knew that you already knew about what'd happened. She sat there and let me go through all of that so-called wedding vow nonsense." He jerked his shoulder away from Thurgood's hand.

"No, she don't know that I know." Thurgood threw up his hands. "In fact, she's probably acting about as crazy and dumb with Dee Dee as you are right now 'cause she don't know that Sharvon told us anything. According to Sharvon, Betty really thinks you don't wanna get married."

"Thurgood, I don't believe you." Freddie began clawing at something on his arm, as though he literally wore his hurt feelings on his sleeves. "You can get outta my house right now. I can't stand a hypocrite, and especially one who's going around the country, trying to tell others how romance and safe sex is supposed to work." Freddie began walking toward his front door.

"Oh, man, please," Thurgood said as he placed his hands on his hips. "You need to calm down. You already taking medicine for that high blood pressure." Thurgood suddenly smiled. "Although, I got to tell you that you really surprised me back at Betty's."

Freddie stopped and spun around. "What are you talking about now?"

"I'm talking about the way you was reacting when my Dee Dee was reading that piece from the Song of Solomon. A man knows what another man is thinking."

"You're crazy."

"Uh-huh." Thurgood smiled. "I'm crazy enough to know that whatever you taking for your high blood pressure ain't stopping Freddie Junior from trying to strike out on its own."

A shade of red Thurgood had never seen before suddenly spread across Freddie's face.

"Don't be embarrassed," Thurgood told

283

him. "Dee Dee can cause a stir in a grave-yard."

Freddie hung his head. "I guess now I'm being a bit hypocritical. I'm sorry," he told Thurgood. "I'm not lusting after your wife. It's Betty I want."

Thurgood laughed. "Man, please. I ain't hardly mad at you. Me and the whole world know that Dee Dee is a fine woman, and a gorgeous one at that."

"She's very pretty," Freddie remarked. "But she's not my Honey Bee."

"Lord, no!" Thurgood blurted. "But I am glad to hear you say that. I mean, there's a lot of playas out here and inside the church that would've had such ideas."

"I'm no playa."

"Of course you are," Thurgood told him. "You've probably been running away and escaping the marriage claws by inches."

"No, I haven't," Freddie admitted. "I've never been within reach of a marriage claw."

"Really?" Thurgood said. He then folded his arms across his chest and leaned against the living room wall. "I betcha when you rode a horse bareback, you tamed that filly, didn't you?"

"I did ride a couple of fillies back in the day, but as soon as I'd feel them bucking, I'd fall off too soon. . . . Word sure got around quick that I was no cowboy."

What Freddie had confessed weakened Thurgood, and it showed as he slowly pushed away from the wall. Although he no longer wore his hair conked, the little gray fuzz he did have stood on edge. "Not even one that you could pay to ride?"

"Nope, I've never had a professional trainer in the art of sex."

"And yet Betty still wants to marry you?" Thurgood shook his head and whistled as he looked Freddie in the eyes. "Man, whatever you need to do to get back on the good foot with my cousin, you need to do it. You can't let nothing, not even high blood pressure, mess up your marriage plans."

Thurgood began thumbing the side of his cheek, as though to conjure up more advice. "If you telling the truth and every woman you ever slept with has stamped your lovemaking skills 'return to sender,' then there's all kinds of things you can use to get your manhood off the trade-in block. If you and Betty think y'all wanna consummate and make things legal, there are ways. I mean, you have the pump. It's a hand pump, so I'm just assuming you ain't been completely idle all these years, so you probably won't have too much trouble with it. And then there's Viagra and Cialis. I'm telling you

285

there's a pill or a cure for just about everything that ails you. We can even come up with something romantic to square away Betty's misunderstanding of where you stand about marrying her."

Thurgood held out his hand to Freddie. "I normally look for a check when I counsel, but since you gonna be family soon, a handshake will do."

"Sure. Why not?" Freddie gave Thurgood a limp handshake.

"Why the soft handshake, Freddie? Didn't I help you?"

"You helped with everything but my cancer."

The two men stood opposite one another, watching smiles fade and concern take their place.

CHAPTER 16

Sharvon's loud voice carried in her normally subdued law office atmosphere. As a partner, she now had a large office overlooking Anderson's historic Sadlers Creek State Park. She also had several staff members to aid her, but at that moment she didn't care about any of that.

"But why did you have to tell him what I did?"

Thurgood had called Sharvon as soon as he left Freddie's and was on his way around the corner to pick up Delilah. He'd recounted the conversation with the trustee. "He didn't tell me not to say anything to you, just not to Betty or my Dee Dee, but my jaw about hit my kneecap when he told me that he had cancer."

"I'm sorry to hear that." Sharvon couldn't find the right words, because the revelation was sinking in too slowly.

"You heard me right," Thurgood snapped.

"The man has cancer, and you're upset because I told him what you'd said to Sasha about him and Betty not having a wedding! The man has cancer, Sharvon."

"I'm not trying to act like I don't care. I do care, and I'm sorry about it. But I needed to tell Cousin Betty myself about what I did which I'd planned on doing tonight." Sharvon's eyes caught a glimpse of someone, possibly a staff member, standing in her doorway. With the phone in hand, she walked over and slammed the door shut. She heard a short yelp but didn't care. "Things have gotten out of hand," she continued. "Don't say anything to her. I'll tell her as soon as I get home."

"You'd better tell Betty something. She deserves to know."

"You can't tell Delilah about the cancer, either. It needs telling in the right manner. I'll figure something out!"

"All of you have gotten me involved way beyond what I signed up for. Freddie don't want me saying nothing to Betty about his cancer. You don't want me saying nothing to Betty about you accidentally running your big mouth, and neither of you wants me to tell Dee Dee. I ain't getting on Dee Dee's bad side. Because if I don't tell Dee Dee, then I don't get no Dee Dee! No excuses, gal. You got until tonight. Around midnight I'm spilling my guts to my wife!"

"Thurgood, I'm only asking that you keep it quiet for a little while longer," Sharvon pleaded.

The insistence in Sharvon's voice caught Thurgood off guard. "For someone who's so sure of herself, you sound scared to death. What else is going on, Sharvon?"

Sharvon put down the phone without answering Thurgood. She'd already promised Leotis several days ago that she'd tell her cousin Betty the truth. He'd promised not to say anything to Freddie until she did. Even during the two evenings this week when they had had an impromptu dinner, she'd enjoyed it so much, she hadn't given much thought to following through with her promise. They hadn't mentioned Ima, either, and that'd given her some hope that perhaps Leotis wasn't as enamored of Ima as she'd thought. The last thing she wanted was to have him distrust her or her word.

Thurgood had just hung up from talking to Sharvon when he pulled into Sister Betty's driveway. Delilah came running outside to meet him, waving good-bye to Sister Betty as she did.

"Thurgood," Delilah said before getting

completely inside the car and pulling on her seat belt. "You won't believe what's happening with your cousin Betty. It's worse than we thought. Your cousin Betty is clueless."

"Tell me about it!" Thurgood snapped. He hadn't meant to be harsh, but it was too late.

"Something tells me that things didn't go any better with Freddie than they did with me and your cousin Betty. Do you wanna go first?"

Thurgood pulled out of the driveway and began slowly driving away. "No, Dee Dee," he told her. "You go first. I've got until midnight, so take your time."

Much to Sharvon's surprise, when she made it home, Sister Betty was gone. She'd left a note saying she was attending prayer and testimony service. She'd gotten a surprise visit from Leotis, and he'd convinced her to ride with him to the church. She'd also written that Sharvon was welcome to join them if she got home in time.

Sharvon's debate about going didn't last long. She checked her watch. It was almost seven o'clock, but she knew prayer meeting didn't begin until seven thirty. "So much is going on around here with all this confusion and secrecy, Father God, that I need to meet you on hallowed ground."

Before she had a chance to change her mind, she changed from her professional work clothes into something more comfortable but still appropriate for prayer meeting. Instead of a pantsuit, which she often favored, she wore a simple peach-colored dress with buttons down the front and a hem to her knees. She tied her hair back into a ponytail and donned a pair of closed-toe sandals.

Looking in the mirror, she said, "The last thing I want to do is have some gossipy church folks talking about what Sister Betty's cousin wore to a prayer meeting."

Sharvon grabbed her car keys and headed out the door, suddenly grinning, reminding herself that there'd still been no mention of that trashy Ima. She'd already decided that Ima had taken herself out of the running by being too loose and flirtatious.

One of the deacons, a short, squatty, coffee-complexioned man named Deacon Belcher, had bad acne and worse breath. He started the prayer meeting with scripture and prayer. Every time he tried to scream the Lord's name to draw the Lord nearer, several folks on the first two pews leaned back, pinching their noses.

Bea sat on the first pew, by the pulpit. She began waving her fan about. "God ain't waiting on no slackers," Bea said aloud. "We better have some juicy, hot buttered testimonies tonight."

"That's right," Sasha said loudly as she entered the sanctuary. Using her cane, she tapped the sides of several pews as she walked slowly down the center aisle. Until she stopped suddenly, Sasha looked angelic in her usual all-white two-piece outfit and white orthopedic Hush Puppies. She aimed her Bible, in one hand, and her cane, in the other, at one of the members.

"Tonight's your night to come clean," Sasha shouted at a young woman. The woman and her three children were sitting on the same pew as Bea. The young woman's children, two boys and a girl, barely looked more than nine months apart. "God knows you've been playing Jezebel, and we ain't buying no baby daddy lies tonight."

Sasha, with her head held high, as though she'd just ordained a princess instead of beheading one, smiled. She eased into the seat left vacant by the sobbing young woman, who'd quickly gathered her small brood and fled the sanctuary. Placing her Bible on her lap, Sasha quickly turned to face those seated behind her. She nodded and glared when she heard a collective sigh throughout the sanctuary from those she hadn't called out . . . yet.

Leotis, dressed in a pair of blue jeans and a plain white short-sleeved shirt, finally entered the sanctuary. Elder Batty, Sister Betty, and two other elders followed. He scanned his members, who sat somberly, as though they were attending a funeral instead of a prayer and testimony service. No sooner had he approached the pulpit than he saw both Bea and Sasha grinning. "What have they done now?" he muttered.

Rather than address at that moment whatever Bea and Sasha had done, Leotis decided he'd let God handle it. There were other immediate concerns, because folks didn't attend prayer and testimony service because they had nothing to pray or praise God about. Leotis nodded toward the organist, who had been sitting there the entire time with his fingers poised above the keys. "Brother Cletus, let us begin with a song."

Once they'd sung their hymns and delivered the welcome address for those attending for the first time, it was Elder Batty's turn to lead the service. He walked calmly to the microphone stand in the middle of the floor and nodded toward Leotis, as protocol demanded. "Praise Him, Reverend."

Elder Batty was dressed in all gray, with suspenders holding up his pants and a wide belt around his fat stomach making him resemble a kangaroo. Pulling on his suspenders, he leaned into the microphone, saying, "You just do whatever the Lord lays on your heart. This ain't no beauty contest, so if you wanna cry and look ugly, that's okay. And we're not looking for professional prayer warriors or testa-lying." The sound of giggles sprang forth. "I was just checking to see who was paying attention." Elder Batty laughed.

Because it was toward the end of summer and people were still on vacation or otherwise occupied, there was barely one hundred people at the service that night. As the service continued, Sister Betty listened to testimonies. Many who attended wanted God's help with their finances, especially with finding a job or getting out of debt. She joined in, touching and agreeing with them, realizing how blessed she was not to have those concerns.

"Lord, I shouldn't have stayed away so long. I could've been here praying, just like I've been doing for years," she murmured as her cheeks reddened. She hung her head for several seconds.

There were also some who'd come asking God's forgiveness. They testified about how they felt convicted because of some unspoken deed or, in a few cases, some outrageous and inappropriate act they'd committed long ago. Several of the church mothers raced over and began covering them with loud prayers and pleading for mercy on their behalf.

Sasha hadn't moved, except to slide a little closer to Bea. "Do you see Mothers Ida Clair and Bossy, who have the nerve to lay hands on someone, and they sinning just as much as them they're praying for?"

Bea sat expressionless, her Bible by her side and her arms folded. "Why do you think I didn't go up there?"

"Harrumph," Sasha replied. "That's the same reason I stayed put. I don't want all them demons interfering with my spiritual walk."

The service had almost ended when Leotis called on Elder Batty to extend an offer to anyone desiring to join the church. "We're a large church with a larger heart and a huge desire to see souls saved," the elder said. "And we desire workers for the Lord. If you've any special skills," he said, smiling, "we can always use a hand. The doors to the church are now open."

Sister Betty felt a touch on her arm. She looked up, and a smile crept upon her face. "Sharvon," she squealed softly. "I didn't know you were here. When did you get here?"

"I've been here for quite some time," Sharvon whispered. "I didn't want to interrupt the service by leaving my seat in the back and coming forward when I saw you and the others first enter."

Sister Betty looked up and mouthed, "Thank you, Jesus," before turning back to Sharvon. "Wasn't this a wonderful service?"

"Yes," Sharvon whispered, smiling. "I really enjoyed it." Sharvon abruptly stopped speaking. Her amber eyes suddenly appeared cynical, and her brown complexion turned muddy as the color drained from her face.

Sister Betty's smile eased from her face when she saw Sharvon was no longer smiling. "What's wrong?" Sister Betty looked over in the same direction that Sharvon had. "Oh, Lord," she whispered.

A few rows ahead, Sasha nudged Bea. "I knew she'd show."

"Who are you talking about?" Bea jerked her arm away from Sasha. "If you talking about Sister Betty," Bea replied angrily, "she's been here all the while. Didn't you see her praying with folks?"

"Who cares about Sister Betty?" Sasha whispered sharply. "I'm talking about the future first lady of our church."

Bea lurched forward and looked down the pew. She did so just in time to see what Sasha had meant before blurting, "What the ham and cheese!"

Leotis wanted to jump out of his seat. Instead, he managed to remain calm enough to rise slowly. He looked dazed, as though he'd seen a ghost, but he knew it was anything but one.

There were almost twenty people heading toward the front of the church, answering Elder Batty's call to join Crossing Over Sanctuary. Ima was at the front.

Elder Batty, his baggy eyes now wide with wonder, glanced back at the pulpit. When he noticed Leotis hadn't budged or spoken, he quickly walked over to him and whispered, "A few Sundays ago," he said rapidly, "didn't Ima already say she wanted to join?"

Leotis finally reacted. He looked up and whispered to Elder Batty, "Yes, she did." With his eyes now locked on Ima, he grimaced, saying, "Pray and pray hard."

While Leotis and Elder Batty remained in

the pulpit with their heads together, whispering, Ima stepped away from the others. With her long sheer white dress covering a pair of white tights, she moved as though what she wore didn't make her stand out. She quickly glanced at her aunt Sasha. Seeing Sasha smiling back was the approval she was looking for.

"Excuse me," Ima said as she sashayed to the front of the sanctuary and stood by Elder Batty, who'd returned to his place at the microphone before looking back at the pulpit. "I'm sorry, Pastor," she told Leotis. "I know testimony service is over, and I hope I'm not out of place."

Ima smiled and quickly turned, not giving Leotis a chance to respond. She looked around the sanctuary, her eyes finding several male parishioners ogling and smiling. "I want to give the Lord praise," she told the members. As she swayed, the long white dress she wore swirled about her feet. "I can't pray like most of you. But I do have a testimony that I just can't seem to put into words." She stopped and peeked again at Sasha, who was still wearing her angelic smile.

Ima turned back to face Leotis. His face was blank, but it didn't stop her. "Is that okay, Reverend?" Ima watched him as he waved his hand quickly, as if to tell her to get on with it or to go away. She smiled and walked over to the organist as those who'd followed her down the aisle found seats to watch the show.

As Ima spoke to the organist, the anger in Sharvon's eyes found its way to where Leotis sat. His head jerked, as though her anger had stabbed him.

"We can just get up and leave," Sister Betty told Sharvon. "There wasn't much left to the service, anyway."

"No way," Sharvon replied. "I'm not budging. God's gonna strike down that trifling witch!"

"But, Sharvon dear," Sister Betty whispered as she tapped Sharvon on her hand, hoping to calm her. "You heard Elder Batty open the doors of the church. The rest of this service will be just an invitation to join."

Sharvon crossed her legs, allowing them to swing, as if she were kicking Ima. "Yes, I heard him."

Sister Betty looked about to see if anyone was watching before she asked, "Well?"

"I think I might just join, after all. It seems like it's a free-for-all in your church."

Ima stepped forward and began to speak again. "This is in honor of God and your wonderful pastor, who has set me on a path

—" Her eyes accidentally found Sharvon. She was surprised she hadn't noticed her before, but Ima didn't flinch. She instead aimed her words in Sharvon's direction, saying, "Toward the goodness that all the Lord has set aside just for me."

With a nod from Ima, the organist began. His long fingers tickled the organ's keys, and he ended with a crescendo, which was Ima's cue to begin to dance. She'd chosen a Tamela Mann selection, "Take Me to the King," written by Kirk Franklin. It had touched Ima from the moment she heard it months ago. Yet the way she chose to live, acting as though God and the world owed her something, and woe to anyone in her path, was the complete opposite of finally giving over all her cares to the Lord. Ima danced as the organist sang.

Leotis suddenly appeared hypnotized as Ima swayed to the music like a beautiful flower welcoming the breeze. Almost in disbelief, he watched as she began running across the front of the sanctuary. Her arms pushed against some imaginary force before she bent with professional flexibility from the waist down into a form, as though she'd learned from the dance master Alvin Ailey. Then Ima leapt, just as much for Leotis as she did for God. She began bounding, with her arms stretched out again, like a gracious gazelle, using the honey-complexioned legs he'd come to admire.

As for the congregation, some stood, craning their necks to see what move she'd make next.

The organist sang, his tenor voice rising and falling in time with his music and Ima's movement. There was hardly a dry eye in the sanctuary. Even Sister Betty wiped a tear, while Leotis remained entranced, standing in awe, with his arms folded and a finger against his cheek, at the way Ima danced.

Sharvon had risen along with the others. But when Ima finished her praise dance and fell to the floor in a heap while the congregation, led by Leotis, clapped enthusiastically, she wasn't there to see it. Sharvon hadn't said a word to Sister Betty before she walked slowly out of Crossing Over Sanctuary and on to her car.

Sharvon sat in her car, taking short breaths. She needed to allow her heart to slow down and to keep herself from dismantling her steering wheel in anger. She looked at the manila envelope lying on the front seat, then picked it up. She hadn't decided what to do with it. "I never did believe Ima's excuse for not marrying that Reverend Lyon

Lipps. If a man of God broke her heart that bad, then why is she going after another one?"

Sharvon held in her hands information on Ima that would destroy her credibility and any chance she had of winning over Leotis. It was just a matter of calling her out. But she needed to maximize that moment when she did it. She could take the envelope and go back inside the church. In front of Leotis and the entire congregation, she could prove Ima was a dishonest cheat. Sharvon unlocked the car door. But she couldn't move. "What if I do this and it backfires? Leotis wouldn't forgive me if I disrupted the congregation, especially if he thought I did it out of jealousy."

Sharvon stared hard when she saw some of the people from the prayer meeting walking toward their cars. "Now the prayer meeting is over." She blew out a breath. She leaned back against the seat, as though she was relieved that she didn't have to do what she'd planned. "If I don't want to answer questions, I'd better drive out of here," Sharvon told herself. "At least Leotis will have Cousin Betty in his car in case that scandalous wench tries something."

Sharvon drove out of the parking lot and down the street. If she'd waited a few minutes, she would've seen Leotis walking to his car, with Sister Betty walking beside him.

She would have also seen that Ima wasn't with them.

CHAPTER 17

Leotis and Sister Betty chatted nonstop about the unusual prayer and testimony service.

"I must say," Leotis told Sister Betty, smiling, "I truly didn't know what to expect when Ima came down to the altar. It hadn't occurred to me that she was wearing a dancer's costume."

Sister Betty turned to look out the window. "This evening's weather is starting to change," she replied. She'd promised God not to interfere when Leotis was about to fall off the romance cliff, and she certainly didn't have anything positive to say about Ima's latest gimmick.

If Leotis realized Sister Betty had changed the subject, he didn't show it. "Who knew she could dance like that?" he asked. "It was like something I saw years ago, when the Alvin Ailey dancers came to Greenville. I've never forgotten that performance. The lead dancer was a Renee Robinson, and, oh my God, the way she contorted her body when she performed 'Night Creature.' " Leotis laughed. "I'm sorry. Here I am, going on and on about modern dance, which I'm certain I've never told you I enjoy so much."

"No, you've never mentioned it."

"Perhaps after Ima's completed the new members' class, she'll consider joining the praise dance team. What do you think?"

Sister Betty quickly turned on the car radio. That he always kept it tuned to the same gospel station was a given. But were it rap, she'd still listen rather than discuss Ima. No sooner did she hear Tamela Mann singing the same song Ima had danced to than she turned the radio off.

"You don't like Tamela Mann?" Leotis asked. "I know Brother Cletus put his touch to it tonight, but I love her voice, and she was so funny in those Tyler Perry movies, playing Madea's daughter."

Sister Betty nodded, wishing he'd shut up. "I hope Sharvon got home all right," she said instead.

"I'm surprised she didn't stay for the entire service," Leotis replied. "If you hadn't mentioned she'd been there, I wouldn't have known it. I didn't see her at all."

"I guess you didn't." Sister Betty had much to say about Leotis's lustful look as Ima danced the dance of the seven veils, pretending it was a praise dance to God. But she said nothing. When they reached her home, she gathered her Bible, saying, "Thank you for bringing me home. I'm a bit tired, so I'm going inside to bed."

"You made it home, I see." Sharvon was coming out of the kitchen, carrying a cup of tea. "I'm sorry I left you there by yourself."

Sister Betty talked to Sharvon as she continued toward her bedroom. "It wasn't a problem. I was surprised and happy you came. I didn't know what time you'd get home from work or if you'd feel like coming out."

Tossing her Bible and hat onto the bed, Sister Betty rushed into her bathroom, trying to avoid any further conversation with Sharvon. Standing over her basin, she hung her head, praying. "Lord, I'm trying to mind my own business, and the Devil keeps throwing folks in my path. But I'm gonna continue to fast and pray until you say enough, Lord. I'm gonna wait on you and my Freddie."

Sharvon went into the living room to drink her tea. Standing by the window, she saw that Leotis's lights were still on inside his home. Tossing back her head, she drained the teacup and sat on the sofa. *I'm being a coward,* she thought. *I need to go right inside and tell Cousin Betty everything.* She kept repeating to herself the need to air everything, as though thinking about it would be good enough to replace actually telling her cousin the truth.

Sharvon heard a beep from her cell phone, alerting her to a missed call. Once she checked her cell phone log, she realized it'd been Delilah calling. She could only imagine what she had to say.

"Hello," Sharvon said after she called back and Delilah picked up. "Sorry I missed your call earlier. It must've been while I was in church."

"You were at church?" Delilah repeated. "That's good, 'cause you're gonna need God's help in setting things straight. Thurgood has told me what's going on, and young lady, it's a mess that's getting messier by the moment."

"I know," Sharvon replied as she began twisting her hair with her free hand.

"Well," Delilah said, "I'm listening."

"Cousin Betty is in her bathroom. When she comes out, I'm going to tell her."

"Oh, the hell you will!" Delilah shot back.

"You keep your mouth shut, 'cause grown folks is already on the case."

It was almost ten o'clock, and although Freddie hadn't gone to that night's prayer and testimony service, he'd sat on his sofa, praying. He'd prayed for as long as he could, petitioning God for the same things concerning Sister Betty that he had over the past several weeks. All that praying had sparked his appetite. His body was tired, yet he still felt a need to prove that he could take care of himself. Between staying and eating at Leotis's and Sister Betty feeding him when they were together, he hadn't filled his refrigerator or his cabinets with the foods he liked or would stay in his stomach.

Against his doctor's orders, he decided he'd drive to a nearby Burger King. *A salad should stay down,* he thought. Arriving there, he found the drive-through lane overcrowded on that warm summer's evening. He parked the car in the lot, and now fully depending upon his cane for support, he went inside.

Freddie had just paid for his meal and was about to leave when Elder Batty and Bea entered. Bea just glared at him before she walked away to find a table, while Elder

Batty walked over to greet Freddie.

"Hi there, Trustee Noel," Elder Batty said with a smile, extending his hand. "I'm so glad to see you out and about."

Freddie looked at him, juggling his cane and his bag, and then he reached out to accept the elder's handshake. "I'm getting along," Freddie told him. "Sorry I didn't make the prayer or trustee meetings tonight."

"No problem. You've got to take care of yourself, and we've postponed the prison concert. We couldn't get permission in time to do it right. And if we couldn't do it right, we knew you wouldn't want to half step on something so close to your heart."

"I feel terrible. I should've sent off those requests months ago," Freddie said sadly. "Those men are going to be so disappointed. I hated that I promised them, and now it's not going to happen."

"Don't worry about that. We've rescheduled it for next March. Reverend Tom already cleared it with the prison. He felt you wouldn't mind if he got involved." Elder Batty smiled. "And besides, with this part-time job I got as a process server, I've missed several, too."

"I almost forgot you go around messing up folks' day, delivering subpoenas,"

309

Freddie teased.

Nodding toward Bea, who was seated at a table, Elder Batty chuckled and said, "I gotta do what I gotta do to make enough money to bring a lady to this fine establishment."

Freddie lowered his head so that Bea wouldn't see him laughing, too. He was certain she was trying to figure out what was happening. "I guess when you get a big case, you gonna upgrade to McDonald's."

"Yeah, I guess so." Elder Batty laughed. "But then what would I do with Bea?"

Elder Batty's smile faded as he touched Freddie's shoulders and said sternly while looking directly at him, "I'm serious about you taking care of yourself. That high blood pressure ain't anything to play around with. That's just a small step before a stroke or a heart attack, and God's given us five good senses to slow down when we need to. And you know you gonna need your strength. That wedding ain't but a few weeks off."

"Well, from your mouth to God's ears," Freddie replied as he looked away, avoiding the elder's truths while wondering why more people close to Sasha hadn't heard there'd be no wedding. But he'd promised God he wouldn't pressure Sister Betty or do anything rash. He'd go home and eat his salad while he waited on God to show him when to straighten things out. Perhaps he would accept Thurgood's help if God led him in that direction.

"Batty, I'm hungry," Bea called out. She finally waved quickly at Freddie, but without speaking. "You said we wouldn't be here all night if we came to a Burger King," Bea whined.

Elder Batty turned around and smiled. "All right, Bea, just give me another moment." He began chuckling. "I guess Bea ain't feeling too friendly toward you at the moment. She's been pissed off about that bedpan you introduced her to."

"Sorry about that little incident, Elder."

"You've got no problem with me. I've wanted to toss a bedpan or two in her direction from time to time. But I've got something else to tell you."

Freddie really didn't want to hear it, but since Elder Batty had taken the incident with Bea so well, Freddie owed him that much. "What's going on?"

"It's about what happened earlier at prayer and testimony service." He snickered and added, "Let's just say our pastor has an admirer who danced for him like Salome did for King Herod."

"Who was that?" Freddie didn't move,

even when he saw Bea rise from her seat with her hands on her hips, throwing eye daggers his way. "Who danced for him?"

"Well, she said it was for God, but wasn't nobody fooled."

"Who?" Freddie's voice had risen, but he reined it in. The elder's grace period was up as far he was concerned. "I really need to get home, so if you got something to say, say it."

"I'm talking about Ima," Elder Batty replied. "What other brazen hussy would do something so ridiculous and sexy in the sanctuary except —" He stopped and nodded toward Bea. "That brazen hussy sitting over there, my Bea. She certainly would if she could and had a chance." He turned and walked away, laughing.

Outside in his car Freddie placed his cane beside him on the seat. Placing his soda in the cup holder, he muttered as though he were not alone. "Leotis's a good man but a fool." He put the car in gear and began driving away, already deciding that his Honey Bee was more important than whatever mess Leotis was about to step in. He was keeping his promise and not interfering in matters that didn't concern him. And at the same time he wondered how his precious Betty, being all up in Leotis's business, could've let something like this happen. *After all,* he thought, *it's not like she's got me reining her in.*

Leotis lay down the phone. He'd just called Freddie to check up on him and tell him about the results of the earlier meeting. He didn't want Freddie to be concerned about the upcoming prison ministry event.

"Where could he be?" Leotis got up and looked out his window, as though he expected Freddie to be standing on his porch. "Please, Father, don't let that man be lying passed out again with nobody there." He looked at his watch. "Eleven o'clock at night. Where would he be at this time of night even if he were well?"

Freddie had tried to keep the salad down. He'd been in the bathroom, vomiting nonstop, since he returned home. He had heard his phone ringing but had been unable to answer. "One more pill to take," he reminded himself as he finally poured a glass of water. He clenched one fist, as though doing so would make the pill stay in his system.

Freddie thought his mind was playing tricks when he heard the sound of his doorbell. "It's almost eleven thirty," he murmured. "Who in the world would come around this time of night?"

Freddie debated whether to answer or not, but the ringing was persistent. Still undecided, he peeped out the window before opening the door. "What in the world are you doing here?" Freddie asked. "Don't you know how late it is?"

Thurgood entered Freddie's house, and without an invitation, he sat.

"Didn't we just chat yesterday?" Freddie said as he stood leaning against his living room wall. "I wasn't really expecting to see you again so soon — and so late."

Thurgood took out a small Bible from his pants pocket. He beckoned Freddie to sit next to him. When Freddie finally sat, Thurgood began speaking. "I haven't known you but for a couple of years. When I left here yesterday, you gave me a lot to think about."

The surprised look upon Freddie's face was genuine. "I did?"

"Yes, you did. I was truly impressed before, when you won that huge mega lottery and decided to give most of it to you and Betty's church to help them in a crisis. I don't know if I could've or would've done that, but it was really unselfish." Thurgood's eyes suddenly began to blink, as if he couldn't believe what he'd admitted. "God rewards unselfishness."

Freddie looked at Thurgood. He could tell there were questions in Thurgood's tired eyes that his mouth had trouble asking.

"I know you're a praying man," Thurgood continued. "I'm a praying man, too. But when I pray, I expect God to give me enough wisdom on how to move or climb mountains. I don't expect God to leave His throne and come down here with a rope or a shovel to help me."

Freddie's tongue finally loosened. "What are you talking about, Thurgood?"

"I'm talking about you and my cousin Betty and how y'all done got God all up in something that can be fixed by the two of you."

"You holding that Bible," Freddie told him, "but you acting like you don't know that it says to wait upon the Lord and be of good cheer."

"That's exactly what it says," Thurgood replied, "but are you happy? Because if you happy, you sure a sad-looking something."

Freddie didn't answer, but he couldn't disagree, either. "So what are you telling me?"

"I'm trying to tell you that if you tell God that you want a house, He ain't gonna build it for you. God will see that you need to get that job, to put aside that money, or get a loan. All you have to do is find somebody to build it or do it yourself, if you can."

"I still don't understand, Thurgood."

"Dammit, man." Thurgood rose off his seat and shoved the Bible back into his pants pocket. "I'm telling you that you asked God for Betty, so now get off your arse and get her. She won't care if you have cancer or high blood pressure or whatever. Besides, with her praying for God to heal you, it's a done deal. You know the woman has favor."

Freddie gave a faint smile. "Thank you, Thurgood, for being here for me. I guess I needed a good ole kick in the butt."

Thurgood sat down again. "I told ya I'd help you. But I realized you waiting on too much help. You got to throw some skin in the game, too."

"I know you're right. I've got one more checkup, and if it goes well, then I'll be totally finished and released from the cancer trial. I'm still feeling a bit tired, though." Freddie paused and took a deep breath. "In fact, I'm feeling exhausted all through my bones, and I'm burping like crazy but can't keep nothing down."

"God is able," Thurgood said softly. He turned and pretended to look at a picture on the wall so that Freddie wouldn't see anything that looked like pity in his eyes. After all he'd just told him, one sad look could let the Devil throw more doubt in the man's life.

"But I'm believing that when I return, there'll still be no need for a stem cell transplant," Freddie then added. "If there's a need for a transplant, then at least they've already harvested my good cells."

"Well, I'm gonna let you get some rest," Thurgood said as he rose to leave. "It's almost midnight, and I've got to get back to my Dee Dee. We've got the relationship seminar coming up." Thurgood winked as he opened the front door. "And she and I have to do our homework."

Freddie stood in his doorway, watching Thurgood walk away, waving while laughing at his own joke. Freddie shook his head and said loudly, "Don't you two study too hard, or you'll break a brain muscle."

The day after Thurgood left Freddie's home and returned to his hotel, Delilah called Sharvon early in the morning and insisted on talking.

"I finally caught up with Sasha," Delilah said. "I explained that you were just confused and had a lot on your mind when you misspoke about Betty's wedding plans. Sasha actually surprised me. She didn't call you out of your name or anything. In fact, she said she was thrilled that the wedding was still on."

"Cousin Delilah," Sharvon snapped, "now you got that old woman thinking I'm crazy. You told me you'd handle it."

"And I did just that," Delilah replied sharply. "Too many secrets can ruin too many lives. Trust me, I know."

"And you're certain that that's all you told her? I need to know if there's more, because I still need to tell Cousin Betty what I've done." Sharvon could tell Delilah was in self-editing mode. Delilah always gave a summary that was too long and complicated matters. It meant that there was something Delilah either couldn't or wouldn't say.

"What you really need to do is to cut down on working so many hours and find you a good man."

"You mean like the one you have?" Sharvon replied.

"Oh, child, please. You can't start with someone like your cousin Thurgood. He's been seasoned and whipped real good by God and life. You need someone who knows just as little as you do, so the two of you can make all the dumb mistakes at the same time and move on."

Sharvon laughed. She hadn't wanted to do it, but Delilah's wisdom always left her puzzled or laughing. "Well, if I run into somebody as dumb as me, I'll be certain to snatch him up."

Delilah laughed that time. "You won't have to run far," she told Sharvon. "Just mosey on over a couple of houses down from where you live."

"Are you talking about Reverend Leotis Tom?"

"I sure am," Delilah replied. "Lord knows, he's as dumb as you when it's something worldly. Every time I'm around him, I can see and smell Similac in his diet."

"Cousin Delilah!"

"Cousin Delilah nothing," Delilah said. "Between you and your cousin Betty, I haven't found another couple of females as underused as you two. But at least Betty's got something on her ring finger. You, young lady, ain't cut your eye teeth, from what I can tell."

Sharvon listened on as Delilah shared her pearls of wisdom on her current state of celibacy and what it was worth. When Sharvon had heard enough, she interrupted. "Listen, Cousin Delilah, I truly do appreciate your eclectic wisdom, but did it ever oc-

cur to you that Leotis just might be interested in someone else?"

The sudden quietness on the other end
surprised Sharvon. Delilah always had a
quick comeback or something to say about
everything.

"Did you hear what I just said?"

"I most certainly heard that foolishness,"
Delilah finally said. "Please tell me that you
ain't falling for that nonsense in your head
that's telling you that Reverend Tom is
interested in Ima Hellraiser, Sasha's way-
ward niece."

"What made you bring up her name?"
Sharvon was curious. Perhaps there was
something more that Delilah knew and that
she ought to know.

Delilah summed it up, as she always did
when she was keeping a morsel under wraps
for another time. "I heard it from Sasha
when we were discussing the dumb thing
you did. I don't know anyone who gets
more of a kick out of discussing somebody
else's crazy plans than Sasha. We got to talking about the foolishness that comes along
with being young, and I couldn't have shut
her up with a sledgehammer to her mouth."

The mention of Sasha's name brought
back the reason why Sharvon had been
upset with Delilah in the first place. She

didn't try to change the annoyance in her tone when she spoke. "Oh yes, I forgot. You told her the truth about Freddie before I told Cousin Betty."

"You can't put no blame on me, because like I told you before, I'm not accepting blame for putting most things out in the open," Delilah shot back. "And especially when they need to be told." Delilah took a breath before she continued. "Anyway, there's nothing Ima can do about getting the reverend, anyhow."

"What makes you say that?" Sharvon almost pushed the phone's receiver through her ears, trying to make sure she didn't miss one word.

"You're sure asking a lot of questions for someone who's trying to pretend she ain't interested in the man."

"What makes you say that Ima can't get Leotis?" Sharvon repeated, ignoring Delilah's honest insinuation.

"She can't get the man, because, according to Sasha, Ima's still got that alienation of affection lawsuit pending against her. The current wife of Reverend Lyon Lipps is coming after Ima. She's claiming Ima knew that the man had gotten married when he was in prison, before he became a reverend. Apparently, from what I've learned, from a source that'll remain anonymous, the current Mrs. Lipps wanted a big slice of his mega ministry dollars to let him go. And it appears that Lyon Lipps figured it was cheaper to keep her, and he let Ima go instead."

"Then why would she continue with a lawsuit against Ima?"

"That's the same question I had," Delilah replied. "I guess she didn't like Ima, and frankly speaking, I can't think of anyone who does. I'm guessing the lawsuit is being continued out of spite."

Sharvon almost dropped her cell phone. She could've stopped Delilah moments ago and told her that she already knew about the lawsuit. How she'd had the manila envelope in her car with the scandalous information on the night Ima had danced at the church, but decided not to out Ima to Leotis and the congregation. First of all, she'd have to explain how she came across such detailed information. Even if she admitted that she'd discovered the lawsuit only by accident when she was researching the background of another preacher whose sordid extra-marital affair was part of another investigation. She'd typed in Reverend Lyon Lipps's name out of curiosity, but she hadn't expected to learn anything damaging. She could've let out a whoop at first, but she quickly calmed down when she realized that if anyone backtracked, they'd seen her pass code next to the research entries. The fact that the information was too good not to print out, even if she did nothing with it, was the excuse she gave herself.

"But my understanding is that Reverend Lyon Lipps chased Ima, and he did ask her to marry him," Sharvon finally replied in an even tone. She didn't want to appear overly interested.

"That may be true," Delilah agreed, "but I guess since he hadn't seen or heard from the woman in so long, he figured his wife had gone ahead and gotten a divorce. She fooled him because he was still married when he became engaged to Ima. Besides, it wouldn't be too hard for his wife to win a court case with Ima's sordid history as evidence. If Reverend Tom knew about it, he'd quickly put an end to any lustful attraction he might have. Everyone knows he's real particular when it comes down to the reputation of his church, as well as his own reputation."

"Well, the way he looks at her every time she's within smelling distance, you'd never know he was thinking about anything holy."

"He's still a man with needs," Delilah told her. "But he's also a man who's not quite on the same level of worldly experience as Ima. So if you feel about him the way I now believe you do, you'd better make a plan to snatch that man and rescue him from the hell pit."

CHAPTER 18

"She-rilla," Sasha snapped, "where in the world have you been?" Living right next door to Bea had its advantages. Both knew the goings-on of the other. "It's almost midnight!"

Thinking she might've stepped outside in the hallway a bit too far, Sasha closed the top of her nightgown. "Get in here. I've got something to tell you."

Bea looked at Sasha and laughed. "What you got to tell me, Sasha? Huh?" Bea leered as she went ahead and stuck her key in her apartment door. "You've got a lot of nerve, Smurf," Bea scolded. "I'm doing all the planning and making up flyers for our business, and you couldn't even stay around the other night to hand them out or put one up on the church bulletin board. Why don't you just go ahead and get in business with that floozy niece of yourn?"

"So I take it that you don't wanna know

what's happening with Sister Betty and Trustee Noel's wedding plans?" Sasha turned to reenter her apartment. She left the door ajar, knowing if she didn't, Bea would knock it off its hinges to hear more.

Bea pushed open Sasha's door and found her seated on her living room sofa, smiling, with a bunch of papers in her hands. "One day you gonna make me lose my religion," Bea told her as she found a seat next to Sasha. "What you done found out? Me and Batty just ran into Freddie last night at the Burger King. Batty ain't told me nothing about no change between Sister Betty and Trustee Noel."

"It's probably because Elder Batty don't know what I'm about to tell you if you just stop pushing me." Sasha laid down the papers she was holding. She spread them out, knowing Bea would see what was on them. "There's going to be a wedding, after all," Sasha told Bea. "And we ain't got a lot of time to pull this reception off."

"Who told you that?"

Sasha sighed and said, "Delilah."

The expression on Bea's face didn't change. She hunched her shoulders and asked, "Delilah who?"

Sasha shot forward. "Listen, Bea, it's late, and I ain't got time for twenty questions.

You know doggone well that besides that hussy in the Bible, there's only one other Delilah we know."

Bea's jaw dropped before she bristled. "Thurgood's Delilah?"

"That's right," Sasha answered. "The very same woman who finally got Thurgood to get rid of that ridiculous conked hair and his clothes of many colors."

"I didn't know she was in town."

"Both she and Thurgood are here having one of those sex shows they advertise as counseling. They ain't fooling me not one bit." Sasha moved closer to Bea, seeing that Bea was more interested in what she had to say than in starting another fight. "Delilah called and left me a message to call her. So I called her soon as I got home."

"But Delilah don't even like you," Bea offered.

"She don't like you, either," Sasha snapped. "But that ain't the point."

"Well, can you get to the point?"

"Delilah told me that what Sharvon said about there not being a wedding was just one big misunderstanding. Delilah said that Sharvon was just concerned that with the trustee being sickly, like before there might have to be a postponement."

"Well, we had seen him in the hospital

that day," Bea replied. "And he has looked a bit sicker than normal." Bea's face lit up. "Well, at least he ain't dead or dying, so we need to stop wasting time and get this reception planning going."

Sasha tapped Bea's arm and pointed to the papers she had spread out on her coffee table. "As you can see, Bea, I'm way ahead on that one. I already called Porky. We got us an appointment to see what our hundred-dollar deposit can get us."

The following morning Bea met Sasha by the elevator in their apartment building. They'd already decided to get as much out of Porky as possible without adding a lot more to their hundred-dollar deposit. With reserved seats on the Access-a-Ride bus, they rode to downtown Pelzer to meet with him.

The two old women arrived armed. Sasha had her cane and Bible. Bea carried her pocketbook and her small notebook. They ambled up the walkway to the El Diablo Soul Food Shanty. Bea stopped and looked at the front of the newly renovated building. She smiled.

"Well, Sasha, at least there aren't citations from the health department plastered all across the front of the building." Bea looked around further before pointing toward the building. "And look at all those lovely fake silk flowers lined up on the windowsills."

"I still believe he set the fire to his own place just so he could get the money to fix it up," Sasha replied. "I wouldn't put nothing past Porky."

Bea glared and pointed her notebook toward Sasha, asking, "Then why are you so willing to do business with the man if he's so shady in your eyes?"

"I never said there was anything wrong with what he did," Sasha replied. "I'm just saying he didn't fool me."

During its almost thirty years on Ptomaine Avenue, the El Diablo Soul Food Shanty had been an eyesore and the source of more food-related illnesses than any other restaurant in Pelzer. It'd remained in business because of the prowess of its notorious owner, Porky La Pierre. Porky had a natural gift for attracting the high and mighty with their low reputations. Church folks would race there after service, looking for the latest gossip or bootleg DVD. No one ever said it was for the cuisine, as Porky loved to call his all-in-one-pot cooking.

"So what's happening?" Porky asked Bea and Sasha after they entered. He raised the dingy chef's cap off his bald head and slid his feet into a pair of his favorite green flip-flops, which he always wore. Porky's brown skin had splotches of something oily all over where there wasn't any clothing. His huge stomach poked out of an equally dingy white apron. "Follow me."

Porky led Bea and Sasha into another room, which had once been his storeroom. He'd had the walls touched up in a cream-colored motif, set off by dark brown panels in each of the room's four corners. "What do you think so far?"

Sasha stood in one spot, saying nothing as she slowly turned around. From where she stood, she could reach over and touch the counter, so she did.

Bea wouldn't keep quiet as she took it all in. "Porky," Bea said, "how many people can you fit into this room?"

"Depends on whether you got them standing or sitting. If they're standing, then you can get about twenty inside. If they're sitting, then just cut that amount in half, allowing for chairs and tables. I recommend you use this room for your cocktail hour. Folks can just walk up to the counter to get what they like. I'm suggesting that you use colorful napkins. That way they won't need paper plates. They can just suck the food off with one of those fancy toothpicks with the umbrella and use that same toothpick to stir their drinks." Porky proudly waved his hands around the room. "You can just feel the ambulance!"

"It's called *ambience,* fool!" Sasha hissed, poking the floor with her cane like she wanted to do to Porky's huge stomach.

Bea began swinging her pocketbook back and forth like she was winding up, ready to throw something.

"I can tell by the looks on your faces that you're impressed." Porky gently pushed Bea and Sasha from their rooted positions and led them through the door to another room, one that he used as his office. "Y'all grab a chair, and let's get down to business."

Sasha regained her composure and took the small wirebound notebook from Bea's hands. She then laid it upon the table. The notebook had colorful tabs separating each section to make it easier to get to each. "We don't have a lot of time, so we are stuck with you," Sasha told Porky. "Bea and me done made our final plans for Sister Betty and Trustee Noel's wedding reception. We expecting it to go off without a hitch, and it'd better not be in that closet you just showed us."

"And don't be trying to cheat us out of what we expecting for that hundred-dollar deposit," Bea added. "We done promised you a cut out of the first ten events we gets to plan after this one. We need Sister Betty's send-off to be all first class."

Porky laid an elbow on the table and began skimming through the notebook. When he finished, he closed it and leaned back in the chair. His eyes began to blink like a broken traffic light, first one and then the other. Everyone in Pelzer knew that it was a sign that he was about to tell a bigger lie than usual. Everyone also knew that Porky couldn't control his eyes when that happened.

With his dark eyes alternately blinking nonstop, he began describing to Bea and Sasha what he was prepared to offer that he considered just as good as first class. "I see you want some whore derbys," Porky said as he scratched cornflake-size dandruff off his scalp. He quickly used the same hand to sweep it off the table.

"Let me see that!" Bea snatched the notebook and looked inside. "That's hors d'oeuvres, stupid." Bea quickly turned in her seat to face Sasha. "You'd think for a hundred dollars, the man would be able to read." She turned back to face Porky, saying, "Just say *or dirbs*. It sounds like *birds*." She shook her head as Sasha began thumping the floor with her cane to get them back on track.

Porky clasped his hands together and continued. With his eyes still in alternate blink mode, he said, "Along with those birds, you want some crabs, lobster meat, and some of them little franks rolled up in biscuit dough."

"Just tell us what you gonna do," Sasha ordered. "It's hot, and we ain't got time to waste here."

"Well, you're in luck," Porky said, smiling. "I've got some of those little franks already in the freezer from before the fire last year, and there's some lobster meat I got in last week from old man Red Brown. Y'all knows him. He's that fella with the teeth looking like claws, who sells fish on the side, when he ain't chasing down a dentist. It ain't real lobster, but it's definitely passable."

Bea and Sasha looked at one another. They began shaking their heads, as though they couldn't believe Porky would try to shortchange them after they'd already placed a deposit.

"We'll come back to those," Sasha said.

"That's right. That part ain't settled. What about the crabs?"

Porky's smile widened. "Oh, Bea Blister," he said. "You still the same ole Bea. You know I keep a bottle of Blue Ointment for such things. I can let you have a bottle for an extra dollar or two and it'll clear it right up. It don't make sense, you spending hours down at the free clinic."

"Bea, please tell me why you had to go and hit him with that metal gravy ladle?" Sasha asked as she and Bea walked to their seats on the Access-a-Ride bus after leaving Porky laid out. "It may take weeks for that swelling on his head and lips to go down. That's gonna cut down on the time we need to get this business off the ground."

"Well, at least now he won't be able to speak or think of such stupid things."

"Aw, he hurt your feelings, didn't he, Bea?"

"He sure did," Bea hissed. "That fool knows I've changed. I'm saved now."

"Well, that much is true," Sasha admitted. "He shouldn't have wanted to charge you for that bottle of Blue Ointment. He should've given it to you for free, like he used to do."

CHAPTER 19

As soon as Bea and Sasha stepped off their apartment building's elevator, they found Ima standing outside Sasha's apartment. Her eyes were red, and one look at her tear-streaked face told them she'd been crying.

Sasha picked up her stride, getting to Ima before Bea.

"What's wrong with you?" Sasha asked Ima. "How long you been in this hallway?"

"I'm going to go on inside and make some adjustments to these flyers I'm revising," Bea told Sasha. "You go ahead and take care of your niece." She slowly adjusted her pocketbook and the notebook in her hands while reaching for her door key, as if she was waiting for them to continue talking in her presence. When they kept quiet, she jammed her key inside the lock. "Sasha," Bea said softly, "we'll chat later." Bea wasn't too upset, because she knew Sasha would tell everything, anyway.

They went inside Sasha's apartment, and within minutes Sasha had given Ima something to drink. Without any coaxing, Ima began telling her what was wrong.

"He hasn't said a word," Ima told Sasha. "I can't figure out the man. I invite him to lunch at an expensive restaurant. He stands me up, and I pretend it wasn't anything. I felt certain that dancing would do it. And now he hasn't called me after I danced my heart out, and he didn't even wait around after the prayer meeting to say a kind word or anything."

"Maybe he's just been busy," Sasha replied. "He is the pastor of a big church."

"Oh, never mind," Ima said. "I should've never listened to you."

"And you said you'd do exactly what I told you to do. And I sure didn't tell you to get up there in front of the entire congregation and channel your inner stripper."

Shortly after Ima's mini-meltdown, where she left crying again, Sasha and Bea strolled to a nearby pharmacy. They walked two blocks out of their way because Bea was still embarrassed from her neighbors seeing her wigless. On the way, Sasha told her what had happened earlier, when Ima stormed out after Sasha accused her of stripping in the Lord's house.

"You were wrong to call what she'd done stripping, Sasha," Bea told her. "You remember when they used to call me Bea 'Baby Doll' Blister?"

"They called you a lot of dumb names, pretty much the same way they do now."

"Hater," Bea snapped. "Anyway, I know stripping, and what Ima did at that prayer and testifying service was hardly stripping."

"Gimme a break, Bea. You couldn't have stripped paint off a wall," Sasha replied. "Ima is fighting a losing battle."

Bea stopped walking and pointed her finger at Sasha. "Then why did you tell her you'd help her snag our pastor?"

"Do you want the truth?"

Bea pulled at Sasha's arm to urge her on. "It would be unusual for you, but I'd like to hear what truth sounds like coming out of your mouth."

"I did it because I didn't want Sister Betty getting the better part of life's deal."

Bea stopped walking and pulled Sasha closer. "What are you yapping about, Sasha? What better deal does Sister Betty have? She's old and lonely, like you, except now she does have a half a man who done gave her an expensive ring." Bea kept listing the differences between Sasha and Sister Betty, finally telling her, "They both rich, and you ain't hardly got a dime between paying rent and buying toilet paper."

Sasha stepped away from Bea and stabbed the concrete pavement with her cane before she lifted it, as if she wanted to hit Bea. Quickly dismissing Bea's rundown, she began walking away, leaving Bea huffing as she tried to catch up. When Sasha felt Bea had chased her enough, which was only a few feet, she told her, "I just didn't want her niece Sharvon to get a chance with Reverend Tom. There you have it. That's the truth, the whole truth, and nothing but the truth."

"That makes no sense," Bea blurted. "What do you care who the pastor becomes involved with? I'd just be happy to see him shut them closet-door rumors for good."

"Why must I have to spell everything out for you, Bea? You're the one that's been as far as the eleventh grade."

"So what am I missing?"

Sasha pointed to a bench and, with her cane, indicated to Bea that they should sit. "Listen," Sasha began. "Sister Betty and Pastor already acting like they're mother and son. He's got her all up in his business."

"So what?" Bea replied. "Neither of them have any family in South Carolina, that is, until Sharvon came to stay with Sister Betty."

"Exactly," Sasha went on. "It was bad enough having Sister Betty have the last word of telling the pastor what thus saith the Lord and him all emotionally tight. The last thing the church needs is for him to get involved with another boring woman. Can you imagine how much more boring our church would be? Folks are already leaving because of the economy or moving away. Sharvon and her dull way of thinking would send them running for the exit door in droves." Sasha looked up toward the sky before announcing, "With Ima in his life, there'd be some sparks, some drama."

For the second time in two days, Bea's jaw dropped. She leaned back on the park bench, looking at Sasha as she straightened her wig. "You know what, Smurf?" Bea snapped. "If I'd have told you everything you just told me, you'd be hauling my butt off to the loony bin. But somehow knowing the way you think, it makes sense that you'd feel that way. But I think you need to come clean and call it what it is."

"What do you mean, Bea?"

"I mean, you're just jealous of Sister Betty," Bea replied, shaking her head.

"Ain't that what I just explained?" Sasha

answered. "Weren't you paying attention?"

Still shaking her head, Bea helped Sasha off the park bench. They began their stroll once more toward the pharmacy. With dueling opinions about what was real and just downright crazy about Sasha's reasoning, they almost walked past the pharmacy. Just as they entered, they came face-to-face with Elder Batty.

"Sasha, Bea," the elder greeted. "How are you ladies this beautiful afternoon?"

"Batty," Bea said, "I didn't know you were coming out my way."

"Well, I was actually headed toward the Promised Land board meeting. I'm representing Reverend Tom."

"Why isn't he heading it, like he's supposed to?" Sasha asked. It didn't matter that Elder Batty wasn't talking to her. "It seems to me like he's been doing an awful lot of shirking lately."

"He's not shirking anything, Sasha," said the elder.

"She's just in a bad mood today," Bea offered. "But where is Pastor?"

"I haven't a clue," the elder replied. "He said he would be gone for a couple of days and that I was to stand in for him at this meeting."

"Are you telling everything?" Bea asked.

"I got a feeling you ain't telling everything."

"C'mon, Bea," Elder Batty told her. "You know me."

"I sure do," Bea replied. "So what is it that you ain't telling me?"

"That's right," Sasha added. "What are you up to?"

No sooner had the elder raised his hand to protest than the bag he held fell and a legal-size envelope fell out.

Bea looked at the envelope and grinned. She immediately knew what was on the elder's mind and gently pushed Sasha aside so Sasha couldn't read the writing on the envelope. "Never mind us." Bea suddenly smiled. "I see you've got something else on your mind. You go ahead and take care of that meeting."

"Thank you, Bea," the elder replied, smiling as wide as she had. "I'll just take my envelope here, and I'll see you later." He picked up the envelope, shoving the contents back inside of it as Sasha tried to lean over to see what it was.

"Bea," the elder said, winking as he ignored Sasha's efforts, "you wouldn't happen to be baking your famous red velvet cake tonight, would you?"

"I'm not," Bea said, nodding toward the bag now in his hands. "But I see I should prepare something tasty and sweet."

"Well, when I'm through processing what needs to get done, I'll come by." Elder Batty then turned to Sasha and asked, "Where's that niece of yours? I've got something for her."

Sasha lifted her cane and began thrusting it at the elder. "You nasty buzzard," she hissed. "My niece ain't participating in nothing you and this she-rilla got going, you oversexed silverback monkey!"

As though Bea and Sasha always carried with them a cheering squad for their madness, some of the patrons began gathering. It was enough of a crowd to cause the elder to rush off without looking back.

"Y'all just plain ole nasty." Sasha shook her head. "I betcha he got something in there to help his imagination." Sasha stared at Bea, looking at her from head to toe. "I can see why he would."

"Hater!" Bea hissed. "You always hopping on those munchkin legs to the wrong conclusion. If you must be all up in my business . . ." Bea raised her hands, as if to ask God, "Why me?" "He always wants a piece of my red velvet cake when he's done gone and had to serve somebody one of them legal subpoena papers. It's more stressful on him than the ones he's got to give it to."

"Whatever, Bea!" Sasha exclaimed, shaking her head, as if she did not believe one word Bea told her. "Let me get what I came for, and I'll meet you at the register. Don't take all day."

"Don't worry about me," Bea called out. "You just make sure you don't pick up any more Preparation H instead of toothpaste."

Several aisles over in the same pharmacy, Sister Betty scanned the various brands of toothpaste on the pharmacy shelves. Her handheld shopping basket was completely full. She'd come to the Promised Land to visit her dear friend, the former congresswoman Cheyenne Bigelow. Cheyenne was now home from the hospital. She'd promised to pick up a few items that Cheyenne needed and bring them to her.

"I certainly never expected to run into you," Sasha said. "I haven't seen you too much in church lately, either, except for the other night at prayer and testimony service."

"Good day to you, too, Sasha," Sister Betty replied as she dropped the box of toothpaste into her basket and began to walk away. "Have a good day."

The clicking sounds from Sasha's cane thumping on the floor caused Sister Betty to walk as fast as her arthritic knees could carry her. She knew Sasha was up to no good, and was certain that whatever Ima had done the other night had Sasha's blessing. She was just about to reach the register when she almost knocked Bea over.

"Well, isn't this something!" Bea exclaimed, acting as though she and Sister Betty were the best of friends. "I'm surprised but happy to see you over here in the Promised Land."

"Why?" Sister Betty sat her basket on the counter and began taking out the items. She wanted to say something more but wouldn't chance undoing all her fasting and praying.

"Well, with the trustee only out of the hospital again, and just a short time before you two trip down the aisle, I figured you'd be doctoring him so he could make it. Ain't neither one of y'all getting any younger, so ya might as well stop the delay."

Sister Betty slammed the basket down on the counter. "Bea Blister, what in the world is you talking about now?"

"I'll answer that." Sasha began to grin; it was slow at first, and then her entire face broke out into a sneer. "You must be falling away from grace," Sasha told her. "It looks like neither the good Lord nor the trustee letting you in on much these days. That'll happen when you being disobedient to God's will."

"That's right," Bea agreed. "It's a good thing you have me and Sasha around to keep you informed about things." She put her hands on her hips and added, "Although I don't know why our dear pastor didn't say nothing, since he was the one who picked up the trustee from the hospital."

Sister Betty said nothing. There was nothing she could say. Either she believed Bea and Sasha or she didn't. "Are you two running your mouths about something you've heard or something you've seen with your own eyes?"

"Oh, we definitely saw your fiancé in the hospital," Sasha replied. "He was in there the same time as yours and ours dear friend Cheyenne."

"I know I ain't making up nothing, and I'm still a bit upset with him, but I'm willing to let bygones go because y'all getting married." Bea straightened her wig and added, "But you need to know it's only because I'm saved. That man of yourn thoroughly got me pissed off that day."

Chapter 20

Sister Betty had called the same car service that had brought her to the Promised Land to take her back home. She'd been relieved earlier, when Cheyenne had begun to doze off during the visit. The unsettling news from Bea and Sasha about Freddie's recent hospitalization had made her too angry and confused to hold a decent conversation. She couldn't wrap her mind around why Leotis hadn't said anything, although with the way things stood with her and Freddie, she could see why he hadn't.

As soon as the car service neared her home, Sister Betty saw Thurgood's rental car in her driveway. She remembered today was the last day of Sharvon's short vacation and figured they were probably inside having a visit. She didn't feel up to company at that moment, but they were her family, and the way things were going, they would be her only family.

Sister Betty had planned on quietly entering her home and heading straight for her bedroom and putting away the things in her bags later. She still didn't feel up to chatting. When she neared her living room, she heard Thurgood praying.

"Father God, you said whatever is bound on earth shall be bound in heaven. I bind chaos, ill will, and bad health in this here home. Cancel the Devil's assignment, Father."

Drawn by the prayer, Sister Betty peered inside the living room. She saw Thurgood, Delilah, and Sharvon. They were holding hands while Thurgood prayed.

"And, Father God," Thurgood continued, "you said further in your Word that whatever is loose on earth is loose in heaven. I loose peace, wisdom, and understanding. Amen."

It appeared she'd come in at the end of the prayer, so Sister Betty wasn't certain what had been said before. Any prayer asking God's peace in her home was welcomed, so she couldn't help but add an "Amen."

Sister Betty had surprised them, but it was Sharvon who reacted first. She dropped Delilah's hand. "I never heard you come in." She took the bags from Sister Betty's hands. "As you can see, we were just praying."

"Have a seat, cousin," Thurgood told Sister Betty. "Me and Delilah don't have a lot of time, but there's some things that need saying."

Delilah walked over and stood between Sharvon and Thurgood. In her no-nonsense way, she came to the point. "Sharvon's got a confession, and you just need to hear her out."

"Cousin Delilah!" Sharvon's eyes narrowed. "We just prayed for God to lead us, and you go ahead and do it your way?"

"How do you know God didn't tell me to do it this way?" Delilah refused to back down. "I'm really getting tired of folks asking God to make a way and then expecting Him to do the shoving."

"My Dee Dee is right," Thurgood chimed in. "God needs you to know and believe that He's there for support and guidance. God already did the only heavy lifting when he sent His son to the cross."

"What is y'all talking about now?" Sister Betty moved away from the others and sat down. Her body and her mind seemed to have aged that day. Between Bea and Sasha and now her family, she wanted to scream, wondering when God would give her the peace they'd just prayed for.

Sharvon took a deep breath. "In a nutshell," she began, "I was so angry with Mother Pray Onn when she was here that day that when I tried to hit her with that magazine, I might've given her the idea that you and Freddie wouldn't be getting married."

"You ain't in a court of law, Sharvon," Thurgood blurted. Pointing at Sister Betty, he ordered, "Tell her straight out what you said, and stop trying to skirt around the facts."

Sharvon looked at Delilah with a sad expression. She sought help, but Delilah turned away.

"I told Mother Pray Onn that there'd be no wedding, just to get rid of her that day." Sharvon sighed. "I'm sorry."

Sister Betty's response was a surprise to them all. "What's there to be sorry about? Sasha only wanted to plan a stupid reception. She wasn't engaged to Freddie. I was. He'd hardly know what you'd told Sasha when he decided he didn't want to get married. He's just full of secrets and lies, and I'm glad the Lord is showing me who's for me and who ain't!" Sister Betty's hands twitched in her lap. She fought to hold back tears.

"Betty, please pull yourself together," Thurgood said. His tone was sharp, angry, because half-truths had stolen the peace he'd just prayed for. He then turned to Sharvon. "You still determined not to tell it all?" Thurgood asked Sharvon. "God has an eternity. The rest of us ain't got all day."

"I'm about tired of this," Delilah told Sharvon. "You got all that book learning and not an ounce of common sense."

Sharvon folded her arms in defiance. She felt cornered, but it was her own doing. "Freddie overheard Mother Pray Onn telling Bea and Leotis that your wedding was off."

Sister Betty leapt off the sofa. "What do you mean, she told Freddie and Leotis? Are you saying that Leotis and Freddie both knew and neither of them said a word to me? The three of you let me sulk around this house for the past several weeks, and none of you had the decency or the courage to tell me that it was something Sasha said and that you started?"

Thurgood decided he'd try to explain things a bit better than Sharvon, who, he felt, had just made a mess. "Betty," he said calmly, "look at it this way. Freddie believed what he heard, and he's been heartbroken and praying to God that you'd change your mind and want to get married."

"What do you mean, Thurgood?" Sister

Betty's eyes grew wild, and she seemed to turn into someone none of them recognized. "You knew that Freddie wanted to marry me, and you didn't say a word?"

In case Sister Betty had thoroughly lost her mind, Delilah quickly stepped in front of her husband, ready to protect Thurgood if she had to. "In all fairness, you never said a word about believing your wedding was called off. You let me and Thurgood go on and on about how we were so happy to be a part of your wedding —"

"All of you, get out of my home!" Sister Betty ordered. She sounded as though a demon had possessed her. "I don't need this!" She began walking in a circle, slapping her hands together, before waving them about. "I want my peace of mind back! I want my peace back." She kept repeating the phrase before rushing out of her living room and into her bedroom.

The wailing sounds from Sister Betty shocked the others into silence.

CHAPTER 21

Sharvon, Thurgood, and Delilah each gave a questioning look and wondered if they'd been transported to some strange reality show without their permission. None of them wanted to follow Sister Betty's orders to leave until they no longer heard the sound of her crying.

"I'm not going anywhere and leaving her like this," Sharvon told Delilah and Thurgood. "She's in no condition to deal with all this drama."

"With all of us out of her sight," Delilah told Sharvon, "it will give her a chance to regroup."

"You go and we'll stay here quietly a little while longer," Thurgood added. "Dee Dee and I gonna hold hands and quietly pray before we go."

A short time later, carrying a small Louis Vuitton overnight bag, Sharvon waved good-bye to Thurgood and Delilah before she got in her car and drove away.

Thurgood and Delilah said a quick prayer and left without checking in on Sister Betty one last time.

"The Betty we saw back there was not the Betty I've known all my life," Thurgood told Delilah as they drove away. "I've a mind to turn around and go back there. I'm not feeling right about leaving her alone in that condition."

"She'll be all right," Delilah replied. "She needs time."

"I hope you're right, because if I didn't know any better," Thurgood said, "I believe she wanted to cuss us out. And I ain't never in all my years of knowing she was under the Lord's direction heard an uncivil word come out of her sanctified mouth."

"She's in love, Thurgood," Delilah said as she looked out the passenger-side window. "Love in the hands of the inexperienced will make them say and do some crazy things."

"Speaking of crazy," Thurgood replied, "I'm wondering if we should've gone ahead and told her about Freddie's health."

"I'm not sure if we should've or not told Betty that Freddie has cancer. I think we've gone as far as we can with meddling at the moment."

"As usual," Thurgood said, "you're right."

"I know," Delilah replied before turning around to face him. "But you're gonna tell her, anyway, aren't you?"

"Only if Freddie doesn't tell her about it first. And it'd better be real soon," Thurgood answered.

"Thurgood," Delilah sighed, "you know who I really feel sorry for?"

"Who, Dee Dee?"

"Reverend Leotis Tom."

"I almost forgot about him and his part."

"Thurgood, Betty feels as close to him as a real mother would. She may forgive us. I'm not certain if she'll forgive him."

Thurgood grimaced. "It looks like Betty's walk with the Lord is under attack from all sides, and from the way she went off back there, I'm not certain how she'll handle him not telling her that he knew Freddie held her responsible for calling off their wedding."

"That may be the least of her problems where Leotis is concerned," Delilah replied.

"What else would she be mad about?"

"She's bound to find out sooner or later that we knew about Freddie having cancer and kept that from her, too. After all, from what we already know, Leotis knew about it before we did."

"Damn!" Thurgood made a U-turn and headed back to Sister Betty's.

CHAPTER 22

"Don't you think you ought to straighten out things with Sister Betty before you wear grooves in your face from smiling so much? She may not want to hear anything about a wedding until you do."

"You just keep driving, Reverend. It's my face, and I'll smile till it cracks if I want to." Freddie pulled down the car's visor and slid its cover so he could see his reflection in the mirror. "God just gave me a new lease on life."

"Amen to that." Leotis broke out into a grin. "I don't know what you told God, but He's certainly shown you favor."

Freddie closed the cover to the visor. He adjusted his seat belt against his bony frame and began to laugh. "Yes, He has."

"You're completely finished with the multiple myeloma trial, and you don't need the stem cell transplant."

"I sho' am, and I sho' don't."

"And for the foreseeable future you'll have to see the oncologist only every three months."

"I sho' do."

"Well, Trustee Noel," Leotis said, "it's almost six o'clock, and I haven't eaten since we started out this afternoon. Would you care to share a meal with me?"

"I sho' don't," Freddie replied. "You can eat after we stop at the florist."

"Why are we stopping at a florist?"

Freddie looked at Leotis and laughed. "You don't need to have dinner with me. You need to hook up with Thurgood Pillar. Right now I think I got more playa tendencies than you."

Leotis waited in his car, smiling as he watched a jubilant Freddie point the florist toward several flower boxes. After Freddie purchased what looked like one huge hand-held garden, they were on their way again.

"You do realize that if you start bringing her flowers like this after you're married, she'll think you've done something wrong, don't you?" Leotis began laughing. "You'll be in for a world of hurt behind some flowers."

"At least I'll have a wife to get mad," Freddie said as he returned Leotis's laugh. "You, on the other hand . . ." He stopped

357

speaking as the smile slid from his face.

Leotis saw it, too, as he turned the corner completely onto his block. It was Thurgood's rental car parked far from the curb in the front of Sister Betty's house. "Hold on, Freddie." He pressed on the accelerator, and within a couple of minutes he'd parked the car in front of her house.

No sooner had Leotis and Freddie still holding the bouquet of flowers raced out of the car and onto the porch than they ran into Thurgood, who'd just stepped outside. His face was expressionless, but he kept wringing his hands.

Freddie tried pushing Thurgood aside so he could enter the house. "What's going on?"

"She'll be fine," Thurgood said as he gently pushed Freddie back, keeping him from getting past.

"Why are you blocking us from going inside?" Leotis stood with both hands on his hips, as though it made him look more like an adult. "You can't keep us outside. Why can't we go inside?"

Thurgood continued to block the door. "Delilah has already spoken with her."

"What in the world was Delilah doing with her that we can't do?" Freddie asked. He paced back and forth several times before trying to dodge under Thurgood's outstretched arms, which were still blocking the doorway.

"They had a woman talk, and since ain't none of us laying claim to being such, we can't go in until Betty asks us to."

"Who says so?" Freddie asked.

"I say so." Sharvon had walked up the steps to the porch, carrying the same bag she'd left with earlier. "You two need to just go on about your business. We can take care of our cousin without your help." Sharvon didn't wait for a reply before turning to Thurgood. "I got here as fast as I could."

"You go on inside. She's in there by herself for now," Thurgood said. "Delilah was in there a little while ago and tried to calm her, and when she couldn't, she told me to keep the car. She's called a cab and gone off somewhere, telling me it wasn't none of my business and to just sit tight until she gets back." Thurgood cocked his head toward the house. "I come out here because inside, things aren't getting any better."

Sharvon began glaring at Freddie. But the scowl appeared tame compared to the eye stabs she then sent toward Leotis. Without saying another word, she went inside and slammed the door, almost decapitating one

359

of Thurgood's fingers.

"Don't take it personal," Thurgood told Leotis. "She's a bit on edge today. Although, it seems she's extra mad at you."

"I seem to have that effect lately." Leotis turned to say something to Freddie, but he'd suddenly disappeared. "What in the world? Where is the trustee?"

"Oh, he sneaked around the side of the house while you were jawing about the aggravating nature you seem to have with women."

"Why didn't you stop him? Sharvon told us to stay out, and you told us, too."

"Reverend, please, that man is in love and is fighting cancer. What's he got to lose by ignoring me and Sharvon?"

Freddie found Sister Betty's side door ajar. He stood outside for a moment to determine if he could hear any voices and from which room they came.

He didn't have to wait long. He could hear the exhaustion in Sister Betty's voice, and he knew her well enough to know that she'd been crying. Freddie inched the door open farther. He heard her voice coming from the direction of her bedroom. He crept down the hallway until he came within a few feet of the hallway bathroom that separated her bedroom from one of the others.

"He should've been the one to tell me, instead of Delilah and Thurgood," Freddie heard Sister Betty say. "What kind of woman did he think I was that I couldn't handle something like that?"

"Who's she talking to?" Freddie murmured as he leaned against the wall for strength. He still carried the bouquet of flowers in his hands, and already some petals had begun falling to the floor. "Is she talking to herself now?"

Inside her bedroom, Sister Betty glanced quickly into her mirror. Her jaw was set, despite the motion of one hand tracing the creases that outlined her jowls. Her face remained expressionless as she bent her neck forward, as if to get a closer look at the dark bags under her eyes. She smiled bitterly, noticing the bags seemed even darker against her brown skin, as though some blind person had given her a make-up job.

With her small hands carving through her wig, Sister Betty smiled wickedly before she suddenly snatched the wig from her head. She sent it flying toward the dresser. And the wicked smile remained on her face, not revealing whether she cared that the wig had landed on the floor or not. She'd already removed her partials when they loosened minutes ago and interfered with her sobbing. It didn't seem odd that she was wearing nothing but a slip and one house shoe. Her short braided hair had already begun unraveling, and now it made her look wild and crazy, the nappy braids resembling tiny snakes like on the head of Medusa.

Suddenly a pout appeared. It'd happened fast, removing any doubt that she'd taken leave of her senses as she addressed the person in her mirror. Sister Betty bit her bottom lip as she lifted a hand and pointed as she began to argue. "Betty Sarah Becton." She gave a curt nod to her reflection. "You've given almost your entire life to service," she told her reflection. "Everybody came first — your church, your friends, your family — everybody but you. And you were happy. God met your every need. You've got more money than you'll ever need, and the more you gave away, the more it kept coming back to you."

Sister Betty spun around, bumping her shin on a chair, and the pain reminded her that it indeed was she who was suffering. She grabbed the Bible off the nightstand and held it out before her with trembling hands. "I know you're real," she explained to God before she began thumbing rapidly through the pages of the Bible. "I won't argue that. But here I am again, standing before you, full of doubt when it comes down to me and what I thought you wanted for me. I know the Word says that you are a jealous God. . . ."

The tears began dropping, and she wondered where they'd come from, because she felt dry and empty. But Sister Betty was determined to say her piece to God. "I know you are a jealous God, and if you strike me dead, then so be it," she said as she held up her Bible, as though reminding God of what He'd said. "In Exodus thirty-four, verse fourteen, you said, 'For thou shalt worship no other god, for the Lord, whose name is Jealous, is a jealous God.' "

Still inside her bedroom, Sister Betty dropped her head and placed the Bible back on the nightstand. Challenging God, she pleaded, "So I need to know who it is that I have put before you." Her knees began to shake; she went to her bed and sat on its edge to continue. "It can't be my Freddie, because I never stopped going to church or serving you. Having him made me want to serve and praise you even more."

Outside her bedroom Freddie cringed at the mention of his name. His head swung from side to side out of desperation. *Oh, Lord, what have I done to her?*

Sister Betty's eyes found the picture of her and Leotis taken on the day when the church broke the ground for the Promised Land development. "Certainly not my pastor," she told God. "You commanded that we serve our leaders, and I've done that. I've done more than that. I — I — I . . ." Her voice began to trail off. "I became his spiritual mother. You told me to do that in a dream!" One small hand pounded the other, and Sister Betty's voice became stronger as she railed against heaven. "I've done everything you told me to do, and yet, you've not removed one stumbling block between Freddie and me."

Sister Betty suddenly felt the blood rushing to her head. Pulsating beats from her heart felt as though they would push through the walls of her chest. Beads of perspiration popped on her forehead as sharp stabbing pains shot up and down one of her arms. She felt disoriented as a weak hand shot forward, desperately trying to grab hold of anything or anyone, but she reached out too late, and she collapsed onto the floor, calling on the one name she always had. "Jesus!"

"I thought I told you to wait outside,"

Sharvon hissed. She quickly moved to the other side of Sister Betty's bedroom door frame, blocking him from opening the door farther.

Freddie hadn't heard Sharvon come up behind him until she tapped him on his shoulder, and at that moment, he'd heard Sister Betty call out the name of Jesus, and she'd complained about him, as well. Now standing there with his strength renewed, he'd had enough of Sharvon ordering him around and interfering in his and his beloved Honey Bee's business.

"You can't tell me when I can and when I can't go inside this house! This ain't your house!" Freddie's voice rose, matching the frustration that'd built up. "I'm going inside that room, and if you try and stop me, you'll find out that I'm just one pistol shot away from removing all the headaches in this house! Now, move out of my way!"

Freddie shoved Sharvon aside and pushed in the bedroom door. Sharvon followed him and gasped when she saw Sister Betty struggling to get up off the floor.

Freddie quickly tossed the bouquet on the floor. He and Sharvon, each with a hand under her armpits, began to lift Sister Betty off the floor.

She shoved their hands away. "I can do

it." She grabbed the edge of her mattress, and after several attempts she pulled herself onto the bed and sat on its edge.

Sister Betty pointed to her wig, still lying on the floor. Sharvon reached it first. She shook it and tried to reshape it before she brought it to her cousin. Sister Betty quickly placed the wig upon her head and tucked in all the natty braids she felt peeking out from under it. Looking around, she found her partials still lying at the bottom of the glass. Reaching inside the glass, she grabbed the partials, shook off the excess water, opened her mouth, and rocked them from side to side until they fitted perfectly.

Neither Sharvon nor Freddie had said a word the entire time Sister Betty tried to regain her composure. She'd put the wig back on her head and the teeth in her mouth, but she still looked crazy wearing a slip and one house shoe. They took turns looking from Sister Betty to each other, wondering who was brave enough to say something.

Finally, Sister Betty broke her silence. Turning to Sharvon, she pushed her shoulders back, crossed her legs, and said, "Sharvon, I want you to leave."

Sharvon's lips fell open to protest, but not in enough time.

"I don't want to hear a complaint or a refusal," Sister Betty told her. "I'm apologizing for putting you out earlier, but for right now, I need you to find someplace else to be."

After sneering at Freddie, Sharvon threw up her hands and silently left the room.

Not wanting to anger Sister Betty any further, Freddie began picking up the flowers off the floor. When he picked up the last petal, he refused to let her see the sadness in his eyes, and without speaking, he, too, headed toward the door.

Sister Betty uncrossed her legs. As she sprang off her bed, the one house shoe she wore flew off, hitting Freddie in his behind. She didn't flinch or apologize. "You stay put, coward."

"I won't go nowhere if you don't want me to go," Freddie said weakly as he turned around.

Sister Betty and Freddie continued talking. She fussed, and he listened, mostly with his head hung, beaten down with her truth. They shared how each had gone to God and their Bible. Both had operated under the belief that God would show them the other's true feelings and that God would fix things.

"I guess I expected God not only to give me something but also to put it directly into my hands, without me so much as lifting a finger," Freddie admitted. "Just tell me what you need."

"I need you to stop being a liar and a thief," Sister Betty accused. She walked slowly toward where he stood with his jaw slack and the flowers in disarray.

"I'm no liar and no thief." Freddie looked at her, his head spinning from how, in seconds, things had changed, refusing to believe what she'd just called him, and thinking that perhaps she was just too overwrought to think straight.

"You lied to me about that so-called high blood pressure," she told him when she was close enough to slap him, should she want to. "And you stole my heart and my dreams."

Freddie was speechless. He dropped the flowers and the facade. "I'm sorry, Honey Bee. I didn't know how to tell you."

"You knew how to ask me to marry you, didn't you?"

"Yes."

"Then it would've been the same way if you could've told me that you had cancer."

"You mean on my knees?"

"If need be," Sister Betty told him. "We could've both gotten down on our knees and prayed about it. You acted as though you didn't know that I had favor with God."

Freddie thought for a moment before he answered. He wanted to weigh his chances of her not going off on him again. He decided he'd trust God to hold her in place. "I hear what you say, Honey Bee. But you didn't act like you had favor with God."

"What do you mean?" Against her will, she could feel her hands balling up, as though she needed to hit or lash out at something.

"I mean that if you were all that certain about having favor with God, then you would've never believed God didn't want us to be man and wife."

It was out there, and no way could he take back the words. The hurt look that spread across her face shook him, and he began to struggle to put together an apology.

"I know that now," she finally said. "Between God reminding me that without Him I'm at the Devil's beck and call and me loving you so much, I thought I wanted to just lie down and die. I felt like I'd never had a Christian walk a day in my life."

"I haven't been led by the cross for as long as you have, Honey Bee, but God sure knew how to get my attention. I wasted all that time pushing you and others away because I'd forgotten that it's our faith that pleases

God. God was just testing me, because He knew I wasn't going to need no stem cell transplants or such. Most of the time when I went for checkups, I was telling other folks to look to God, and here it was I'd come home and pop a chemo pill and do just the opposite."

Freddie stopped and led Sister Betty to one of the chairs in her room. He gathered what was left of the bouquet and handed it to her. "But when it's all said and done, this is what's left of my heart when you're not in my life, just pieces of something once so beautiful."

Sister Betty took the flowers and looked them over. She stood and tossed the flowers with their broken stems and torn petals into the wastebasket. "I'm not taking no chances, so we're gonna have to start all over again."

Freddie's timid brown eyes suddenly glowed. "You mean, just the two of us?"

"Yes," Sister Betty replied. "I'm not babysitting grown folks no more. If they can't get out of their own fixes, then they'll have to learn to pray their way through."

"Do you think we should put our foot down with Leotis and Sharvon? I know they're walking around, feeling a bit guilty about something. Maybe we'll let them know that they may be pastor and family, but we've got our own lives to live."

"And maybe we just don't tell them nothing. Let them figure it out, like we had to. I mean it when I say that I'm focusing on God and you. Them others gotta make their own way," Sister Betty insisted.

"So what should we do first?" Freddie asked as he sat down next to her. "You just tell me, and I'll hop right on it."

"Well, Freddie Rabbit," Sister Betty teased, "we could start by planning this honeymoon properly."

"That's a great place to start," Freddie said, laughing. "At least we can concentrate on that and not have to worry about the wedding reception."

Sister Betty's hands flew up to her head. "Oh my goodness, I forgot about that. We still have to stop Bea and Sasha."

Freddie began laughing again while he patted her hand. "Don't you worry about that," he told her. "It's already taken care of. I'd been working on something with Batty, and I didn't have a chance to tell you about it before we had our little . . ." He stopped and took her other hand and continued. "Before we had our little misunderstanding."

"Well, can you tell me now?" Sister Betty looked at the way Freddie held her hands.

He held them tight, as if he thought she'd use them to hit him if she didn't like what he had to say.

"I'll tell you, but I don't want you to get mad or nothing. Just remember that I had gone ahead and done some of the grunt work while you tended to Leotis."

Sister Betty pulled back, but not enough to get her hands out of his. "Grunt work? What does that mean?"

"It means that when I tell you what I and Batty did about Bea and Sasha's meddling, you'll be grunting from holding your stomach tight from laughing."

Somehow Sister Betty didn't know whether to believe him or not, but she didn't want to start again with doubts.

At the same time Freddie doubted she believed him, but he didn't want to start again with a fight.

While Sister Betty and Freddie were in her bedroom, going back and forth, trying to tie up the loose ends of their wedding planning, Leotis was at home, looking out of his living room window and wondering what was going on inside Sister Betty's home. When he'd stood earlier on Sister Betty's porch, Thurgood needed to use a bathroom and Leotis offered to let him use the one in his house.

"Thanks for letting me use your bathroom," Thurgood said when he returned to the living room. "I'd have held my pee until my eyeballs turned yellow before I went inside my cousin Betty's house."

"Not a problem," Leotis replied without addressing Thurgood's colorful descriptions or outlook on life. "I don't hear any loud noises or see police cars pulling up. I guess the trustee is safe inside."

"Too bad the same thing can't be said for you," Thurgood said, rubbing the back of his neck as he stood.

"Do you think somehow I'm involved in whatever is going on over there?" Leotis pulled the window curtains shut before adding, "You must be joking, because I've done nothing."

"Oh, really?" Thurgood replied. The temperature inside the living room suddenly plunged when he made eye contact with Leotis. To also show he was serious, Thurgood planted his feet in a wide stance. "Well, then, let me count the ways." Thurgood began his sermon slowly. He would take his time so that Leotis could understand it all. "My cousin Betty was always open with you, and yet when it came down to choosing what was best for her, you chose to keep the trustee's secret about his cancer."

"He asked me to do it!" Without thinking, Leotis covered his ears with his hands so no further accusations could enter.

Thurgood jabbed his finger at Leotis's chest, but without touching him, and rebuked him. "I know you a reverend and all, and you got a habit of judging folks that sin differently from you, but I'm asking you to keep your mouth shut until I'm finished." Thurgood retreated several feet out of Leotis's personal space, his eyes in a locked position as he delivered his verdict. "All this nonsense with my cousin Sharvon — you pretending to like her like she's your sister — that's a load of crap, and you know it. Before you came along, she focused on nothing but being the best damn attorney my family ever had. And then you step up with your ripped muscles and pretty looks, your pretty hair, fast track-running routines, and your fast-talking mouth full of sermons for the spiritually challenged, and now she's walking around, arguing not only with juries but with herself, too."

Leotis rolled his neck as though preparing to fight. "You are a guest at this moment, Thurgood, and I'm a reverend who's heard enough —"

"That's really too bad, because despite what you've heard, I've not said enough," Thurgood interrupted before swallowing hard. Then he lit into Leotis again, this time with a steady, lower-pitched voice and furrowed brow. "That simple but pretty woman child, Ima, is not your soul to save all willy-nilly. Anyone inside of God's circle who's called to preach and who stays prayed up oughta discern a hurt person when they see or hear one. Ima's go around hurting other people because she's been hurt, and I'm not talking about just recently, looking for love in all the wrong places and from all the wrong people. I've known Sasha Pray Onn and that bunch of scalawags she calls a family for as long as my cousin Betty has. That girl Ima grew up in a world of hurt. It don't take a rocket scientist to figure out that when you put a pretty flower in some manure, it's either gonna be a gorgeous blossom or a stinky one, and in Ima's case, she's managed to be both."

"I've done nothing to Ima!" His mind conveniently dismissed the way she'd kissed him quickly and where she'd placed her soft lips, and how much he'd liked it.

"Yeah, well, from where I'm perched" — Thurgood pointed his finger again at Leotis — "you ain't done nothing for her, either."

Leotis was determined to show that this was his home. He wouldn't take insults in his own house without repercussions, so he walked quickly to his front door. He opened it and pointed toward the street, telling Thurgood, "I'm sure you know what this action means."

"Sure I know what it means," Thurgood replied. "It means you want this whole neighborhood to hear me yell how unholy you've been acting. You want everyone on this block to learn how your semi-immature womanizing has disrespected my cousin Betty's relationship and God in the process."

"You're judging me! How are you going to stand here in my house and judge me with accusations that you know nothing about?" Leotis slammed the door and started toward Thurgood, stopping an arm's length away. "You who spent years in and out of prison and used a gun to do your dirt before you claimed salvation has the nerve to judge me?"

"Listen here, Leotis. I'm talking to you man-to-man and not deacon to reverend. Let's not get things twisted, and please don't come all up in my face, talking crazy, just because I had permission to piss in your bathroom." Thurgood moved aside, leaving

Leotis with his mouth agape. "I'm just a man who tells it like it is."

CHAPTER 23

Delilah's long blond tresses spilled down one side of her head as she leaned across the table inside Le Posh. She smiled at several of the other churchwomen. They sat at a nearby table, wearing vogue designer dresses and jewelry, and they acknowledged her by saying "Praise the Lord. God bless you, Sister Delilah." Many others around the room had simply nodded and waved when she entered the restaurant. Like the other women, she, too, had dressed to impress. And impressed she had. Delilah's genetics defied the age on her Medicare card.

"How long are you going to read that menu?"

Delilah looked up and began to smile. "Not long." She nodded toward the door. "I was just waiting for our other guest to arrive."

Ima entered Le Posh and was relieved to

see that it wasn't as crowded as before. When the waiter escorted her over to where Delilah sat, Ima put on a fake smile. It was curiosity that'd brought her there when Delilah had all but ordered her to come, but once she saw Sharvon was there, too, her smile faded and the real Ima came through.

"I thought you said you wanted to talk to me and buy me dinner," Ima hissed at Delilah. Without looking at or mentioning Sharvon, she added, "I do have more important things to do than participate in one of your group sessions. I even took the express bus to get here, because my car is acting up."

Sharvon didn't say a word; she cocked her head and gave a "What the hell?" look to Delilah.

"Just sit down, Ima," Delilah ordered as she ignored Sharvon's questioning stare. Knowing there were others watching them, she smiled the entire time.

Normally, Delilah wouldn't dare relax her elbows on a table in such a ritzy place, but this time she did and she rested her chin upon her hands. "In about five minutes the Upstate First Ladies Club is going to meet. I'm not a first lady, but I know these women from some of my seminars. I told them I needed to be here to listen so I could help them at our next meeting."

Sharvon was the first to speak. "So what does this have to do with me? I'm no first lady."

Removing her hands from under her chin, Delilah sat back. "You're not one now, but you want to be."

"Well, that's hardly my problem or goal," Ima lied, smiling at the obvious state of discomfort Delilah had placed Sharvon in.

"Actually, it *is* your problem," Delilah told Ima. "You wanted to be a first lady about a year ago, but it seems the original first lady beat you to the title. And don't sit here and pretend you ain't still trying for the gold."

"I guess she told you," Sharvon murmured.

"Don't be tossing stones, Sharvon. You could get some nasty cuts living in that glass house of yours," Delilah warned.

Delilah straightened her shoulders and began talking softly, changing her manner as she began to speak. "You two think you know all there is about being the wife of a man of God. And I don't care if it's a small church or a megachurch. It takes a special anointing for a first lady to succeed in the role. Many women are not anointed. Some women have selfish motives and want all the glory but don't want to put in none of the work. Being the first lady is much more than fashionable hats and designer clothes, fancy cars and homes.

"You have to be a woman of high moral fabric. You have to know when to speak and when not to. A first lady needs to be thoroughly versed in psychiatry, and most had better know how to take care of their men at home. Most of the women you see here tonight found out the hard way." Delilah suddenly fell silent, as did all the others in the room.

A tall and slender, fortyish-looking, beige-skinned woman rose from her seat. She had large cornflower-blue eyes and wore little make-up, yet she looked as if she had walked straight out of *Glamour* magazine. Looking directly ahead, as though she knew all eyes were upon her, she walked into the center of the room, where a small table had been set up. A handheld microphone lay on top.

The woman reached into her Leiber dandelion suede gator handbag, a handbag that looked all of the fifteen thousand dollars it'd cost, and withdrew a pair of glasses. After donning the glasses, she quickly scanned the papers in her hands before laying them aside.

"Now, *she's* got it going on," Ima whispered. "Those collection plates must be overflowing for sure."

Delilah remained silent, and Sharvon shook her head at Ima's ridiculous conclusion.

The woman looked over at Delilah and nodded, acknowledging her presence. "Allow me to introduce myself," she began. "My name is Althea Love. My husband is the head bishop, Arthur Love, overseer of Jehovah Jireh Temple in Piedmont. Of course, that makes me the first lady."

Vigorous applause followed before she waved her hand for it to cease and began speaking again. "Although we all are familiar with and know our sister Delilah Dupree Jewel-Pillar, she has brought along guests today." She turned slightly and looked at Sharvon, who'd turned in her chair to face the center of the room. "Allow me to introduce Ms. Sharvon Becton. Ms. Becton is a partner at the prestigious Singer, Berry, and Becton law firm, which is not too far from here."

Sharvon nodded when she heard the obligatory applause. She turned and smiled at Delilah but was surprised to see that Delilah remained stone-faced. She quickly turned back in her seat to face the woman who appeared ready to introduce Ima.

First Lady Althea pointed to Ima. "To the

left of our beloved Sister Delilah is her other guest. Please welcome to our meeting today Ms. Ima Hellraiser. Ima is the niece of Crossing Over Sanctuary's church mother president, Mother Sasha Pray Onn."

Unlike the applause Sharvon received, whispering began and ended, with just a few of the women lightly tapping their hands together, as if trying to wave off something nasty. The difference in enthusiasm appeared noticeable to First Lady Love, and she said, "C'mon, ladies. Is this how we show agape love to our guests?" That time the applause was louder, but the disdain remained on some of the women's faces.

Sharvon was surprised at how she suddenly felt sorry for Ima, who suddenly looked pale and embarrassed. As much as Ima had done and said some things Sharvon felt were meant to get under her skin, Sharvon didn't appreciate the obvious lack of respect coming from the so-called women of God.

Delilah still said nothing. Her gaze remained upon First Lady Althea.

One of the women read the minutes from the last meeting, and then it was time for the women to suggest topics or review current issues that'd not been resolved.

"I definitely feel as though what I brought to the table at our last meeting was not resolved," a voice from the floor announced.

"Yes, First Lady Magbee?" First Lady Love moved aside so that the woman could come to the table and use the microphone.

First Lady Magbee rushed over and grabbed the microphone. With one hand on her ample hip, she narrowed her eyes and began from where she'd left off while still seated. "And you can believe, I don't aim to leave here today with it remaining the same."

Both Sharvon's and Ima's mouths dropped, and they even managed to give one another a strange look of disbelief.

It was Sharvon who first spoke up, whispering, "What in the world could she be upset about?"

"I'm thinking the same thing," Ima replied, shaking her head. "Look at her."

The woman, short and squatty with a pretty face, wore enough heavy and expensive jewelry around her neck and wrists to never have to go to a gym to work out.

First Lady Magbee continued. "I've been telling all of you we need to come clean. I know I'm not the only one who's sitting up in church every Sunday and smiling as though everything is okay."

The eyes of most of the women fell upon Sharvon and Ima. They quickly looked away, as though to say, "We have no idea what this woman is talking about."

First Lady Magbee went on to reiterate how she needed the first ladies to tell their congregations the truth. "Every week we're standing by the door with our illustrious husbands, smiling while we watch either their baby mamas sticking out a hand for a supposed handshake or some money or one of their men on the side doing the same. I'm sick of it!"

Again, all eyes fell upon Delilah's table, where Sharvon and Ima sat gape-mouthed. Delilah still hadn't said a word or made a move.

First Lady Love gently took the microphone out of Lady Magbee's shaking hand. "I don't believe this is the sort of conversation we need have in front of our guests," she reminded Lady Magbee. "I'm certain our sister Delilah had other things she wanted discussed with these young women, who, as I understand it, aspire to be first ladies, too."

Lady Magbee held a jewelry-laden hand out in front of her before she turned and snatched the microphone back. "And I don't believe this is the sort of conversation that should be kept a secret in the damn closet, along with your husband!"

Sharvon and Ima sat almost head-to-head when they moved their chairs in closer to see and hear better. Delilah still remained silent, except now she was smiling.

All the way back to Pelzer, Ima and Sharvon tried to outdo each other as they discussed the woes of the first ladies at the meeting.

"Have mercy," Sharvon blurted. "I've been in a ton of courtrooms. I've heard all sorts of testimonies, and some things have been major surprises —"

"Yeah," Ima butted in. "But I know you ain't never heard no mess like that. How they gonna sit up there and brag about how long they chased the man and wore him down, using every trick in the book, and then complain? In fact, I'm still shocked that those ungrateful women would air their dirty laundry and yet couldn't forgive their husband's indiscretions after they got all that hush money and gifts."

"Well, I've got my pride, and there aren't enough gifts in the world for me to put up with all that nonsense," Sharvon commented. "When two of them nearly went to blows when it came out that their husbands were truly low-down with their down-low activities, I was almost ready to order some popcorn. Unbelievable!"

Out of nowhere Sharvon and Ima suddenly gave each other high fives and laughed.

With the exception of earlier ordering them into the car because they'd wanted to stay and watch a couple of first ladies throw down, Delilah had hardly said a word. Every so often she peered into the rearview mirror at them. She'd start shaking her head at Sharvon and Ima, sitting in the backseat, trading observations of what they'd called "dumb moves by supposedly smart women."

"It wasn't like all of them still had youth on their side or were particularly good-looking," Ima continued. She kept jiggling in her seat and thumping her head, as though she were the crazy one. "I just don't get it. The way they told it, they all had the fine homes, their kids in boarding schools, and got a little sexual touch-up every once in a while from their whorish husbands. It's not the ideal situation, but I don't know of one that is."

"Perfect or not," Sharvon said, "if those men felt like they weren't ready to marry, then those desperate women now sitting and complaining, with their titles of first lady, shouldn't have chased after those men in the first place. I'm certain they got some type of signal from their husbands' hesitancy or behavior before they got to the altar."

No sooner had the words left Sharvon's mouth than Delilah finally spoke up. "Bingo!" She quickly reached beside her and grabbed two books, flipping them over into the backseat. One nearly popped Ima upside her head. "You two got the first lesson. I need you to read this book I just gave you so you can quickly learn the second one before you really are caught in a mess. God is not going to change His plans just to fit yours. Stop trying to use a plan B when God's plan A is so much better and predestinated." Delilah then began humming before she murmured, "Ain't no truer saying than youth being wasted on the young."

Sharvon and Ima each took the paperback books, turning them over, as though looking for a key to unlock their insides.

Sharvon began reading the title on the front cover. "*Tell Prince Charming to Keep that Slipper —*"

"*I'm Standing on My Own Two Feet,*" Ima added as she read the last part of the book's title. "Who in the world is Elder Olivia Stith-Bynum? I've never heard of her," she

388

told Delilah.

"Sometimes when I'm holding a workshop just for women, and single women in particular, I have Elder Stith-Bynum as a guest speaker, or I'll have the women read her book for our discussion," Delilah explained. "You just make sure you two read it, 'cause I got Betty's wedding coming up, and I don't have time for the craziness you two are laying on folks. I'm hoping when you've finished with it, you'll put the brakes on your nonsense."

Delilah took a breath and added, "I ain't asking you two to become good or best friends. I ain't that crazy and as dumb as you are acting, and neither of you are that crazy, either. I'm just saying that for the sake of your self-esteem and that you not feed that male ego beast that's roaming between the reverend's ears and his thighs, that you do better for yourselves."

Ima leaned over closer to Sharvon than she'd ever wanted and whispered, "What did she just say?"

Sharvon tilted her head in Ima's direction and whispered, "She said we should cut it out trying to get Leotis. Get our heads out of our backsides, and for us not to expect to share make-up tips or clothes."

The car remained quiet as Delilah pulled

off Highway 85. It was easier to drop off Ima first at her apartment near the Promised Land before heading toward Sister Betty's house. It was obvious by the numerous boarded-up homes, rusted car remains in driveways, and other blight that Ima didn't live in the best of neighborhoods. Sharvon reacted to it by biting her lower lip, and she was about to cower in the backseat, as though she didn't want anyone to see her, but she caught Delilah's disapproving look as she watched her reaction in the rearview mirror.

Knowing Delilah would want her to say or do something to take away the embarrassment from Ima, Sharvon asked, "Do you mind if I use your bathroom?" She was certain Ima would say no and they'd both be off the hook. But Ima told her that she could.

The two women got out of the car, and Delilah watched as they went up the walkway to Ima's apartment. The apartments were all one-story garden units, and they were surprised when Elder Batty opened the door and came out.

"What in the world were you doing in my hallway?" Ima asked as she rushed him.

"I just needed to serve these papers," he told her. "I've been trying to catch up with you for some time." He turned quickly, and after seeing that Sharvon was with Ima, he added, "Sharvon is an attorney. Maybe she can explain things to you."

Ima pushed out her leg to trip him, and Elder Batty hopped over it and scuttled away, tipping his hat toward Delilah as he jumped into his car and sped away.

Sharvon felt convicted. The fact that she knew about the lawsuit had her already too much in Ima's business. She turned away. "Never mind," she told Ima. "I can wait until I get home."

Ima seemed preoccupied. She'd already ripped open the envelope before Elder Batty had gotten into his car. She would chase him down if need be. Seeing the shocked look on Sharvon's face, Ima began smiling. "Well, glory to God," Ima blurted. "Prayer does work."

It wasn't the reaction Sharvon had expected, so she had to ask, "Is everything all right?"

"It's more than all right," Ima replied as she shoved the papers into Sharvon's hands. "You're not my attorney, and I can't say that we're really friends, but doggone it, I got to share this news."

Delilah continued to sit and watched the two women. She observed first the look of surprise on both Ima's and Sharvon's faces. Delilah then watched Sharvon hand the papers back before both women broke out in laughter. Since she and Sharvon already knew what Batty had been trying to deliver for some time, Delilah felt positive that it was a document informing Ima that the lawsuit had been dropped.

While Ima was doing a happy dance in front of her apartment, her aunt Sasha was ten blocks away, feeling miserable inside of hers.

With her lips curled, Sasha began stroking her wrinkled neck as she leaned back and stared at Bea. "This is all your fault, Bea. You just had to go and hit Porky with that metal spoon. Now what are we gonna do? He's threatening to sue, and we don't have nowhere to hold the dang wedding reception. I don't know what possessed me to go into business with your neurotic and violent self. I oughta punch you in the throat and cut you up for fish bait."

For the past fifteen minutes Sasha had been fussing and threatening Bea. Ever since she'd found out that Porky put out the word that he would come after them and take every dime they could make from the business that hadn't started yet, she'd given her false teeth a workout.

Bea let Sasha have it again with her same old threat. "Keep yelling at me, and I'll stuff your munchkin butt in a pillowcase, tie it down with a rock, and toss you into that pond over yonder to join the other bottom-feeders."

Before Sasha could answer Bea's threat with another of her own, her doorbell rang. "I ain't expecting no company."

"It's probably security coming up here to tell you to shut your big mouth," Bea told her. "You gonna learn to have a little class yet."

Sasha went to her door, and standing on her tiptoes, she looked through the peephole. She came eyeball-to-eyeball with Batty.

"It's Elder Batty," he said. "I just want to know if Bea is in there with you. I got to tell y'all something."

Any hint of gossip was enough for Sasha to open her door to Jack the Ripper. "Come on in," she said. "She-rilla is in the living room."

As soon as Batty stepped inside Sasha's living room, Bea gave him a wide-eyed look and asked, "What are you doing knocking on Sasha's door? What's going on with you and her?"

"Oh, hush up, Bea," Sasha told her. "There ain't nobody living or dead that want your leftovers."

Grabbing Bea about her shoulders, with his eyes sparkling, Batty laughed, telling her, "Girl, please. Don't nobody want us . . . but us."

Not quite believing him, because she had strayed from time to time, depending on how far behind she was with her bills, Bea shoved him away. "What you got to tell us?"

"First of all," he began, "I got y'all's hundred-dollar deposit back from Porky. I laid an extra hundred on him to calm down him and that lump Bea gave him." He grabbed Bea around the shoulders and hugged her to him again. "I don't know what he said or did, but judging from that king-size knot on his bald noggin, he won't be doing or saying it again." Elder Batty turned Bea loose and began laughing and holding his stomach.

Elder Batty stopped laughing long enough to reach inside his pocket and peel away five twenty-dollar bills from a wad of cash. He winked as he gave them to Bea.

Bea smiled just at the moment Sasha began flailing. "Why you give all that money to Bea? Some of that is mine."

Sasha jumped off the couch and came at Bea, but Batty took one hand and, with no effort, lifted Sasha up and gently placed her back on her sofa. He peeled off two fifty-dollar bills and gave them to her.

"What's going on?" Bea asked. She wasn't happy to see Batty give away money that she could've fleeced off him, but she'd settle that later. "What's the plan, man?"

Elder Batty then took from his back pocket an envelope. He opened it and gave each woman a sheet of paper. "Y'all back in business."

Bea and Sasha read the papers Elder Batty gave them over and over. They looked at one another, and neither blinked or smiled.

"What is this?" Bea asked.

"Yeah, what you trying to pull?" Sasha asked. "Because whatever Bea be doing to get you to do things, I ain't doing."

"For one thing," Bea snapped, "you couldn't. And for another, don't nobody want a tough sausage when they can have a tender steak."

Elder Batty covered his ears and looked from woman to woman. At that moment he could've knocked Freddie out for getting him involved in some of Bea and Sasha's insanity. But Freddie was one of his best friends, and he was the best man, so he'd suck it up and do what was necessary, and besides, it wasn't his money he was spending. It was Freddie's.

"You know this is B.S.," Bea told Batty. "This won't be no B.B.S."

"I know, Bea," Batty replied. "This is only yours and Sasha's business. All I did was to have it incorporated and put down a deposit at Le Posh in Anderson so y'all could have your debut wedding reception for Sister Betty and Trustee Noel. I even got them to do the decorating so folks will be talking about how classy an affair it is. Anybody walking in there that day, bringing their invites, will know right away that it was all B.S."

Tears sprang to Sasha's eyes. She hopped off the sofa and raced over to where Batty sat by Bea. Sasha pushed her dentures to the side and kissed Batty hard enough to draw the pus out of the big pimple on his jaw. She then leapt up before Bea could snatch her by her neck and raced off to her bedroom.

Aside from wanting to hit Sasha for swabbing down her man with her bald gums, Bea was speechless. She sighed before finally telling Elder Batty, "I ain't never had no one do something this kind for me. I still don't know why you did it, but I'm glad you did."

"You know I'd do anything for you, Bea, and especially for that red velvet cake you're gonna make me when we get off this couch."

Bea began laughing. "Well, come on, then. I should have enough ingredients to make you a small one. It'll have to be quick because I need to get started on the invites and get them in the mail."

"I'm way ahead of you," Batty whispered. He pulled out another piece of paper and handed it to her. "They're already in the mail."

Bea scanned the names on the paper. "These are mostly all the people we figured Sister Betty would want to come to her wedding. You even have a few I haven't heard from or about since they left the church years ago." Bea stopped and looked Batty up and down. "Why did you go ahead and do all the heavy lifting? Now me and Sasha won't have much to do."

Elder Batty began grinning and wringing his hands. He quickly averted his gaze before he turned around to face her again. "I don't know why you can't figure out, Bea Blister, how I really feel about you. But all I want you to do is look radiant on that day so I can imagine what you'd look like if you ever decide to put aside your playgirl ways and make an honest man of me. I know we tried it once before, but we can make it work this time, if we both give up a few things and take up a few others."

Bea got up from the sofa. She headed toward Sasha's bedroom door, beckoning Elder Batty to follow. "I don't believe one word of what you just said, but it sure sounded nice to hear."

Elder Batty began laughing again. "You see, Bea," he said, "I told you didn't nobody want me or you but me and you."

CHAPTER 24

It was as though God owed Sister Betty and Freddie for all the misery they'd suffered. The fall weather on their wedding day was perfect. A colorful assortment of orange, brown, green, and yellowish leaves clung to the branches of the trees, as though they didn't want to miss one moment of the festivities before slowly drifting to the ground.

Three shiny 2012 silver and black stretch limousines took up most of the space in the church's main parking lot. A gilded-edged reserved sign stood at the mouth of the parking spot normally occupied by Reverend Tom. Today the spot had been set aside for the late-model Bentley that'd brought Sister Betty to the church. Freddie had told Delilah and Elder Batty to spare no expense, and they had followed his orders to the letter.

Inside the church the decorations were

simple yet classy. The wedding planner had had navy blue, fuchsia, and white ribbon bouquets attached to the sides of the first three rows. Several other pews had black-and-white ribbons and were for the surprise guests Freddie had brought in as a special gift for his Honey Bee.

In another part of the church Sister Betty waited along with her bridal party. Her nerves were causing her to weep and munch on saltine crackers to keep from vomiting. She kept Sharvon busy retouching the little make-up she'd allowed and sweeping the crumbs gathering on the bodice of her dress and on the floor.

However, the bride and her attendants weren't the only ones who were nervous. Others were both nervous and secretive.

Leotis was in the room adjacent to his study, trying to entertain the guests Freddie had hidden there. The plan was for no one in Crossing Over Sanctuary to find out about them and go blabbing about it.

Months ago Freddie had told Elder Batty Brick and several of the other deacons and trustees about his planned surprise for Sister Betty. He wanted some of the former members from the Ain't Nobody Right but Us — All Others Goin' to Hell Church to be invited. Reverend Knott Enuff Money had pastored the church, and the overseer, Bishop Was Nevercalled, had moved on after Reverend Money changed the church's name to Crossing Over Sanctuary and then retired. Reverend Tom had taken over as pastor from then on.

Elder Batty had been an original member, along with Bea and Sasha. He'd used whatever means necessary to get Bea to talk about their old church congregation and where they were presently. He'd always done it in such a way where she never knew he was fishing for information. It'd been easy because Bea loved to gossip, and she did provide other distractions, her red velvet cake being one.

Because the pastor's study was toward the rear of the church building and away from the din of the sanctuary, the chatter from the surprise guests went unheard and unnoticed.

"Man, what happened to the buff dude that had everyone call him Deacon Mellow Yellow?" a man said, laughing as he stood back on his heels and looked another man over. "But you still looking okay for a dude now hugging fifty, so tell me, Deacon Laid Handz, man, where have you been hiding, and what the heck have you been up to?"

Deacon Laid Handz had been the head of

the deacons' board for several years before he had to leave. He'd put his hands to some of the young female members one time too many, and his safety, as well as the church's finances from a possible lawsuit, were always jeopardized.

"Oh, I've married and settled down," Deacon Laid Handz replied, showing the band on his ring finger before pressing both hands to his rather large belly. Years ago he was the narcissistic, handsome playboy deacon with the snow-white teeth, clear light-skinned complexion, and curly black hair. Now he looked older and fatter and, judging from the run-down heels on his shoes, a lot poorer. "Brother Tis My Thang, I can't believe it's you."

"I'm still the man," Brother Tis My Thang replied as he snapped his fingers, making the letter Z formation. "I'm still handling my organ on Sundays for the choirs, and I'm still the talented, take-no-prisoners man now, at forty."

Deacon Laid Handz cocked his head and scratched his jaw as he gave Brother Tis My Thang a questioning look.

"Oh, you don't hafta say it. I know that look," Brother Tis My Thang told him. "I've been out of the closet for quite some time. It was so many church folks packed like sardines in it that I decided I'd rather be straight." With that last statement, the man turned around, laughing, and went off to chat with some of the other guests, saying, "I can't wait to see the look on Sister Betty's face when she sees me."

While it was customary for the bride to arrive late, today Freddie had chosen to break that custom by being late himself. Thurgood and Elder Batty had left some time ago to pick Freddie up from his house, and no one had heard from them yet.

Just as Leotis was about to lose hope that the wedding would happen, and had resigned himself to the fact that he'd have to deliver the bad news to Sister Betty, Thurgood raced through the door with Elder Batty and Freddie right on his heels.

"Where have you guys been?" Leotis asked, lifting one eyebrow. "This wedding was scheduled for twelve noon. It's almost twelve thirty-five."

Freddie began shuffling his feet and kicking at the floor. "I thought I could've depended upon this one," he said as he pointed to Thurgood, "to pick up the cruise tickets and keep hold of the passports until he could give them to my best man."

Thurgood coughed slightly, as though he'd something in his throat. "I ain't gonna

403

be but so many 'this ones.' Now, I told you I'd been running around, trying to help you out, and I just simply misplaced the dog-gone things."

Elder Batty hurried from his corner and stood between Freddie and Thurgood before things escalated. Smiling, he placed his arms around the men's shoulders. "Y'all do remember that this is supposed to be a joyous and happy occasion, don't you?"

The relaxation was noticeable as their stances returned to normal.

Thurgood lifted the ring box from his inside pocket and opened it to show the ring. "Just so you can see it again and know that it's safe," he said slowly as he closed the box and handed it to Elder Batty. From his other pocket he fished out an envelope with the passports and cruise and airline tickets, giving them to Elder Batty, as well. "Now, let's go and get you married before you ask me if I made those reservations in Fort Lauderdale for tonight."

Thurgood began laughing as he turned Freddie aside and gave him one last look. "Well, like I told you before, for a man who doesn't have my sense of style, you still look pretty good." Thurgood had wanted Freddie to wear a neon yellow tuxedo with a black sash, but Freddie had protested, telling

Thurgood that he'd no intention of standing at the altar looking like a dumb, emaciated bumblebee.

It was Freddie's turn to laugh and lighten the moment. "I may not have your sense of style on this day," he told Thurgood, "but come Halloween, I may use that idea of wearing a neon yellow tuxedo with a black sash getup."

"That's all I'm asking," Thurgood replied. "I just want you to dare to be a little different on this auspicious occasion."

"Yeah," Elder Batty added, "go ahead, Trustee. Act a bit suicidal on your wedding day."

"If you guys are finished trying to keep this man from getting to the altar, we can get started," Leotis announced. "The bride and her party need escorting down the aisle. I've already sent the surprise guests inside to take their seats."

Leotis then turned to Thurgood. "I'm sending word to the ladies that it's time to get this show on the road. Thurgood, you wait at the back of the church, like we rehearsed, so you can walk Sister Betty down the aisle."

Leotis turned and nodded at Freddie and Elder Batty. "Freddie, get ready, and, Batty, go in the other room and get the surprise groomsman. I can't wait to see the look on Sister Betty's face."

Sharvon took a deep breath as she waited at the back of the church to enter the sanctuary. She touched the ring of pink roses woven into a headband that sat upon her head. She wore her hair in long ringlets and swept to the side. Sharvon began fidgeting as she held her bouquet of red and pink roses and baby's breath in one hand and ran her other hand over the bodice of the mauve-colored, long silk gown with its high, uncomfortable neckline. She and Delilah had wanted to wear something shorter and a bit more revealing, like a V-neck cut, to make their look more modern and even a little sexy. They'd also tried convincing Sister Betty that adding a teardrop diamond necklace would distract folks from looking at their bosom, if that concerned her. But her cousin Betty insisted that everyone wear the same high-neck style.

Sharvon saw her escort approach. He looked every bit as handsome in person as he did in the pictures she'd seen of him at his grandmother's funeral. She reached out to accept the hand he offered. "Thank you," Sharvon told him. "I know my cousin Betty will never forget this."

"I wouldn't have missed my godmother's wedding for all the money in Las Vegas," Chandler told her. "I just hope she'll forgive me for telling her I wasn't certain if I could make it since my wife, Zipporah, wasn't able to come."

"I know what you mean. It's not easy trying to put one over on Cousin Betty," Sharvon replied. "I also think it was so sweet of Elder Lamar to fly in, take your place, and pretend he was Freddie's groomsman for the rehearsal dinner last night."

"That was good of him, but I did fly him first class to make it up to him. But I still have one other big concern."

"What's that?"

"I'm praying Sister Betty won't see me and scream out, 'June Bug!' "

"She still calls you June Bug in public?"

"Yes, sadly she does."

Sharvon began chuckling. "You better hope I don't do that, too. I think it's hilarious."

Delilah heard the laughter behind her and looked back in time to see Sharvon with Chandler. She nodded her head at them and smiled. "You look beautiful," she told Sharvon.

Unlike Sharvon, Delilah had rebelled down to the last fitting, but she finally gave in. Now she stood in front of Sharvon in her long, formfitting navy-blue matron of honor gown, her blond hair cascading down her back and a woven ring of blue forget-me-nots upon her head. Her bouquet had the same flowers, but with sprigs of baby's breath dispersed throughout. "Lord, I hope I can get through this without strangling," she told Elder Batty as she clutched his arm. "This neck choker is killing me. I can hardly breathe."

Elder Batty said nothing but smiled appreciatively and tapped her on her arm to comfort her.

The music signaling the wedding procession to begin filtered in from the sanctuary.

Batty looked over his shoulder and told them, "Let's do this."

Thurgood had already entered the outer corridor, where he kept Sister Betty out of sight until the official wedding march music played. "It sounds like things are starting. Are you nervous?" He'd asked Sister Betty that same question several times while they'd been standing there.

"I think you are more nervous than I am," Sister Betty teased. "Calm down. Aren't you the one who is the marriage expert?" She gave him a quick tug on his arm and kissed him on his cheek. "I can't thank you enough for doing this for me."

"Oh, gal, please," Thurgood said as he returned the kiss. "I've been waiting to give you away for quite some time. I couldn't be happier."

There was a rap on the door. It was one of the church ushers, who'd come to get them. Thurgood and Sister Betty followed behind the usher and stopped when they came to within a few feet of the sanctuary door.

They heard the bridal entry music and shuffling sounds as the guests stood to their feet.

Sister Betty didn't think it would happen, but she could feel it coming on. She felt every negative feeling she'd either heard or read about when it came to the wedding jitters. Her small white pillbox hat, with its tulle veil that was short in the front and long in the back, began constricting her as though an anaconda had her head in its grip. She could feel the onset of gas building in her stomach and seeking an exit, and then she began to hiccup.

Thurgood began tapping her on her back to stop the hiccups. It didn't work. He even whispered, with a deep voice, in her ear, "Boo!"

The organist replayed the bridal entry

music three times before the guests began chattering, Freddie began sweating, and Leotis began waving his Bible around. Sharvon looked at Delilah, and neither gave a hint of what to do.

And then they entered. Thurgood, in his tuxedo, walked beside Sister Betty, holding her by one arm as she smiled nervously. Sister Betty, walking slowly, held a huge bouquet; it was made of red roses and white and cream lilies, with a spray of white silk ribbons holding it together. She also wore just a little make-up, including barely any of the red lipstick Delilah had insisted she have. There was a shimmer coming off her clip-on diamond and pearl earrings, and her feet felt comfortable in the slip-on rhinestone-covered beige pumps. Her wedding dress was simple yet elegant for a woman of her age. Sister Betty had described it to Sharvon, who'd hired the best seamstress in Pelzer. So on this day, Sister Betty wore her dream dress. It was made of lace over charmeuse and had rhinestone and crystal beading. It was a dress that floated as she walked, hiccupping softly, down the aisle.

As they neared the altar, covered with lilies, roses, and carnations, Sister Betty smiled. She felt nothing was real. How could it be? She was an old woman who'd hit heaven's jackpot. She looked at Freddie, standing tall and confident in his tuxedo, smiling broadly, and without reaching for his sprig of hair, which had fully returned. She felt the hiccups cease and her breathing becoming normal as Thurgood placed her hand in Freddie's before turning to sit on the front pew. And just as thoughts of Ma Cile came to mind and how her best friend would've approved of it all, she saw June Bug. She fought back tears and the urge to yell, "June Bug, you came," and she remained at Freddie's side, smiling at him instead.

Freddie looked at his Honey Bee. He was happy that the vows had not yet begun. He couldn't have spoken the words "I do." She'd taken his breath and speech away.

Leotis performed the wedding ceremony perfectly. Sister Betty and Freddie had decided not to repeat any personal vows but to let God command their marriage ship, and they'd go wherever it sailed. There were no sudden outbursts when Leotis asked if anyone knew of a reason for the couple not to marry.

They exchanged their wedding vows, and each placed a ring on the other's hand. When it came time for Leotis to say, "I now

pronounce you man and wife," so many ap-
plauded that neither Freddie nor Sister
Betty heard him add, "You may now kiss
your bride."

Freddie quickly looked at Thurgood, who
sat grinning like he was about to watch his
student graduate. He pursed his lips, nodded at Freddie, and waved him on.

Freddie lifted Sister Betty's veil. He licked
his lips, as Thurgood had instructed, and
with one arm under the nape of her neck,
Freddie went in for the kiss.

Those around the altar heard Delilah's
sigh of relief. She winked over at Thurgood
as they both prepared to see if the couple
had learned everything they'd suggested.

Just as Freddie placed his arm in a position to tilt Sister Betty back a little and kiss
her further, she sprang forward like a
bobblehead doll and kissed him so hard,
they both could've landed on the floor of
the altar and at the foot of the cross. The
sanctuary exploded in laughter and praises,
but that didn't embarrass or stop the old
couple from their deep-sea tongue diving.

"Leotis, do something," Sharvon whispered. "It's embarrassing."

Leotis looked at Sharvon and laughed. He
moved closer to her and whispered, "What

you need to be doing is taking notes." He winked and moved back into his position.

Chapter 25

The newlyweds and the bridal party had not yet arrived to the Le Posh ballroom. They'd gone directly from the church to a nearby photographer's studio to take the bridal party pictures.

Of course, Bea and Sasha decided to make good use of the bridal party's absence to promote their new business. Sister Betty and Freddie had asked their guests to contribute to multiple myeloma research instead of giving wedding gifts. That meant there'd be plenty of room for Bea and Sasha to set up their business presentation on one or two of the empty tables.

Standing at the front door to Le Posh, Bea and Sasha did their best to make sure their debut event went off without any unnecessary drama.

Bea, wearing a fiery red, curly wig, a dark green gown with silver glitter, and her comfortable flat shoes, collected the invites.

She wanted to make sure those on the separate list she'd given Elder Batty were allowed in. Some folk who thought she'd never amount to anything needed to see the new and improved Bea. It didn't matter if they knew Sister Betty or not.

Sasha stood on the other side of the door, wearing a small-brimmed hot pink hat with a veil that fell to the side each time she moved. Her dress was the same color as Bea's. Each time Bea let a guest enter, Sasha would greet them, saying, "Welcome. This is a B.S. affair," after which she'd press one of their business cards into the hand of the shocked guest.

Bea finished setting out their packets containing printed brochures and began to smile. "Thank ya, Lord," she whispered. "These look so elegant and classy." They had used gold parchment paper and had had the brochures rolled up like scrolls, with green satin ribbons tied in a bow around the middle. They wanted their B.S. to stand out.

Sister Betty's next-door neighbors, cousins Patience Kash and Joy Karry, arrived, smiling from ear to ear. The two missionaries had been overjoyed from the moment they received their invites. With their new private investigation firm floundering from a lack of clients, they appreciated Bea and Sasha's efforts to promote their business. Anytime they could attend an event where church folks were invited, the possibilities for discovering dirt were enormous.

"We can't wait to see what B.S. has in store this evening," Joy told Sasha, with Patience nodding her assent, before they left to find their seats.

The thirty large round tables seated ten guests each inside the Le Posh ballroom. Every table had been decorated with mauve, fuchsia, and navy-blue linen, and big white bows had been tied behind every chair. The place settings were elegant and contributed to the ambience of the occasion. The Noritake Crestwood cobalt platinum dinnerware and the various sizes of forks, knives, and spoons, along with several gilded-edged champagne flutes, confused many of the guests.

None were more confused than the former members of Sister Betty's old church. Reverend Knott Enuff Money swept his Jheri curl aside and looked at Bishop Was Nevercalled.

The bishop simply hunched his shoulders, saying aloud, "Lord, bless whatever it is we're gonna eat this evening, and may the serving of the food carry as few calories as possible so all the fat folks here won't suffer diet failure. Amen."

Brother Tis My Thang ran his fingers through his perm and gave a low whistle, which ignited the false bravado of Deacon Laid Handz. "I'm so glad they set a lovely table," the deacon told the others as he fished through the shrimp boat placed in the center of the table. Taking one of the knives, he speared a bun from the bread basket, cutting it in half before spreading a thick layer of cocktail sauce on the halves and placing several pieces of shrimp between them. "This makes me feel right at home, because this is how I eat every night," he lied.

The others at the table were determined to show that they, too, had as much class as the affair called for. Following Deacon Laid Handz's lead, in between bites of their impromptu shrimp sandwiches, one by one they began lifting the lemon-water finger bowls to their mouths, raising pinkie fingers as they sipped, instead of using the lemon water to clean their hands.

"It is so good to see all of you again," Ima called out to her old congregation members as she approached the table. "Reverend, Bishop Deacon, Tis — you all look wonderful." Ima gave them her best smile, hoping to replace the sour expressions that'd suddenly appeared on their faces. "Do you mind if I join you so we can catch up?"

"Catch up?" Deacon Laid Handz jerked his head and looked around the table at the others. "Did she just ask us to play *catch-up*?"

"She sure did," Brother Tis My Thang said, rolling his neck. "I'm sitting here wondering why the police didn't catch up with her from the time she set me up for borrowing money from the building fund."

"I was just thinking along the same lines," Bishop Was Nevercalled chimed in. He'd long ago lost his bad stuttering habit, and he was ready to blast Ima for something she'd done and he hadn't responded to. "I'm lucky some of our congregants didn't catch her like I did with Minister Love in the fellowship hall, exchanging kisses. She'd better be glad I was as saved as I was. I'd have called the entire congregation together and turned them in if my stuttering wouldn't have taken up the entire morning service."

Ima put a hand on one hip and smirked. "So then the answer to my question about joining you and catching up is . . ."

"Oh, hell to the naw!" the table chorused.

Nonplussed, Ima took her hand off her

hip and looked them straight in their eyes. "Y'all got a lot of nerve trying to signify on me. All of you together are too dumb to fall down by yourself." Ima's look dared all of them to move before she finished. "I'll be over there among some of the classy folks at this reception. You scrubs call me when you can cast the first stone." Before any of them could finally respond, Ima turned and sashayed away, flipping the shawl she carried back at them, a move they could interpret any way they wanted.

The band Elder Batty had hired for the reception was outstanding. They were five men and one female vocalist from Crossing Over Sanctuary's gospel jazz band. It was the cocktail hour, and they played soft hymns and the vocalist sang slow songs while the guests enjoyed appetizers of shrimp, lobster puffs, and assorted pastries.

Several guests walked around and mingled, while others traded lies about how close they were to the newlyweds, but most knew they were there to observe and report.

While the band played, Ima sat off in a corner by herself. She hadn't stood out as she normally would. Wearing a plain green dress with the hemline to her knees, her hair pinned back, and very little make-up, she appeared removed from everything happening at the reception. The cold shoulder she'd gotten a moment ago had hit her hard. *Too many chickens coming home to roost at one time,* she thought.

Ima found an unoccupied table near the back of the room, away from the band and most of the guests. She sat with the shawl to the dress she wore modestly covering her lap and legs. With her head down and the palm of one hand supporting her chin, she opened the book she held. It was the book Delilah had given her the last time she'd been at Le Posh, when she learned the life and role of a first lady weren't what she'd thought.

"That book must be real good to make you want to bring it to a wedding and read."

Ima placed a finger on the page before closing the book, and looking up, she saw Leotis smiling. "Yes, Reverend," Ima said with a blank expression. "It's just that good." She quickly put her head down again and reopened the book.

Leotis tilted his head to see what she was reading. When he couldn't, he slowly came around to where she sat, until he was standing behind her and looking over her shoulder. "Elder Olivia Stith-Bynum. I've heard of her. I believe she's the head of the E.S.T.H.E.R. organization," he told her as he began reading the title aloud. "*Tell Prince Charming to Keep that Slipper — I'm Standing on My Own Two Feet.*"

Leotis looked puzzled as he added, "I didn't think you went in for her type of self-improvement techniques with a fairy-tale twist." Leotis folded his arms as he strolled around Ima's chair and again came face-to-face with her. "Not that I'm saying there's anything wrong with you and that you need improvement. It's just that I definitely see you as someone who is very comfortable with the emotions of *Sacred Love Songs,* which is why I haven't asked for my CD back."

"Shouldn't you be off somewhere, asking God to give you more discernment, or whatever it is that you're lacking?" Ima quickly moved her chair closer to the table and placed the book on it before she continued reading.

His eyes danced as he leaned in and teased, "Have I done something to you?"

That time Ima slammed the book shut, nearly catching her finger between the pages. She pushed her chair back, and one of its legs banged, catching the toe of Leotis's shoe. Ima had a severe glint in her eyes meant to send chills through him. "You want to know whether or not you have done something to me?" Ima stood and folded her arms across her chest. "Yes, you have done something."

"What have I done?" Leotis's voice became almost childlike as he questioned her. "Just tell me what I've done."

"You've wasted my time!" Ima squinted her eyes, sending piercing green disdain his way. She then picked up her shawl, which had fallen on the floor, grabbed her book, and strutted away, never looking back and leaving Leotis stunned.

Leotis quickly looked around to see if anyone had overheard or seen what'd happened. A thunderous applause rang throughout Le Posh, and he was glad to see it wasn't because of what had just happened between him and Ima. Instead, several members of the bridal party had entered the ballroom. He straightened his shirt collar and his jacket. He didn't have time to ponder what the problem was with Ima.

Chandler entered Le Posh with Sharvon on his arm. He took her to the middle of the dance floor, twirled her around, and then they sat. The next ones to enter were Elder Batty Brick and Delilah. Delilah let go of the elder's arm and quickly whispered in the ear of Brother Casanova, the emcee for the reception. He smiled and nodded.

Elder Batty Brick then took Delilah's hand, and they did the same twirl as Chandler and Sharvon had before they, too, found their table. The only ones who hadn't entered yet were Thurgood and the newlyweds.

"Ladies and gentlemen," Brother Casanova said, "there's a slight delay. Please proceed and have a wonderful time. I'll return shortly." He then motioned to the band to play, and the vocalist began singing.

Leotis walked quickly over to the table where Chandler had just gotten up, leaving an empty chair next to Sharvon.

"You look beautiful," Leotis told Sharvon. His eyes darted about, as if he expected to get a brick upside his head or to be caught doing something wrong. Ima's new attitude, the way she'd dismissed him, had caught him off guard, and not in a good way. Talking to Sharvon and finding out what had happened to the newlyweds and Thurgood would take it off his mind. And she did look beautiful and almost angelic, classier than normal.

"Thank you," Sharvon replied. She quickly looked past him to see what was happening on the dance floor.

Leotis noticed she kept her eyes on the dance floor. Several couples had begun to dance as the band played and the vocalist sang "My Funny Valentine."

"Would you care to dance?" Leotis extended his hand to Sharvon. "It'll give us something to do until the newlyweds arrive." As soon as the words left his mouth, he felt the hairs rise on the back of his neck.

"Move out of my way, Prince Charming," Sharvon snapped. "Go hold yourself until the newlyweds arrive." Sharvon pushed back her chair, which almost caught Leotis's shoe, as had happened when Ima did the same move. "When you feel you've gotten yourself together," Sharvon hissed, "don't call me, because I'm sure it'll be temporary."

Sharvon walked away, grabbing the hand of Elder Lamar, who'd just sat down and begun munching on an egg roll. The food flew out of his hands as Sharvon dragged him onto the dance floor, and despite his friendship with Leotis, he couldn't have looked happier.

Leotis's hands flew to his face. He couldn't feel any scratches or marks, but she'd just verbally slapped him hard enough to give him a concussion. "What is going on with these women?"

"You look lonely," Delilah whispered as she snuck up on the reverend.

"I'm fine, Sister Delilah," Leotis said. "It's

just been an unusual wedding."

"Oh, the wedding was just wonderful, and the only thing unusual was the inexperienced bride and groom." Delilah chuckled, dismissing the astonishment on Leotis's face. "Pick your face off the floor before you trip over it. C'mon. Let's dance a little."

Leotis looked at Delilah and suddenly began laughing. "Why do I feel you helped to build the brick wall that's suddenly been erected in my life?"

"I most certainly did have a hand in it," Delilah confessed. "Me and the Lord need you to stop and observe your ways before you and others get hurt." Delilah took his hand as she led him onto the dance floor. "Reverend Tom," she said, "you have a good heart that's wrapped up in a man who wants nothing more than to do God's will. Unfortunately for you, there're two natures that's in a battle. If you keep going the way you are, that fleshly nature gonna overtake you and undo all the good will and work you've done. And despite you thinking you know it all, those two women aren't for you to mold or to shape. Stay in your lane so God can continue to use you."

"You are something else, Sister Delilah." Leotis began laughing, and before he could say another word, the band turned up the tempo and the vocalist began singing Chaka Khan's song "I'm Every Woman."

"You see," Delilah told Leotis, laughing, "that's confirmation right there."

"Move! Get out of my way! Let's go!" Those words came from all four corners of Le Posh. Women of all ages raced out onto the dance floor. Delilah pushed the reverend back to save him from the stampede.

Ima slammed her book onto the table, and by the time she reached the dance floor, Sharvon was there, too. They, along with the other women, began dancing all kinds of moves as they mangled the melody to what nearly every female alive called their freedom anthem. And when they finished mangling that one, they started destroying the melody to "I Will Survive" when they sang it a capella.

Determined to take advantage of possible business with the eager women, Bea and Sasha waded in with business cards in hand. They almost became cripples; the women mowed them down each time Bea and Sasha tried to press a business card into their hands. Bea's dress had a rip, and Sasha didn't know where her hat had disappeared to.

"Ladies and gentlemen," Brother Casanova announced, "I've just received

426

word that a limousine has just arrived. Like you, I can't wait, either. So without further ado, it is my privilege and honor to present to you Mr. and Mrs. Frederick Noel."

The guests jumped to their feet and began applauding. "It's about time," someone yelled out, as though they needed to see the couple again before they believed the wedding had actually taken place.

Bea and Sasha hurried and made sure they stood nearby so, no matter how messed up they now looked, they could take a bow after the newlyweds entered.

Thurgood, still wearing his tuxedo, entered as soon as the ballroom doors opened. His eyes quickly found Delilah, and seeming pleased, he began smiling broadly at her.

Thurgood straightened his bow tie and adjusted his sash before he strolled over to where Brother Casanova stood. Thurgood whispered, "I'll take it from here." As soon as Brother Casanova handed the microphone over, he scratched his head and walked away.

"Have y'all enjoyed yourselves?" Thurgood nodded around the ballroom like the seasoned pro that he was, indicating that he needed to receive an answer. As soon as several people remarked, "It's been wonderful," Thurgood pulled a sheet of paper from

427

his pocket and began reading.

"To all our dear friends who truly love us, and to those who just showed up at our wedding to gawk, my Honey Bee and I want to thank you from the depths of our hearts."

Thurgood stopped reading and smiled. "Oh yeah, this is really from Trustee Noel. Trust me, my cousin Betty ain't had nothing to do with this."

"Thurgood, cut the dramatics," Delilah shouted. "Get on with it."

"Yes, Dee Dee, you're right, as usual." Thurgood looked down and continued reading.

"I've decided that I don't have the time to do things the way most would when they get married. Instead, I'm whisking my Honey Bee away, and it ain't nobody's business where I'm taking her. And I'm sure Thurgood knows how to keep his big mouth shut, as well as Delilah, who'll somehow tempt him to spill the beans.

"Speaking of Delilah, it may be unusual, but she'll be standing in for my wife and tossing the bouquet. Of course, old Thurgood ain't allowing nobody but him to feel up on his wife's thigh for the garter. He'll be searching for days, because my Honey Bee is still wearing hers and I'll be the one taking it off.

"There's plenty of food to take home in those Jiffy bags secretly stuffed in your pockets and pocketbooks. We also hope y'all enjoy and take pictures of that seven-layer wedding cake. There's a reason there's no bride and groom figures on the cake. It didn't make sense to have it, since me and my Honey Bee wasn't gonna be there.

"We'll be back when you see us. In the meantime, Reverend Tom and the rest of you, keep on praising God and doing well by one another, especially when it comes to forgiveness. You never know how your credits toward the Kingdom are stacking up, and I, for one, have a lot to make up for.

"Finally, I gotta tip my hat and toss Honey Bee's wedding veil to Bea Blister and Sasha Pray Onn. Only those two thorns in our sides could've put together one heck of a B.S. wedding reception, whether we wanted them to or not."

Thurgood shook his head, laughing, and began folding the paper to put it back into his pocket. Before he could say another word, the guests began clapping and laughing, too.

And, of course, Bea and Sasha raced out onto the middle of the floor, looking crazy with their ripped dresses, Bea's wig turned to the side and Sasha's bun undone. They were deliriously happy and pranced around, yelling, "That's us. We're B.S."

EPILOGUE

In the Le Posh ballroom, Sharvon and Ima decided to join in the fun, and this time they'd include Leotis.

Ima was the first to approach him. She threw her book and shawl onto the seat of a chair, and with her finger, she beckoned him to come to her. Of course, she'd made Leotis wait until the band played MC Hammer's song "U Can't Touch This!" If she hadn't embarrassed him before, she'd make certain he got the point now.

After the music was over, Leotis was near exhaustion from trying to understand and keep up with Ima's latest mind-blowing moves and welcomed a chance to sit. But then Sharvon raced over, and with a wide grin, she yanked him off his chair just as the band began playing En Vogue's "You're Never Gonna Get It."

An hour later the reception in the Le Posh

ballroom was over. Delilah and Thurgood were exhausted. The last of the guests had finally left, and they needed to get back to their hotel and pack.

Delilah chuckled and then sighed. "They should be almost to the airport by now and then off to Fort Lauderdale to catch the cruise ship to Jamaica tomorrow morning. I wonder how things are working out for them."

Thurgood stood and began stretching his long arms and laughing, too. "Well, if they're going to do everything we suggested, they'll probably knock themselves out and sleep for the rest of their honeymoon."

"This may sound crazy," Delilah said. "I feel like an old mother hen who just let her chicks out for the first time and hopes they don't end up in a stew pot."

Thurgood began rubbing his hands before he pulled Delilah close. "You know, Dee Dee, I just had an idea."

"Is it what I'm thinking?"

"Yep."

"Do you think they'll be mad?" Delilah asked softly. "But we do deserve a vacation, too. And besides," she added, "Jessie and Tamara won't mind if their parents and grandparents stay away a little longer and have some fun."

Thurgood chuckled. "Well, I'll tell you what. We don't have a chauffeur, but we still got that Bentley until tomorrow. Dare we keep it an extra day and hope they won't be upset, or dare we take that vacation to Jamaica and then on to Mexico? What are the chances they'll think we're spying?"

Delilah's gray eyes sparkled as she teased, "I'll take that double dare for two hundred, Alex."

Miles away the white stretch limousine carrying the newlyweds sped down the highway toward the Greenville-Spartanburg airport. Freddie and Sister Betty hadn't stopped grinning since they left the Bentley with Thurgood. They were acting like schoolkids, laughing and holding hands, finding it hard to believe they were finally man and wife.

"Do you think our guests will be mad?" Sister Betty asked as she sipped sparkling cider and admired her new wedding band. "I'm thinking some folks might be a bit upset that they didn't get to see us before we left for our honeymoon in Jamaica and Mexico."

"I don't know if they will or not," Freddie replied. "I really don't care, because we left them in good company and with plenty of quality food and entertainment. The oncologist said I was doing splendid and I shouldn't worry about a thing and should enjoy the honeymoon."

Sister Betty smiled. She hadn't given a thought to her new husband's health since they'd made up and placed everything in God's hands. She was back on her faith mission, and that was where she intended to stay. "For as long as God allows," she whispered to Freddie. "One day at a time."

Freddie kissed her and said, "This is our honeymoon, and no negative vibes or pity parties allowed." He reached beside him and picked up the little microphone on the back wall where they sat. "Driver," Freddie said, "can you please press the play button on that CD I gave to you?"

"Yes, sir," the driver replied.

Suddenly from all the speakers throughout the limousine Sister Betty heard the sweet sounds of one of her favorite vocalists. It was Bishop Paul Morton out of New Orleans.

"I know I'm no singer like the bishop," Freddie told her. "But I'm gonna always try and do right by you and make you happy." And in that moment, Freddie joined in with Bishop Morton, singing the love song simply titled . . . "Finally."

Sister Betty had never heard Freddie sing

like that. He was almost on key, and even during the speaking part of the track, he kept the pace. The sincerity overwhelmed her. She took a deep breath, as though she wanted to inhale everything about the moment.

As soon as the song was over, the old couple kissed again, and with a twinkle in his eye, Freddie laid his head back in the crook of Sister Betty's arm, then closed his eyes for a moment before he began smiling again.

After a few moments he sat up straight and reached for his glass. He took a sip of the sparkling cider and smiled so wide, it looked as though his teeth would pop out of his gums. "Betty honey," he said, laughing, "you know how we're supposed to already be in a praise mode when we enter the church?"

"Of course, I do, Freddie, but what's that got to do with whatever it is you look like you about to do?"

"I'm just saying that today begins the rest of our life together, and I don't see no reason to wait until we get to the hotel tonight or to that cruise ship to begin the honeymoon."

"Freddie, what's wrong with you?" Sister Betty began smiling as she laid down her glass and a twinkle formed in her eyes. "Whatever it is, I'm willing to give it a try."

Freddie spoke into the microphone again. "How long before we get to the airport?"

"It's going to be about another five minutes or less, sir."

"That's about all the time I need," he murmured before telling the chauffeur, "I want you to play the second track I gave you."

Suddenly pulsating drumbeats reverberated throughout the limousine. It felt as though an earthquake had hit. Freddie leaned forward and flipped off his jacket. He took one look at Sister Betty and began jigging in his seat before waving his hands in the air as he'd seen teenagers do on the television.

Freddie closed the curtain that separated them from the chauffeur's peering eyes.

"Betty Noel, are you still wearing that garter?" Without waiting for her answer, he began singing along at the top of his lungs to the song that was playing, "Let's Get It Started," by one of his now-favorite groups, the Black Eyed Peas.

A READING GROUP GUIDE
SISTER BETTY SAYS I DO

PAT G'ORGE-WALKER

ABOUT THIS GUIDE
The suggested questions that follow are included to enhance your group's reading of this book.

DISCUSSION QUESTIONS

1. Has God ever blessed you with something that you'd thought never possible? How did you react? Did it increase your faith?

2. Discuss the difference between having faith and exhibiting desperate behavior.

3. Do you have the patience to wait on God? If yes, why? If no, why not?

4. How do you interpret the message of the Song of Solomon?

5. Sister Betty's faith floundered at a moment when she thought she had understood God's purpose for her life. Have you ever had cause to second-guess God? What did you do to receive clarification beyond prayer?

6. Trustee Freddie Noel's life went through

a major transformation. Did it make you think more or less of him? Do you believe love has an expiration date in someone's life? Was it inappropriate for him to desire love and as much intimacy in the twilight of his life? Do you feel his cancer caused him to react differently than he would have had that illness not happen?

7. Sharvon and Ima are both single and both beautiful. They are ten years apart, and one is college educated and the other was educated on the mean streets of life. Discuss their behavior when it came to Reverend Leotis Tom. Did their backgrounds make a difference?

8. Reverend Leotis Tom spent much of his youth dedicated to the belief that he was anointed and set aside. What made his reaction to Ima and Sharvon not only inappropriate but also amateurish for a man so judgmental and intolerant of others?

9. Are there any characters who you would like the author to bring back? Who?